BASQUE MONEY

BOOK 2 OF THE SeaOx SERIES

BY
TERRENCE (T) MAULT

 **FriesenPress**

Suite 300 - 990 Fort St
Victoria, BC, Canada, V8V 3K2
www.friesenpress.com

Copyright © 2015 by Terrence (T) Mault
First Edition — 2015

All rights reserved.

No part of this publication may be reproduced in any form, or by any means, electronic or mechanical, including photocopying, recording, or any information browsing, storage, or retrieval system, without permission in writing from the publisher.

This book is a work of fiction. Names, characters, places, and incidents either are products of the author's imagination or are used fictitiously. Any resemblance to actual events or locales or persons, living or dead, is entirely coincidental.

ISBN
978-1-4602-6127-9 (Hardcover)
978-1-4602-6128-6 (Paperback)
978-1-4602-6129-3 (eBook)

1. Fiction, Action & Adventure

Distributed to the trade by The Ingram Book Company

Table of Contents

Dedication vii
Acknowledgements viii
Prologue ix

Chapter One
Escape to Bermuda 1

Chapter Two
Phone Sex 4

Chapter Three
Missing Her Man 8

Chapter Four
Styled For Bermuda 12

Chapter Five
Pelling's Rules 16

Chapter Six
Beach Babes 19

Chapter Seven
Lisbon Investigation 22

Chapter Eight
New Playmates 26

Chapter Nine
Bermuda Investigation 29

Chapter Ten
Marta and The lieutenant 32

Chapter Eleven
George Yaro's Connections 35

Chapter Twelve
Exercise Can Get You Killed 40

Chapter Thirteen
Suicide and Murder 52

Chapter Fourteen
Gulfstream Jet at Your Service 57

Chapter Fifteen
Bidding for a Winery 66

Chapter Sixteen
A Person of Interest 71

Chapter Seventeen
Gulfstream Takeover 75

Chapter Eighteen
Who is Ursula? 81

Chapter Nineteen
Money Matters in the Caymans 86

Chapter Twenty
Ava Sails The SeaOx to St Jean de Lux 93

Chapter Twenty One
Ursula's Assignment 100

Chapter Twenty Two
Pelling in Control 108

Chapter Twenty Three
Murder at Sea and the Pompous Cayman Cop 110

Chapter Twenty Four
Death on Departure 118

Chapter Twenty Five
Dereliction of Duty 124

Chapter Twenty Six
Basque Banking 129

Chapter Twenty Seven
A Heart To Heart Talk 140

Chapter Twenty Eight
Destination Undecided 147

Chapter Twenty Nine
The Rome Diversion 153

Chapter Thirty
Rendezvous at the Utrecht Chateau 160

Chapter Thirty One
ETA Issues Sanctions 170

Chapter Thirty Two
Ruth's Millions 173

Chapter Thirty Three
Andre and Elspeth Reunited 175

Chapter Thirty Four
The Party's Over 179

Chapter Thirty Five
Elspeth's Vivid Dream 185

Chapter Thirty Six
Do What You Have To So You Can Do What You Want to 190

Dedication

For Patricia, the beautiful Diva of our wonderful family.

Acknowledgements

The manuscripts of Basque Money and the first book, The SeaOx, would not have been completed without the time consuming and diligent editing of Patricia. Thank you darling. Our daughter Cathy wrote the bios under my picture on The SeaOx and Basque Money. Thanks Cathy. Thanks also to our daughter Darcy, your support was very much appreciated. The scenes in the books in George Town would not have been as real if not for that fabulous January we spent with my brothers, Joe and Robert on seven mile beach so expertly hosted by my lovely sister Margaret and her husband Gilbert Plamondon, both retired Cayman bankers.

Prologue

First of all, I assume you have read the first book in this series, The SeaOx, and for that I thank you.

If not, thank you for buying this book. This simple guide and the synopsis will be useful in the transition to Basque Money, book two.

Characters

The SeaOx: 44' Hans Christian Pilot House sailboat purchased from Hamburg Marina by Andre Laurent.

Andre Laurent: 44 year old single Canadian who buys his dream sailboat and begins his new lifestyle.

Ava Haas: partner in Hamburg Marina who sells the SeaOx to Andre Laurent and contracts to teach him the boat on a shake-down cruise to Oostend, Netherlands, London, England ending in Le Havre, France.

Elspeth Vander Riis: wealthy Utrecht widow who is in love with Andre Laurent and looking forward to rendezvous in the near future at her Paris apartment. Mother of twins: Mathijs and Marta.

Mathijs Vander Riis: (Mathijs pronounced Mattice) is called Tice and is back from a finance course in New York and set to begin as a broker in the Paris office of Merrill Lynch. He has brought a flight attendant home to the family chateau in Utrecht as a guest.

Marta Vander Riis: Mathijs and Marta are twins. Marta is a language professor at the Utrecht University. She flies her own airplane. She has a thing for Lieutenant Robert Bizet.

Lake A-4 Renegade Amphibian aircraft: Marta's pride and joy.

Sylvie Bern: flight attendant and Tice's guest at the Utrecht Chateau.

Lt. Robert Bizet: single, Sûreté detective who is a friend of the Vander Riis family.

Henk Veldhoen: chauffer and servant of the Vander Riis family.

Sergeant Alain Moline: Lieutenant Bizet's right hand man.

Teddy Pelling: ETA assassin who reports to Raoul de Vascos, his control. He hijacked the SeaOx, kidnapped Elspeth Vander Riis, then shot and wounded Sylvie Bern.

Ruth Meikle a.k.a. Ruth Ann Werner: High priced Paris call girl and financial planner whose clients are: Teddy Pelling, Pierre Turin, Raoul de Vascos and George Yaro.

Ida Tesh: childhood girl friend of Ruth who looks so much like her, they get mistaken for twins.

Raoul de Vascos: Pelling's control and nephew of Esau Navarra, a member of the ruling council of the Basque terrorist group, the ETA.

George Yaro: trusted accountant of the ETA and a favorite client of Ruth.

Gulfstream V: George Yaro's private jet.

Pierre Turin : Merrill Lynch broker in Paris branch. His best client is Elspeth Vander Riis and his newest is Andre Laurent. Turin will lose Elspeth's account to Mathijs, when he begins his career in the Paris office of Merrill Lynch. Turin was responsible for Andre's interest in Elspeth.

The Bijou: 50' Beneteau sailboat Pelling and Ruth purchased in Bordeaux to escape the Sûreté and ETA by joining a small flotilla of Beneteaus being delivered to Charleston, South Carolina via Lisbon and the Azores.

A Synopsis

The series of the SeaOx begins when Andre locates one of these unique Hans Christian sailing yachts in Hamburg, Germany. He had been searching for months for this particular model: a 44' Pilot House Model. He knew only 16 had ever been built. Ava Haas, the broker, was living aboard the boat when Andre arrived. It had been listed for sale for months, but Ava hoped it would never sell, as she wanted to buy it herself. Andre read the boat's history. It had been shipped via freighter from Taiwan where it was custom built in the TA SHING yards. It stayed in a warehouse in Hamburg awaiting the launch as soon as the owner recovered, but he never did and his estate administrators listed it for sale. Ava launched HCPH-13-94 at her marina and began living aboard. Andre bought the boat and named it the SeaOx. Andre contracted Ava Haas to teach him the boat on a shakedown cruise to Oostend, over to London and back to LeHavre, France. They became intimate friends, left the SeaOx at LeHavre and drove into Paris for a short stay. They parted at Orly airport when Ava flew back to Hamburg with Andre's promise to sell her the SeaOx if he decided to quit his lifestyle aboard and move ashore.

Andre sailed the SeaOx to Nice, France and left if at Baie Des Anges marina while he drove to Paris to meet Pierre Turin in the Merrill Lynch office. His brokerage account had been transferred there from Montreal. While in Paris, he met and fell in love with Elspeth Vander Riis and, after a week together at her apartment, they decided to cool off their new relationship and rendezvous back there in one month. Andre sailed the SeaOx back to LeHavre and stopped for provisions at Brest. A big mistake, as he was hijacked by Pelling, continually drugged, bound and held hostage on the SeaOx. He was forced to sign a transfer of ownership of the SeaOx to Pelling. Pelling forced him to cash in his brokerage account and drove Andre to Paris to pick up the cheque. After cashing the cheque, Andre was forced to call Elspeth to announce his arrival. Pelling drugged him once more, stowed him in the trunk of their rental car while he kidnapped Elspeth and drugged her. He drove both back to the SeaOx and tied Elspeth in the master berth and Andre in the V-berth in the bow. Andre and Elspeth were unaware of the other's presence. Pelling arranged to pick-up the ransom and return to the SeaOx with it. Pelling took Elspeth in a drugged state to the airport and left her in a restaurant booth. He called the chateau and advised that Elspeth had been released and her location. Pelling was unaware he had been followed back to the SeaOx by Lieutenant Bizet and Marta Vander Riis flying high overhead in her amphibian. They landed and explained to the marina manager who they were and why they were there. The manager said they had just missed the captain of the SeaOx and a drunk lady pass by the office moments before. The lieutenant insisted they board the SeaOx. They rescued Andre Laurent and retrieved the ransom and posted a police guard at the SeaOx. They flew a very disoriented Andre back to the chateau in Utrecht. Elspeth was picked up at the airport and driven to her chateau by Tice. Both Andre and Elspeth were sedated by the family doctor. When they awoke in the morning, they were relieved to both be alive. When Elspeth told her story, Andre was thunder struck. Pelling had given Elspeth a note supposedly written and signed by Andre, saying Pelling was his partner and Andre had shown him Polaroid pictures he and Elspeth had taken of their lusty week together. Pelling would not molest or harm her if she would give him one million guilders for her safe release. Elspeth said she was devastated at Andre's treachery. Andre was flabbergasted and stunned at the devious and evil Pelling. When he told his story, he denied any knowledge of this letter. Elspeth told him she believed him and produced a document from Pierre Turin which she had requested (her due diligence about her new love) about Andre Laurent. Still, Andre was in an impossible spot and asked Lieutenant Robert Bizet to arrange for him to take a lie detector test at his office in Paris. The following morning, Pelling shot Sylvie Bern while she and Tice were playing tennis. The bullet creased her shoulder and knocked her into Tice who caught her and carried her quickly into the chateau. They bandaged her wound and sent for the family doctor. Elspeth was badly frightened as Pelling had warned her if the ransom wasn't paid, he would kill her twins and then her. Obviously, as Slyvie resembled

Marta, Pelling thought he was shooting at Marta. When Pelling called now demanding one million US dollars, he asked did he kill her daughter or just wound her. Elspeth said she was wounded and she would gladly pay the new ransom to keep her bargain with him. He would call again with further delivery instructions on the money.

The story continues with Pelling intercepting the new ransom by killing the UPS delivery person. He takes refuge at a farm he and Ruth are renting in Bordeaux. Ruth will meet him there but brings a client along, Raoul De Vascos, Pelling's control who has convinced Ruth he has orders to liquidate Pelling and recover his money. Ruth has a last minute change of heart and helps Pelling escape. Pelling sets the Sûreté onto Raoul and has him arrested with a promise to Lieutenant Bizet that he will send enough information to convict De Vascos of murder. Pelling and Ruth purchase the Bijou which provides an escape from France to the US. The route of the small flotilla of sailboats stops in Lisbon with onward stops in the Azores, Bermuda and finally, Charleston, South Carolina. However, when in Lisbon, Pelling is sighted by Andre and Ava and decides to abandon the Bijou and leave by air in disguise. Andre alerted Lieutenant Bizet who has the local police take the co-owners of the Bijou into custody as suspects in a number of murders and terrorist activity. Andre kept watch on the Bijou awaiting the arrest of Pelling and his blonde companion.

THE SEAOX ended with Andre Laurent witnessing Pelling and Ruth attempting to escape. He went aboard Pelling's sailboat and shot Pelling in the right wrist and the left knee. He drugged both of them, tied them securely and applied tourniquets to the terrorist's wrist and leg. He left them unconscious for the Lisbon police to arrest. However, when the police finally boarded the Bijou, no one was there. They reported they saw a lot of blood on the stair steps and floor boards and obvious evidence of a struggle, but nothing else. When Lieutenant Bizet arrived from Paris in the morning, he was given this news and passed it on to an astonished Andre and Ava.

Lieutenant Bizet's investigation into Pelling's disappearance led him to believe that the early flight to Bermuda was the most likely escape route. Bizet returned to Paris and Marta. Andre Laurent and Ava Haas sail the

SeaOx back to Bordeaux. Elspeth Vander Riis is shopping in New York. Mathijs and Sylvie are heading for a healing holiday in Mustique.

I hope you enjoy the continuing story: Basque Money.

Terrence (T) Mault, Author

BASQUE MONEY

BOOK 2 OF THE SeaOx SERIES

BY
TERRENCE (T) MAULT

Chapter One
Escape to Bermuda

The jumbo jet landed so smoothly at Hamilton Bermuda International Airport, the passengers didn't realize they were on the tarmac until the engines whooshed into reverse to assist the braking process. The passengers began to stir. The announcement to "Stay in your seats with your seatbelt fastened until the plane has docked" was ignored, as usual, as some began to stand up and reach for their belongings in the overhead compartments. When the airplane docked minutes later and the door was opened to the warm Bermuda air, a wheelchair was positioned adjacent to where Pelling was sitting. The attendant deftly assisted him into the chair, and began wheeling him toward the entrance. His red-headed niece followed close behind, a single overnight bag on her shoulder. The attendant asked for their luggage claim tickets, then went to retrieve the suitcases. He was gone only ten minutes before returning with the matching bags. Ruth asked if he would drop the bags at the carousel listing the hotel services. When they reached the carousel, Ruth arranged for the hotel limo to pick them up.

As Pelling was carefully being helped into the rear seat of the Hotel Limo, he and Ruth noticed a young couple being led from the airport in handcuffs and escorted into a police van.

"You don't suppose...do you?" Ruth whispered into Teddy's ear.

"I doubt it," was Teddy's reply, but he had the same thought when he saw the young couple protesting about mistaken identity. *Just as soon as they strip search him, they will see he doesn't have a bullet hole in his left knee, and if they had any brains at all, they will see his right wrist is fine when they cuff him.*

Teddy Pelling checked into their Hotel on the shore as Argus Trask. He was uncomfortable figuring the ETA had now cast a net for him since he was responsible for having his control, Raoul de Vascos, captured and incarcerated. The Sûreté would be on to him after Andre Laurent had wounded and drugged him and his long-time girlfriend and left them tied aboard their sailboat, the Bijou, at the Lisbon docks. Laurent had spotted Pelling earlier at a marina tavern and called Lieutenant Robert Bizet in Paris to have the Lisbon authorities take Pelling and Ruth Werner into custody. However, the drug given them wore off quickly and they were able to get loose, disguise themselves as an old man and his niece and leave Lisbon for Bermuda on a late flight. When the Lisbon police came aboard the Bijou they found blood on the steps and floor boards, an empty syringe, the smell of cordite and evidence of a struggle but nothing else.

Pelling, still dressed as the old man Argus Trask, decided to leave a false trail. He booked passage on a ship leaving the following morning. He sent the cash for the tickets to the ticket office by courier who returned to the hotel with the tickets. Upon receipt of the tickets, they checked out and headed for the bus terminal by cab. In the bus station washroom, Teddy did a quick change back into his real self, carefully putting the old man disguise away in his makeup case along with the Argus Trask passport. He changed his trousers and shirt then gamely limped out to meet with Ruth who had rented a Lincoln convertible which they drove from the station to look for a new place to stay. On the way, Teddy suggested they stop so she could remove the red wig and carry on as a natural blonde.

"I'll just brush my hair out and put this wig in my case".

Teddy indicated a parking area up ahead where Ruth parked and changed back to her usual look. They drove all over the Island and finally came back to where they had started their drive. Pelling decided to register at the Beach Villas, three blocks from their original hotel. After checking in as Linus Svendsen, he ordered pizza and beer from room service, for their evening meal.

Ruth left their villa after dropping off her bag and went in search of a drug store. When she returned, she brought bandages, sterile soap, a hair color kit, and flesh colored knee and wrist protectors.

Teddy decided his hair color should be a middle brown and, while Ruth was busy applying the contents of the color kit to his hair, she suggested she visit a salon to have her mid-length blonde hair cut short to her scalp, like the Irish singer, Sinead O 'Connor.

"That will just turn you into a short haired blonde. You would still qualify if anyone is looking for a blonde, but if you were to cut your hair close to your scalp then dye it a middle brown, or black for instance, you would completely change your appearance".

"Teddy, your hair has been so short and so many colors this past month, you won't even notice the change."

"My real passport shows my hair color as light brown so it's not a stretch to have darkened it. Any descriptions of me by Laurent or the Vander Riis family would describe me as being a blonde. I'll get a wig of shoulder length brown hair I can wear in a pony-tail. I have three passports I can use: Klaus Bergen and two in the name of Linus Svendsen Sr. and Jr., which just needs my photo. I'll have a passport picture taken of Linus Jr. then I'll complete the passport. Raoul was an expert at forged passports. I learned from a real artist when I first started working for him. Your passport won't need any adjustment at all. Like most women, you just changed your hair style."

After the dye-job was completed on Pelling, Ruth changed the bandages on his wrist and knee. She washed the entry and exit wounds with the disinfectant soap, patted iodine on the rapidly scabbing wounds and wrapped new gauze on both the wrist and under-side of the left knee. The bullet had entered the front right side of the knee above the joint and exited on the left side behind the knee and above the calf muscle. It had already scabbed over. After Ruth applied the clean bandages, Teddy pulled the flesh colored brace up over his knee, covering any trace of the wounds. He had Ruth pull the wrist protector over the bandage, hiding that wound. Teddy stood, flexing his injured leg by swinging it back and forth and was pleasantly surprised, feeling no pain. The wrist was another story. Whenever he made a fist, he got a painful reminder not to. Pelling figured he could now wear shorts or a bathing suit, appearing to anyone who noticed as just another tourist who went at it a bit too hard on the tennis courts.

Chapter Two
Phone Sex

"Hello Ida, honey. It's Ruth. How are you, sweetie?"

"Well, hello yourself girl. Good to hear from you. I got your fabulous parcel yesterday.

Wow! Is it my birthday or something? All this lovely money. Yummy! What did you want me to do with it?"

"It's for you, darlin'. One of my special friends wants to meet you and party with us. He sent you the ten thousand from Lisbon to entice you to come play with us. We had to skedaddle out of Lisbon and arrived here sooner than we indicated. Can you come to Bermuda sooner, like tomorrow? Teddy has a wicked leer on his face, so the sooner the better, my sweet. Book a villa at the Beach Villas, that's where we're staying. We'll move in with you when you get here. When can we expect you?"

"I can leave in the morning if I get a flight. As soon as I hang up I'll book at the Beach Villas and, with this pile of money, I won't have to bring a thing with me, just a bikini and something to travel in. Wow, I am so looking forward to this trip. Give me your phone number and I'll call right back after I make the arrangements. Incidentally, is Teddy the Teddy you've known forever?"

"Yes, doll. We are at 872-232-6506. Talk with you soon, bye now."

Ruth set the telephone back on its base as she turned toward Teddy Pelling.

"Ida knows a bit about you from our girl talk over the years. She has always wanted me to arrange a threesome with you. She's thrilled and I'll bet right this minute she's likely working herself over with one of her toys, pretending it's us, sweetie. After she gets herself off, she'll call and book a villa here, then make reservations. I bet she calls within the hour, and when she does, I'm going to have lovely phone sex with her after I have a hoot. Do you want to join us or wait until tomorrow for the real thing?"

"The phone has a speaker, right? So sure, I'll have a toke with you, then listen in, and see how it goes."

Ruth busied herself by rolling a couple of joints, lit one and had a long pull, before she got up and handed it to him. She went into the bathroom, dropped her clothes on the floor, and slipped into the terry-towel house coat before making her way back to the living room. Teddy handed the lit joint back to her as the telephone rang.

"Twenty minutes, I don't believe it. Hello?" Ruth said.

"Hi again, pussycat. All set! I'm booked on the early morning flight to Bermuda. It leaves here at 6:50 and arrives around noon. My villa number is 15. What number are you?" Ida said.

"We are in the second one down the beach from yours; number 17. So, are you getting excited lover?" Ruth asked.

"Yes, I'm getting psyched, so tell me what we will be doing together when I get there?"

"Darlin' Ida, I'm going to put us on speaker phone now so you can say hello to Teddy, actually, he's going by the name of Linus Svendsen, and is our plaything and benefactor."

"Well, finally I get to meet you Teddy or should I call you Linus? How are you? Stingy-old Ruthie has been keeping you all to herself for too long." Ida said.

"Good to meet you, as well, Ida. Call me Linus please, and I'm looking forward to your visit," Pelling said.

"Will you guys meet me at the airport or should I get there on my own? Like, take a cab, check in, then casually meet you guys on the beach?" Ida asked.

"Yes please, kitten. We'll be waiting on the beach in front of V15 around 1:00 P.M. Wear a bikini so we can both ogle that fabulous bod of yours."

"You sound real smarmy, Ruthie. Just what are you two up to right now, anyway?"

"We smoked a joint and it's starting to get to me. I'm ready to ravish you, Ida my love. I just said to Teddy, the first thing I thought you'd do after we hung up, was yourself, even before you made the bookings. But, because you called back so fast, I know you haven't had time, right?"

"Linus, you can tell Ruthie knows me all too well. And, normally I would have got out my toys, but I wanted to save all of the good stuff 'till I got there. So how about you? Describe our playmate to me over the phone. That way I can have sex with both of you. I'm sitting here on the edge of my bed in a silky shorty robe over my naked bod. I haven't smoked up, but just listening to your steamy breathing is making me all warm and fuzzy and my nipples are getting real perky," Ida said.

"And, what lovely nipples they are kitten. I'm starkers too, but wrapped up in a terry-cloth bathrobe. Our handsome fella is standing right in front of me, slowly taking off his shirt and shorts. Just wait until you see his lovely… muscles. His gotch are tented out front…yummy. Here, let me pull them down lover. I'll kiss it so you can hear. Yum! Kitty-cat, I hear you starting to purr; are you there… already?" Ruth asked.

"Yes! And, Teddy dear…I can't wait to have you everywhere possible. And I do mean everywhere!" Ida said.

"We will definitely party Ida, but I really do need to take care of Ruth right now, so, stay on the line for a bit."

Ruth spread the terry robe on the couch and got on all fours, burying her head and raising her rump to him. He knelt on his right knee and kept his injured left knee in a stiff position. Holding on to Ruth's slim waist, he moved slowly into her until she became comfortable with the intrusion.

"Teddy, I can hear your action and the sounds are absolutely intoxicating. Wow, it's like I was right there with you…oh… my …yes."

"Very close…Teddy, honey…so excited; you're…so darn fine…oh…lover. Oh, yes, there…there, ooh…Bruno…you're going to make me explode," Ruth said.

"Earth to Ruth! Earth to Ruthie! You got your cookies, Kiddo, 'cause you really lost it there, sweetie. You called him Bruno as he was getting to you."

"Uhh...yeah? Did I? Teddy, honey please, just whoa for a second...let me turn onto my back. There, let me wrap my legs around you...I need you some more."

"God Ida, you have no idea how great he really is," Ruth said.

"I'm so damned envious and I shouldn't hear anymore, so I'm going to take a bath," Ida said.

"Honest...we both can't wait until you yet here sweetie...ooh...Ida, he's...he's...again...yes...Bruno...yes."

"Okay you guys! That's it...that's all I can handle right now...I'll see you on the beach tomorrow afternoon. After my bath I'm heading straight to the airport," Ida said.

Chapter Three
Missing Her Man

A day had passed since Lieutenant Robert Bizet left for Lisbon and Marta hadn't heard from him. She finally decided to call Robert's assistant, Sergeant Alain Moline. Marta felt foolish trying to explain that his boss hadn't called. Sergeant Moline said he had been in contact with the lieutenant and the apprehension of the suspect had been unsuccessful. The lieutenant was busy interviewing air crew of the Lisbon to Bermuda flight which they think Pelling had escaped on. The sergeant didn't make apologies for his boss's inconsiderate behavior, however, he did promise to tell his boss that she had called when next he spoke with him.

After she hung up, Marta felt like a teen-ager who had spent a weekend with a lover who promised her his undying love saying he'd call, then never bothered. After a few slashing outbursts at herself for her impatient petulance, she partially convinced herself that she had called Robert's office out of concern for his welfare, not her own.

Her relationship with Robert Bizet was just a few weeks old but she had attempted to get his attention ever since they first met. She and her twin, Mathijs (Tice) witnessed the murder of the owner of the café where they were dining on a chilly Paris evening two years ago. There had been a student rally earlier that evening, which turned into an angry protest march that surged through the street where the café was located. Part of the mob leaders came into the café and demanded service. The owner could not accommodate the crush of the boisterous mob and refused to serve them, at which time one of the group drew a pistol and shot him.

The mob dispersed quickly at the sound of gunfire. The twins went to assist the fallen owner, but he was already dead.

Marta recalled how later that evening, she and Tice identified the shooter and an accomplice by looking through the known-terrorist-photo-albums at Sûreté headquarters. Detective Sergeant Robert Bizet took their eye-witness accounts and thanked them for their help. That weekend both perpetrators were arrested and the Vander Riis twins picked them out of a police line-up. Detective Bizet informed them that the men they identified were members of the ETA, the terrorist arm of the Basque movement.

Detective Bizet thanked the twins for stepping forward in this matter but felt it his duty to advise them of the possible consequences of testifying against the ETA in open court.

Marta remembered it had only taken Tice and her a short strategy session before she spoke: "Thank you for the warning, Detective, but we feel compelled to testify against this cold-blooded murderer and intend to see him punished."

At the trial they did just that. The gunman was found guilty and sentenced to death. His accomplice was given a long jail sentence. During this time Detective Bizet had a number of occasions in which he warned the twins and their widowed mother that they might be targeted for retribution by the ETA. Robert Bizet liked the twins. He admired their tenacity at the trial and took a special interest in them. Whenever the twins or their mother, Elspeth, were in Paris they would invite him to lunch. For his part, the detective would discreetly arrange to have plainclothes police follow them to provide unobserved protection.

Tice informed his sister and mother what he had learned on a lunch date with his new detective friend. Tice said he had been teasing Robert about being a no-show at many of the invitations from the Vander Riis' accusing him of being a workaholic without a life outside his job. Robert answered that he actually had a life beside his job in the recent past. He'd planned on getting married and settling down until his world was upended. Robert admitted he had become obsessed with his work after the horrific tragedy he had witnessed when his car exploded with his fiancé inside: ETA retribution for his anti-terrorism police work. Knowing this, the Vander Riis family agreed that a lesser man probably couldn't have continued in this line of work. However, Robert Bizet's resolve and strength of character allowed him to continue chronicling terrorist activity, with special emphasis on the ETA. This total dedication to his work earned him a promotion to the rank of lieutenant at the age of thirty.

Marta watched the friendship between Tice and Robert grow and, when Tice was hired by the Paris branch of Merrill Lynch and sent to New York to take his brokerage training at 1 Wall Street, they kept in touch by telephone once a week during his training. During their last call, Robert advised Tice that he had been granted the authority to recruit, train, and assemble his own anti-terrorism squad. His superiors insisted he take a holiday before he began this new project.

Tice told his family that Robert didn't know where he would go for a holiday, so he invited him to their chateau in Utrecht. Before Robert accepted he wanted to know if Elspeth or Marta would mind if he came for a visit. Marta blushed now, remembering what Tice answered. He told Robert that his mother would be away and even if Marta had other plans she would cancel them as soon as she heard he would be coming for a visit. He teased Robert and added, "I think Marta fancies you. What the hell she sees in you, I can't imagine. She will jump at the chance to fly Baker Charlie Nova to Schiphol to pick us up."

Marta set her sights on Lieutenant Robert Bizet and their relationship began on that weekend. Tice had teased her before Robert arrived saying, "You seem excited about Robert's visit. What you see in a single guy six feet tall, handsome, and passionate about his job I'll never know," Marta smiled at the memory.

She phoned her mother and had a nice long gab session. Elspeth suggested Marta get stoned or have a few too many, then go shopping the following day. After saying goodbye, she ran a hot tub. While the tub was filling, Marta poured herself a good long brandy, took a joint and matches to the bathroom. She lit a number of candles, dropped her clothes onto the floor before stepping into the swirling, tepid water. Marta stood naked looking in the surrounding mirrors at herself as she lit the joint. She put the joint into the ashtray on the edge of the tub and eased into the water. It took only two or three good pulls on the joint to get her high.

Marta let herself relax in the swirling water and imagined Robert with her. The brandy and the toke began their magic as she became very aware of her body. Marta began to caress her breasts, then, finally moved slowly toward the center of the large tub and the jet of bubbles coming from the bottom. Marta toweled off, retiring to her bed slightly drunk and very high. She revisited her pleasure until the spasms quieted and she fell asleep thinking of Robert.

Chapter Four
Styled For Bermuda

Teddy Pelling and Ruth Werner were dressed in new outfits purchased at separate shopping outings that morning. Ruth was wearing a light blue muu muu with big white flowers emblazoned on the material. She wore it off the shoulder which showed the fine lines of her neck and her new razor cut, which was dyed middle brown. She finished at the beauty salon at 9:00 A.M. and had prearranged to meet Teddy at this popular beach restaurant for breakfast. Teddy Pelling was decked out in white tank pants and white loafers. He wore a low necked orange muscle shirt. His long brown hair was done up neatly in a pony-tail. They looked at each other approvingly and after complimenting one another, Ruth said, "I wonder if Ida will recognize me. I look so different."

"You'll look the same to her in your bikini, Ruth. Besides, listening to her lusting for you last night on the telephone, has me convinced she wouldn't care if you were bald."

"Hmm...Yeah, you heard correctly. She is really sexy. Ida can turn me on and I do the same for her. My awesome muscle-bound-hunk, you are about to get a very lusty workout from both of us. I'll have her first my friend, then I want to watch you two get it on. After that, it will be a free-for-all, or should I say three-for-all!"

"Sounds like a fun plan to me!" Pelling answered.

As they were about to leave their table to pay their tab, a middle-aged, attractive, well groomed gentleman in a tan tropical suit came smiling to their table and spoke to Ruth.

"Well, well. I thought it was you, Ruth. How delightful to run into you here in Bermuda. How are you?"

Ruth was prepared for such an eventuality because she imagined she might run into one of her better clients at any time.

"How nice to see you George. George, meet my friend Linus. Linus Svendsen, George Yaro. George, make sure you call me when you arrive back in Paris."

"Yes, yes, of course. I'm staying here at the Belmonte Towers. Please call me at the Penthouse. I'll leave word at the desk that you are to be put right through to me. Now don't disappoint me, dear friend. I will be expecting your call."

"Of course I'll call. Thank you for stopping to say hello. But, we really must run. We're going to be late meeting a friend who is flying in from the States," Ruth said.

As the pony-tailed well-built young man, with a slight limp led Ruth toward the cashier's area at the entrance to the restaurant, George Yaro remained by their table watching them leave.

"I take it George is one of your select clients?" Pelling asked.

"George Yaro is a very wealthy industrialist from Argentina who has many business interests around the world. He has been a client for about five years now."

"The way he sounded, talking with you, I got the impression that he knew you would call him."

"Well, George is special, and you're right love, he knows I'll call him. After I do, Teddy, I'll definitely go and visit him. I'll bet you a large amount of money that he insists I bring you along." Ruth said.

"One of those, is he?" Pelling asked.

"George does have some quirks, that's for sure."

"Quirks?"

"When he visited me in the past he has brought nubile young ladies and sometimes a muscular young man. On his last visit he brought a young dance couple from Argentina who enjoyed performing sexually, then enthusiastically shared their exuberance with us. George has been one of my most generous benefactors, Teddy. As a matter of fact, I'd guess he is directly responsible for more than half of the money I have been able to accumulate for us."

"Is he in love with you?" asked Pelling.

"Better than that, Teddy. He's a very close friend," Ruth answered.

"Interesting!"

On the walk back to their Villa, Pelling and Ruth discussed plans to recover their millions from the numbered account in the Cayman Islands. Ruth said she would be able to determine just how much the police were interested in her by asking George to make discreet inquiries. Pelling, however, didn't like that suggestion at all.

"Ruth, I don't give a damn how good a friend he is! I've stayed alive by trusting no one," Pelling said.

"Come on Honey! You've trusted me all these years and we're still tight and very rich! Aren't we?" Ruth asked.

"Damned near cost me my life too, when you got greedy thinking Raoul would be a better bet. You will not tell George anything about me, until I check him out up close and personal," Pelling demanded.

"Have it your way my nervous friend, but George will want to check you out as well, 'up close and very personal', if I know George Yaro," Ruth said.

"So what! Even if he has the greatest connections in the bloody world, he won't find anything about Linus Svendsen," Pelling said.

"But Darling! If he does check you out and can't find anything about you, isn't that going to cast a cloud of suspicion over you?"

"That's covered! I'm working on a special project to do with the money laundering activities of terrorist organizations and I'm not at liberty to divulge any more information than that," Pelling offered.

"You continually amaze me, Teddy! Alright then, when George asks about you, and he will, I'll just say I've known you for longer than I've known him, and you do secret shit for different Governments and make limo-loads full of money doing it," Ruth replied.

"Fine! But that's all you tell him! I'm going to put my bathing suit on and walk in the ocean surf, then lie on the sand and work on my tan," Pelling said.

"Just don't lose that lovely head of hair my sweet!" Ruth said, with a smirk on her face.

"No problem. I'm only going to wade in the surf to strengthen my knee. Come join me later if you want to," Pelling said.

"It's still a couple of hours before Ida gets here. I think I'll just sack out for a while. I'll come find you on the beach when she ought to be here."

When they reached their villa, Teddy went to the bathroom, stripped, hung up his clothes and put on his bathing suit. He applied a tanning oil to his body and before he left the villa he put his money, cashier's cheques, passports plus their loose cash into a runner's belt he acquired while shopping that morning. The millions in cash in the two Gucci bags he had transferred to one bag, which was secure in the Villa office safe.

If, for whatever reason, Ruth decides to bolt, she would go empty-handed, then she would have to go through a number of hoops before she made an attempt at retrieving our millions in the Caymans. This George Yaro character worries me! Where have I heard that name? There have been plenty of opportunities for her to have contacted him. She's such a great actress, so how can I know for certain? I don't believe in coincidences. To me, they are danger signs in disguise. Ruthie is probably waiting to set up something with good ol' George as soon as I leave the villa. I'll do some checking when I get back. Right now, I'm for a little exercise and some rays!

Chapter Five
Pelling's Rules

Ruth watched her well-built friend make his way to the beach.

Wow! Is he gorgeous or what? Wait until Ida sees him...she'll get real excited...I can't wait! What in hell is he carrying a pack sack around his waist for? Ah...of course, he probably has our passports in it, along with our money. He's unbelievable! Teddy baby, do you really think I would just take off with the little money I have, get a new passport and go after the big money myself? If this is his big worry, he really is a head case! He's real uptight about George, that's for damn sure. Teddy seems to have forgotten that I know how he's earned his living. If I did have the guts to take off, he would head straight to the Caymans, lay in wait for me to appear at the Royal Bank and I'd be toast, for damn sure. No siree, I'm sticking close to you, Teddy, and taking my chances. But George, old friend, you are an angel! I'd thought about contacting you just in case, but didn't, and now here you are! I don't really think Teddy is amenable to getting it on with a guy, then again, who the hell really knows Teddy Pelling? I guess I know him better than anyone. He just turned eighteen when my brother Oscar, his high school wrestling coach, brought him to Mykonos to meet me. I was working in Paris as a financial planner and gathering a clientele of wealthy men who paid big money to sleep with me. Business was great. Oscar thought I could help Teddy with his inheritance. Poor Oscar, he was head over heels in love with Teddy and told me he planned to seduce him. Teddy was six feet tall with the muscular body of an Adonis. We got it on, big time. Oscar was insanely jealous and a rift broke out between us. Teddy decided to fix the problem. Oscar was swimming early one morning and ventured out too far and suddenly drowned. Teddy was snorkeling in the area but unable to give assistance.

So, along with the money from his parents, both suicides by drowning, Teddy was co-beneficiary with me in Oscar's estate. I looked after everything while I continued to teach Teddy how to please me sexually. Wow, was he ever a good student. Teddy ended up with almost four hundred thousand US dollars. He gave it to me to invest as I saw fit, keeping ten thousand dollars for his personal use. He then dropped a bomb shell. He was going to enlist in the French Foreign Legion as he needed special training for the work he planned to do after his five year stint. I tried to talk him into enrolling in a military school. Hell, he could afford any school, but he joined the Legion. I had dinner with him every year on his birthday and when his term was up at the age of 23 he was a larger, harder version of that eighteen year old I met in Greece. He told me he was working for a security firm and travelled the world. He would bring me a couple hundred thousand dollars two or even three times a year and has been easily my best client. He always said, or was it a warning? "I don't care what you invest in and I don't care about the return **on** the money I've given you. My only concern is the return **of** my money when I want it." I kept a large amount of our portfolio in T-Bills just in case. I must say I've done exceptionally well with our money as it's now worth over twelve million. All of it coming from "pillow talk" and in a lot of cases clients telling me to buy this or that stock. I did the transactions with four banks rather than with brokerage firms. I suspected Teddy was working on the dark side to earn that kind of money. Then when Raoul de Vascos became a client after George Yaro introduced us, it wasn't long after that Raoul told me he was an official in the ETA and Pelling worked for him. Raoul gave me a heads up whenever Teddy completed an assignment saying Teddy would be along soon with a large amount of money. Raoul knew I was looking after Teddy's money and he knew how much he had paid him over the years, but he has no idea of the total of our partnership. Raoul thinks Pelling has a couple hundred thousand in safety deposit boxes around Europe and almost a million with me. I do not talk about my clients and am always discreet. I continually ask Raoul when he will be giving me some of his money to invest. This has always changed the subject away from Teddy Pelling's money. Anyway, I think I'll go check in with George.

"Good Morning this is the Belmonte Towers."

"Good morning, my name is Ruth and I would like to speak with George Yaro please."

"Certainly, madam! Mr. Yaro is expecting your call.

"Hello George, it's Ruth calling."

"Thank you for calling, mon ami, are you and your handsome friend able to come to a private dinner party this evening?"

"Do you have other guests who will be there?"

"Not if you don't want any, mon ami."

"Hmm...George, I'd love to come, but I'm really not sure about Linus, and we have another friend joining us today from America."

"I will arrange a very private party for the four of us then, mon ami. Tell me, will your American friend like me?"

"George, you didn't even ask me whether my American friend was male or female!"

"But it does not matter, eh Cher? Please come to the penthouse at 8:00 P.M. and we will have a splendid meal served and then we can all get acquainted. Please do not refuse me!"

"I'll see if I can talk Linus and Ida into coming and I will call you again between 5 and 6 this afternoon. Oh George! I do so want to see you. I may need your help with something."

"I will expect your call then, mon ami. I am at your service, as always, and looking forward to meeting your American friend and getting to know Linus".

"Thank you George, I will call."

"You know, Cher, when I spotted you sitting there in the restaurant, I thought, what an attractive lady. What an attractive couple. Then I recognized you...but your hair is different...how lucky for me that I did. Mon ami, are you in some kind of trouble? What can I do to help?"

"Oh George, thank you! I promise to call you later today. If my friends agree to come and the evening goes well, you know what I mean, I'll tell you. Otherwise...well, I'll call you later, I promise."

"Okay! We leave it at that for now...I await your call."

Chapter Six
Beach Babes

When Ruth joined Teddy on the beach, he was talking with a very shapely young lass who couldn't have been any more than seventeen. Her bikini consisted of thongs attached to three modest sized triangles of cloth, the largest of which did its best to cover her triangle of pubic hair. Her hair was shoulder length, black, with two border braids that framed her drop-dead looks. Her eyes were bottomless, black-brown in color and far too wise for her age. She'd been in the sun enough to tan her light complexion an almond color. Ruth learned later that she had come walking up the beach, spotted Teddy sunning and just plopped her towel down next to him.

So what's new about that? Ruth asked herself. I remember how Ida and I were at that age. Only difference was, we used to hunt as a pair. It confirms my suspicions about Teddy though, who has been on a lot of beaches since we met. The ladies just come to him like bees to a blossom and the dude is so cool about it too, which makes him twice as attractive. I'll be nice to her and see if I can help him catch her in his web.

"Hey, Ruth, this is Ursula. Say Hi!"

"Nice to meet you Ursula. I love your bikini. You are a knockout!"

"Hi yourself, Ruth, Thanks. I couldn't take my eyes off you as you walked toward us. You are the sexiest lady I've seen, ever!" Ursula replied.

"You are sweet, Ursula. Do you live here or are you just vacationing?" Ruth asked.

"I was just telling Linus: I go to school in New York and am home on holiday, staying with my guardian, who lives here most of the year," Ursula said.

"I see, and how is the hunting going so far?" Ruth asked.

"Actually, this is only my second day strolling this beach, and well, I thought when I spotted Linus, it might be my lucky day. But, I guess, mmm, he's taken, right?" Ursula asked.

"Relax, Linus and I are very close friends, Ursula, and we're expecting another pal of mine to join us in the next few minutes. Linus hasn't met her yet, but I know he's anxious to do so. So, sweet thing, please don't rush away. Stay and play with us please, won't you?" Ruth asked.

"Mmm, well, if you're okay with it? I mean, are you?" Ursula wanted to know.

"Sweetie, I'd be a dunderhead if I didn't know why you stopped to talk with this gorgeous hunk. Linus likes the attention and take my word for it, he does have an awful lot to offer. So, please stay. I really mean it. You are welcome to join our party," Ruth said.

"Well, if you're sure. Wow! This is going to be a blast!" Ursula said with wide grin.

Teddy was the first to spot Ida striding through the sand toward them with very little on but a magnificent smile.

She wore a bikini much like Ursula's, but what Teddy was noticing was how much Ida looked like Ruth. Ida was lithe in figure and rather more endowed, but they could be twins.

As soon as Ida drew near, Ruth jumped to her feet, embraced her, and after they looked into each other's eyes, they kissed each other welcome. Teddy and Ursula were now up on their feet, brushing sand from their legs, and smiling at the welcome.

"Ida, meet our new friend, Ursula, and of course, you know who Linus is. Say hello!"

Ida looked puzzled, but only for a moment, as she stepped into Teddy's space, encircled his bulk to give him a welcome kiss. She stayed in close enough to feel him against her belly.

"Finally I get to meet you. You look even better than my fantasies of you. Ursula, you sweet thing, don't frown like that! Didn't they tell you how much we all like to share?" Ida said.

"Ah, yeah! Ruth explained we could all get acquainted and party together. I did hear you right, Ruth, didn't I?" Ursula asked.

Teddy answered for all by confirming how he was all for sharing.

"Ursula, we're going to Ida's villa just over there to relax, have a drink and party some. We'd really like you to join us as our guest. You're completely free to participate in our fun, or not. But, please, we'd really like you to join us. Okay?" Teddy said.

Chapter Seven
Lisbon Investigation

Lieutenant Robert Bizet, using an office in the Lisbon Police building, hung up after talking at length with Sergeant Moline at the Sûreté Headquarters in Paris. The Sergeant updated his boss with the latest reports from the Interpol Notice Program who are responsible for the transmission of International "All Points Bulletins" to and from the 176 member nations. Bizet had circulated the descriptions of Pelling/Studer and his blonde companion in the form of "APBs" in Interpol Zone #2 (which included most of the cities on the west coast of the Netherlands, Belgium, France and Spain). The response to these "all point bulletins" came directly from the Interpol Headquarters located in Lyon, France but, so far, no "sightings" had been reported.

It became evident to Lieutenant Bizet that Pelling was a man of many names and faces. The Sûreté, so far, had matched his description with two other identities: Rolf Studer and Klaus Bergen. Andre Laurent had wounded him in the left knee and the right wrist, thinking those wounds would incapacitate the terrorist until the Lisbon police arrived at his sailboat, the "Bijou" to arrest him. Not only did Laurent admit shooting Pelling, he told how he drugged him and his blonde companion. Laurent said he had tied both of them securely then added tourniquets to Pelling's wounds, hoping he wouldn't bleed to death before the authorities arrived. *So, how, in the name of Blazes was he able to escape? Robert wondered. Andre told me he was absolutely certain he left both of them "out like lights", around two AM, but when the Lisbon swat team went onboard two and a half hours later, they didn't find anybody. Just evidence of a struggle.*

However, we now have Pelling's blood type, presently being analyzed at the Lisbon police laboratory.

Lieutenant Bizet had alerted the crew of the early flight from Lisbon to Bermuda to check their passengers for a young couple, matching the description of Pelling and blonde companion. The airline sent word to the Sûreté that a suspect couple was arrested when the flight from Lisbon landed in Bermuda.

Lieutenant Robert Bizet figured the Lisbon flight, which left at 5:00 AM, would have been Pelling's best bet for escape. They had ample time to make that connection to Bermuda. The lieutenant got a negative sighting response from the Lisbon-to-New York flight which left at 7:00 A.M. and had not yet received anything positive from security at the Maritima Gare, who were checking the passengers on the three departing ferries that morning. Nothing in this case has been easy. Pelling's arrest would have been a major catch in the net set for this ETA agent. The airline dispatcher, when asking the cabin crew on the Bermuda flight to discreetly check for Pelling and his blond companion, neglected to mention that Pelling had been shot and wounded in the right wrist and the left knee.

Had the crew been told this, I'm sure they would have been able to temper their suspicions about the look-alike young couple. It occurred to the lieutenant that the crew had a number of options to observe the suspect and thereby determine if he was wounded. Not conclusive proof, mind you, but it would have avoided the embarrassment that followed. The suspects were arrested and taken from the baggage claim area in handcuffs, protesting their innocence. He thought: *Why wouldn't they? When I spoke with the Bermuda police, the first thing I asked was how bad the gunshot wounds were!* "What gunshot wounds?" *came the answer. Because no wounds were found, the shaken young couple were immediately released with an apology from the arresting officers and the airline, who quickly offered them compensation: a free open ticket to fly anywhere the airline flew. No doubt, the Sûreté will hear from the Airline about this fiasco! I checked, and my directive to the airline did indicate wounds to the left knee and right wrist. So, it's their omission!*

During his telephone conversation with his sergeant in Paris, they discussed every possible way out of Lisbon open to the fleeing Pelling and the blonde. Both policemen agreed they had covered all possibilities. Pelling had given them the slip. Lieutenant Bizet thought a third party might have come to the rescue of Pelling. If this were so, they could still be in Lisbon or they may have split up. All the Sûreté had to go on was their descriptions, given by Andre Laurent, which was confirmed by the yacht salesman in Bordeaux, France.

"Whoa, just a minute here Sergeant! Back up a bit. If he did get on that Bermuda flight, he would have had to have assistance boarding and walking because of the gunshot wounds, especially to the left knee. He could have been in disguise of some sort. Damn it!" Bizet said,

"Sergeant I'd like you to go back over the passenger list on that Lisbon to Bermuda flight. This time, make a note of all the passengers who needed assistance pre-boarding at Lisbon and deplaning in Bermuda. Get their passport particulars, if possible, or as much info as you can. Would you please, also, get the names and addresses and schedules of the air crew on that flight and find out when they are due back here? I'd like to interview them. Get back to me with this information ASAP Sergeant, will you please? One more item: Please send the paperwork to the Lisbon Special Squad attention Detective Juarez and claim the 50 foot Beneteau sailboat "Bijou" that is tied up at slip 11 at the Lisbon Marina by the Maritima Gare. Claim it for the Paris Sûreté as confiscated property used in a terrorist operation."

"Okay Lieutenant, I'll get right to it...anything else?"

"No, that's it for now Sergeant"

The lieutenant walked out the front of the Police Building and requested a ride back to the marina where the "Bijou" and the "SeaOx" were tied up. Once there, he asked the constable assigned to him to wait for him while he went into the marina offices and spoke with the staff.

He was back within the hour finding his driver fast asleep in the front seat. He rapped hard on the passenger side window, rousing the constable, who reached over and opened the passenger's door.

"Please drop me off at the Harborside Hotel, I think I'll call it a night, constable."

Once inside his hotel room the lieutenant poured himself a drink of scotch and soda over ice. Sitting on the side of the bed he took a good swig from the drink and reached for the telephone.

"Ah... Marta, I'm so glad I caught you at home. I miss you very much, but I can't say how long this investigation is going to take here. It will depend on what Sergeant Moline turns up for me at that end. What have you been up to?"

"Oh, not very much! A little shopping. We have only been apart a few days and I miss you terribly, Robert. Can I fly myself to Lisbon or should I just sit and twiddle my thumbs like some policeman's wife? My God, that sounded awful shrewish. I'm sorry, I'll be patient and wait until you get back, handsome. Darn it, I want to see you, so bad."

"As soon as I hear from Sergeant Moline and I know more, I'll call you back immediately and let you know."

"Are you getting closer to Pelling, Robert?"

"He appears to have disappeared off the face of the earth, but only because I think we are looking for a description of someone who has changed his appearance and is using another passport. The sergeant is checking this possibility. When you and I hang up, I'm going to call our office to see what he's turned up."

"Alright then Robert, I won't keep you. I'm going to stay right here at mother's apartment until you return. Good Luck! Be careful and keep in touch." Marta said, and hung up the phone.

Robert discarded his shirt and tie and drank the last of his scotch. His thoughts about taking a refreshing shower were interrupted by the ringing telephone.

"Lieutenant, its Sergeant Moline. I called the airline and they faxed me a list of the crew and the passengers. The crew returns to Lisbon tomorrow morning. On the passenger list, there is an asterisk beside four names who required assistance pre-boarding Flight 299 leaving Lisbon and deplaning in Bermuda. The flight attendants doing this task were also responsible in picking out the suspect couple who were arrested and later released. The names of the four passengers requiring assistance are listed along with their ailments. I'm afraid none of these passengers match the description of Pelling, sir, but I made arrangements with the airline for you to meet with the two flight attendants when they land tomorrow at 9:15AM."

"Thank you for this Sergeant. Please fax that information to my office here at the police barracks."

Chapter Eight
New Playmates

Sergeant Alain Moline left Orly airport on the afternoon flight to Bermuda, shortly after Lieutenant Bizet telephoned to explain his suspicions of the elderly man named Argus Trask who required wheelchair assistance pre-boarding and deplaning the Lisbon to Bermuda flight.

The sergeant's orders were simple: Trace the old man and his niece and interview them to confirm that they were who their passports said they were.

Lieutenant Bizet flew back to Paris immediately after his investigation was completed in Lisbon. Bizet settled himself in his window seat and was thankful no one occupied the other two seats in his row. He closed his eyes and reflected on the interview with the two flight attendants he interviewed. One of them was an outrageous flirt. Bizet thought: *That old adage must be true: When you are in love it shows and the ladies come hitting on you from all directions.* He couldn't wait to see Marta again. When his plane landed at Orly at the dinner hour she was there to meet him.

※ ※ ※

Pelling thought to himself: *That was indeed the most intense grouping I've experienced. The stunning school girl, Ursula, plops her towel down beside me on the beach and introduces herself. Before I can figure out how to get her back to our Villa, along comes Ruth and invites her into our party. Almost made me forget about Ida, thinking about playing with Ruth and tasty Ms Ursula. Almost, that is, until Ida comes strolling up. Now I'm really*

26

intrigued. Ida and Ruth look so much alike, they could be twins. Ida and Ruth kiss hello and Ruth introduces Ursula who is pouting and looking like a third wheel. Ida closes in on me, I get a hug and a midsection probe from her as she whispers 'wonders to come' in my ear. Ida turns to Ursula and assures her that she is welcome to join our party. Ruth and Ida walk Ursula toward Ida's villa and I follow. Now I've been involved in some terrific sexual encounters, but this one promised to be unforgettable. Ida and Ursula both wore thongs and Ruth a skimpy bikini and, as we arrived at the Villa, all I could think about was adding Ida and Ursula to my list of conquests.

After Ida made us drinks and Ursula rolled a few joints, we all smoked up, after that it didn't take long before bathing suits came off and we all got busy.

Ursula, while high, lost all inhibitions and teased me into a coupling and implored me to be gentle as she was very new at sexual activity. While we were enjoying each other, Ruth and Ida were renewing their friendship vigorously remembering each other. Ruth came over to console the badly rattled Ursula and took her over to her couch while Ida attacked me. Wow! I didn't think there was anyone as fine as Ruth but...Ida is almost too much of a good thing: more generously endowed than Ruth but otherwise very similar. Ida got very personal about what we were doing to each other and told me what she liked and how she liked it. We got totally involved giving each other pleasure. What a party. I looked upon this threesome as a lusty encounter whereby I got all the goodies available. Not the case, according to Ruth, who told me later that Ida wanted an encore and Ursula said that it was the most intense sex she's had so far experienced. Great, everybody got cookies...later, Ida and Ruth both explained it this way: 'Teddy, the party started with the sexual anticipation so thick you could slice it with a knife. Like a wolf, you are looking at us lambs licking your chops and not realizing that we are looking at you like a gorgeous hunk of meat that we are about to feast on.'

Now, you gotta love a win-win situation like that, I say.

Immediately after the party they all showered together, washing and toweling away the ammonia-like scent of their lusty sex play. Teddy returned abruptly to the real world when he was dry and listened to Ruth relay the invitation to dinner at George Yaro's penthouse. A warning flag went up in the back of his head immediately, putting him on alert. Ruth explained to Ursula and Ida just who George Yaro was. He was her most important client, a very wealthy business man from Argentina who had been a regular of her 'Escort Business' for almost five years.

Ursula was the first to speak.

"You guys are just unreal and I really hope to see lots more of you, for sure. I have to get home and check in with my guardian. I'm real sorry, but I'll be back on the beach tomorrow, for sure."

"What do you want to do Linus?" Ida asked.

"I was planning on keeping a low profile, but, if you both want to go, I'll tag along."

"Good! I'll call George to confirm we'll join him for dinner at his Penthouse. He'll be so pleased."

Hmm, was all the response Linus could muster.

Ursula refused a ride home, preferring to walk back along the beach to where she'd parked her guardian's car. Linus said he was off to stretch his legs, after which he was going back to their villa to change for dinner.

"Now handsome, don't you go getting picked up by any more sexy ladies. We have a long interesting night ahead of us."

Pelling ducked quietly out of Ida's villa and saw Ursula walking along the water's edge. He walked quickly toward the villa he shared with Ruth, then kept on going, staying in the shelter of the shrubbery along the walk path. Teddy Pelling didn't believe in coincidence and wanted to see just where Ursula was heading.

She left the beach a few hundred yards from their villa and got into a Mercedes 380 sports car. Teddy made a mental note of the license plate but didn't know quite what he'd do with the information.

Pelling thought: *This whole bloody day was one big coincidence including an orgy of bacchanalian excess.* He had no problem with Ida and her planned visit, however, the sexy, very willing Ursula was another matter. A bored, attractive, horny youngster out for a sexual adventure? Maybe, but Teddy was suspicious. If she was a plant, who the hell planted her? The only candidates were Ida and George. Teddy was on double alert as he walked back to Villa number #17, the gears in his survival mechanism grinding in his ears.

Chapter Nine
Bermuda Investigation

Sergeant Alain Moline thought to himself: *Now, this is more like it. This is what I call interesting duty. Just look at the color of that water! I might even get a chance to get some sun while I'm here. Got to keep focused on the job at hand, though! Don't want to disappoint the lieutenant.*

The airliner levelled off, floated momentarily above the runway before touching down on the tarmac with only a faint objection from the tires, Sergeant Moline wondered at the amazing task the wheels of a jet airliner performed at touchdown. They went from full-stop to top speed in seconds, carrying huge tonnage, only to be braked to a full stop in a few hundred feet further on down the runway. One would think that blowouts on landings would be a regular occurrence. Not so. They had happened, but only rarely.

It was seven o'clock Bermuda time and he had much to do. The limited information the lieutenant obtained from the two flight attendants in Lisbon wasn't much to go on, but it did provide him a place to start. His first stop was the limo-service that the wheelchair-bound Argus Trask and his niece hired at the airport. After that, the sergeant planned to check into his hotel and change into lighter weight clothes. He was very fit, but the humidity was making him perspire and feel uncomfortable. He estimated he would be able to get the answers to the lieutenant's questions in two days. He could be able to be back in Paris this Thursday. After picking up his bag at the luggage reptile he made his way to the rental car area.

* * *

Ava Haas noticed Andre Laurent was more comfortable now that they were sailing the SeaOx on their way back to Bordeaux. She had the wheel at the steering position in the pilot house. The SeaOx was making a steady six knots under full sail. At this rate, she estimated they would enter the Bay of Biscay ahead of their estimated arrival time. Andre was below making their evening meal. Ava was concentrating on her mental navigation when she caught a whiff of the smells wafting up the stairwell. *What is he preparing, I wonder? I can't place it but the aroma is marvelous!*

Ava was relieved that they were sailing again. That stuff back at the Lisbon marina had concerned her, to say the least. *Andre could have got me killed as well. Andre the gentle sailor has, on two occasions now, become one truly scary guy himself. After he told me how he shot the guy who hijacked the SeaOx, I thought: Good Grief man! You're going to spend time in prison. So what, that could leave me with the SeaOx because he'd, no doubt, have to sell her to pay the lawyers. Andre said he had to incapacitate Pelling until the police came to arrest him. Andre said he didn't think twice about shooting him because he'd promised himself, if he ever met up with him again, he would shoot the bastard first and ask questions afterward. Macho talk. It was just pay-back, I guess, but then he said it was all he could do to restrain himself from killing Pelling. Did he really mean what I heard him say? That's when I realized Andre must still be haunted by what Pelling did to him. Andre told me, after what happened to him, that he could understand how a woman felt after she had been raped. He supposed a rape victim could learn to overcome the violation by confronting it and dealing with it, but in his case, he could only deal with what he could piece together from his drugged memory. He was left to imagine what else had been done to him. If Pelling tries to find the SeaOx now, he'll have to chance the open ocean. I believe this boat won't be safe until Pelling is dead. Lieutenant Bizet thinks the Sûreté are getting closer to an arrest and now this new venture of Andre's into the life of a wine maker seems a strange turn for a sailor to take. Why he wants to be a grape farmer I don't know, but I'm not in favor of anything that ties him down and takes us away from this boat and sailing.*

The subliminal thought she had had on other occasions flashed in her mind at that moment: *I see myself sailing alone on this marvelous sailboat. Now, I wonder, is Andre really a soul-mate? I love the sea and realize I must have been born pelagic.* Ava came abruptly out of her reverie when she heard Andre call to her:

"Ava, do a 360. Check for traffic. Put her on Auto, and come for dinner, please."

Chapter Ten
Marta and The lieutenant

Marta did not care that Robert asked his assistant, Sergeant Moline, to call him at her mother's apartment. She was glad to have any time with him that he could manage and encouraged him to conduct his work in her sumptuous surroundings. She knew she must let him decide. Sometimes he would leave abruptly for his office in order to check something to do with what he was working on. She tried to be of some help to him but she realized his way was that of a very diligent loner. He told her often how he liked to be in her company, but she suspected she was a distraction to him and his work. She wanted him close but she put her selfish interests aside, suggesting he do whatever was necessary to capture her mother's kidnapper. She realized, as well, none of her family was safe until this frightening terrorist was caught. She listened intently to Robert while he brought her up to date on the case. He had taken a long warm shower to wash away the effects of the flight-lag from Lisbon. Marta joined him in the shower after her desire to be close to him got the better of her good intentions. Later, she ordered their dinner brought in from their favorite cafe.

Marta told Robert of her shopping spree and a local flight she took just for the sake of flying again in her Lake amphibian. She walked around in front of him in an animated manner, which she knew he liked. Robert cocked his head to one side, listened, watched and smiled at her recital. He loved the way she moved. Watching her walk away always captivated him as he fixated on her cute behind. Robert encouraged her by asking her questions, which she answered in her delightful way. Marta could have been a wonderful actor as she was such a brilliant mimic.

"Tice and I would do Monty Python skits until we would crack each other up. Mother encouraged us and tried in vain not to laugh, but most of the time we would get to her. So you see, we got rather good at these little skits. Tice and I did one impromptu skit in drama class and our coach stuck it in a review we did. We were darn good at impromptu stuff by the time we got to college when we kind of let it cool, but we'd occasionally perform the odd skit at parties for our friends. So, now you know you're not hanging out with just another pretty face, but rather, a lady of some artistic accomplishment," Marta explained.

"I am a lucky guy to have such an intelligent accomplished and lovely young lady as a special friend. Still, it is hard for me to get past your pretty face and the remarkable package you come in. Please don't think me a dullard when you catch me staring at you. I'm just captivated by you," Robert said.

"What a sweet thing to say, but then again, you are a trained policeman with exceptional powers of observation." She smiled at him over her shoulder as she sashayed out of the room, swinging her behind in an exaggerated manner.

* * *

At ten o'clock that evening the sergeant called from Bermuda with his report.

"Something's not right here, Lieutenant. I've traced Argus Trask to a beach Hotel. He paid cash when he registered there with his niece and then immediately booked passage on a freighter bound for Charleston, South Carolina, which left early the following morning. Strangely, nobody in the hotel saw them leave for the ship."

"Very strange indeed, sergeant did you inquire at the freighter office about them?"

"Yes, I did, Sir! I was told a courier delivered the fare in cash for their tickets, which they issued and sent back to the passengers at the Hotel with the same courier. This is the part that doesn't add up, lieutenant: They never showed up for the sailing."

"Sounds like they wanted people to believe they left on the freighter doesn't it?"

"Yes sir, it does. When I asked, "Did Argus Trask and Anna Werner book passage on one of their ships?" the clerk looked it up and confirmed they had. I had to really probe to get the information from him that they never did get on the boat."

"If my hunch is correct Sergeant, our Argus Trask will have vanished along with his niece Anna Werner. The courier of the cash for tickets will be your next call, Sergeant. My guess is the courier picked up the cash at the hotel desk and returned the tickets to the same hotel and that's where the trail will end. Check it out first thing in the morning and call me back, will you please? Do you have a copy of the description of Pelling and his blonde companion with you?"

"Yes Sir, I do!"

"Good! Take it with you and get a comparison of the redheaded niece and Pelling's blonde accomplice from the courier and limo driver as well as the hotel clerks who checked them in. See if they think they could be the same people. Then, I want you to pay a visit to the Bermuda police headquarters and ask them to circulate a description of Pelling and the blonde.

Even if Pelling and Anna Werner are our suspects, they could be long gone. However, my hunch is he's still on that island somewhere, healing his wounds."

"Anything else sir?"

"That's all for now Sergeant, you've accomplished a great deal so far. Good work! I really think we're on to him now!"

"Please call me at the office and give me the number of a fax where I can send you information."

"Yes Sir! Goodnight sir!

Chapter Eleven
George Yaro's Connections

When the call came into George Yaro's penthouse apartment at the Belmonte Towers, he had been reading a report faxed from ETA headquarters in Bilbao. It contained instructions to be on the lookout for agent Pelling (AKA Corporal) and his blonde companion who disappeared from their yacht "Bijou" located at a Lisbon marina. The instructions came from Yaro's contact in the ETA, Esau Navarra. George Yaro was asked to make inquiries and to check out the passengers who boarded Flight 299 in Lisbon bound for Bermuda. The descriptions he was given of the elderly Argus Trask and R. Anna Werner couldn't be Linus and his very good friend, Ruth as Trask was old and Linus Svendsen was young.

George said to himself: *Sheer luck to have come across Ruth, my dear friend, having breakfast at that popular beach restaurant. And in the company of such a spectacular looking fellow.*

George was delighted Ruth was here in Bermuda. He expressed his pleasure in an outward display of affection as he was watched with aloof patience by her companion, whom she introduced as Linus Svendsen. George, going on about finding her so far from Paris, was miffed when he wasn't asked by either Ruth or Linus to sit with them. In fact Ruth had, abruptly, ended the reunion saying they were late for a date with another friend, who just flew in from the States. As Ruth and Linus made their way to the exit, it suddenly occurred to George how the physical description of Pelling matched Linus and how Ruth could easily fit the profile of the blonde companion. It was her strange hairstyle acquired just this morning plus the slight limp of Linus that got George thinking.

He remembered the first time he met Ruth Meikle in Paris. He was taken to her apartment by a mutual business acquaintance, Pierre Turrin, a Merrill Lynch stock broker he had dealt with on occasion. Pierre suggested he meet his young lady friend who was starting her own financial planning business and seeking new clients with money to invest or spend on her escort business. George remembered he had been charmed by the gorgeous young lady and left the next morning sexually satisfied and fifty five hundred dollars lighter. He deposited five thousand into his account with her and paid her fee of five hundred dollars for the sleep over. On his very next visit one month later they had a very in depth conversation about her business plan. He convinced Ruth to charge one thousand for her sexual favors and to buy a certain stock with the money in his account and to absolutely purchase some for herself. That was the beginning of their friendship. Ruth's fee was now twenty five hundred per night and her personal fortune was in the millions earned mostly with his help. Ruth never divulged the total or that Teddy Pelling was her partner. George had always presented himself to her as an industrialist from a wealthy Argentina family. He was wealthy but got so working as a trusted accountant of the ETA, the Basque terrorist organization. George was miffed at Ruth for being so rudely dismissed and wondered if she really would call him.

* * *

Back at his penthouse, George turned his attention to the call from Esau Navarra who had issued instructions to all ETA agents and contacts to search for agent Pelling, who was responsible for turning Navarra's nephew, Raoul de Vascos, over to the Sûreté.

A five million dollar bounty was placed by Tio Esau on both Pelling and the blonde call girl, Ruth Meikle. His thoughts were interrupted when his phone rang.

"Hello George, it's Ursula. I made contact with them. I picked him up on the beach. The target, Pelling, his friend Ruth and her friend Ida asked me to party with them at Ida's Villa on the beach."

"You can tell me all about it later tonight. What injuries does Linus have?" George asked.

"He has a bandage on his left knee covered by a pull-on tensor knee brace. His right wrist has a similar tensor sleeve covering a bandage. Too much tennis he said. Neither of these injuries slowed him down one bit in the sexual department. Actually George, the guy is just short of spectacular. Thank you very much for this assignment. He's using the name Linus Svendsen, she is R. Anna Werner and Ida's last name is Tesh. They asked me to accompany them to your dinner party tonight, but I declined, saying I had to report in and have dinner with my guardian. I passed for 17, George. It was apparent they thought they were ravishing a tender, but very horny schoolgirl. Your friend Ruth is an especially talented lover as I'm sure you are aware. We are supposed to hook up on the beach again tomorrow. What do you want me to do now?"

"This is terrific work, Ursula! I want you to come here to the Penthouse at 1:00 am, but call first to make sure they have left. We have to play this just right, little one. There is a lot of money at stake. They are believed to have millions stashed somewhere. The ETA has put a bounty on them and we're going to collect. We want to do everything we can to recover his money first, then collect the reward money. If, in fact, they are our suspects, Ruth's friend Linus is extremely dangerous," George cautioned.

* * *

The dinner party at the Penthouse floor of the Belmonte Towers hosted by George Yaro didn't go as he had anticipated. He envisioned a lively atmosphere, with his two chefs and two servers attending to him and his three guests, making sure their glasses were topped up with fine wine and everyone had all they wanted of the Chateau Briand, after which, he assumed they would pair off or play in a group, just like he had done on many previous occasions when he visited Ruth. Instead, there was tension in the air. Too many questions came from his three guests, especially Linus.

"You flew from Paris to Bermuda nonstop, you said. How long did it take you?" Pelling asked.

"Four hours and twenty minutes. Takeoff to landing," George answered.

"What is the range of your jet?" Pelling asked.

"About six thousand kilometers at cruising speed," George said.

"I have my own jet license and I do fly, but usually I leave that to my pilot. He was with the Argentine air force before he came to me," George said

Ruth asked George where he planned to fly next from Bermuda.

"Well, my business here is completed and now I'm looking for some fun. Then I guess, back to Buenos Aries for a short stay then back to Paris. Why do you ask? Do you have a suggestion about the fun?"

"Yes, actually I do, George!"

"Wonderful! What shall we do?"

"Linus is still undercover and basically in hiding for another three weeks. We would like to fly to the Cayman Islands where I have a little nest egg stashed. We will pay for the cost of the flight, if you could be coaxed into taking us there, George?"

"Of course we can go. Forget about paying because this is a pleasure for me to do. Will we all go then? Ida as well?" George asked.

"Yes, Ida will join us? Right Ida?" Ruth asked.

"I have never been to the Caymans. Flying there in a private jet makes me feel like a celebrity," Ida said.

"I will need your passports by noon tomorrow, so we can get all the necessary paperwork out of the way quickly. We could be ready to leave at 4:00PM, if this is satisfactory." The three guests turned to one another, and then all nodded their agreement.

"Good! We will have our evening meal in the air. You have made me very happy including me in your fun. Ah, we will have a great party, no? Can you accompany me to Argentina for a short stay before leaving for France, or would you like to come straight back to France from the Caymans?" George asked.

"Can we just take it a step at a time, George? We can decide in the Caymans what our next destination is. Is this Okay?" asked Linus.

"Of course, of course! I'll fly you wherever you decide after the Caymans."

Pelling excused himself and went to the bathroom. He washed his face with cold water and looked at his reflection in the mirror, thinking: *If anyone could make a wish for the fastest, safest, easiest and least expensive way to get us to our money in the Caymans, this guy would be the answer.*

This is too fucking easy! Too accommodating! Alarm bells were clanging in his head. *The passports won't be a problem, unless R. Anna Werner is on some sort of "hold for questioning" list. Paranoia?* Definitely not! Just his survival instincts clicking in. *If and when we get in the air, I'll feel more in control. I can't really make up my mind who George fancies more: me, Ida,Ruth or all of the above. Probably me and Ida from what Ruth told me about him. I didn't get a satisfactory answer to my questions about why he was here in Bermuda, though. Real Estate business, was all the answer he gave, no particulars whatsoever. The guy's a master at changing the subject and he always changes it to topics of a sexual nature. Ida is in pig-shit heaven, up dancing with him again. Dancing? More like upright sex. Can't get over how much she and Ruth look alike. Like twins, except Ida has those exceptional tits. Never thought I'd ever see much better than Ruthie, but Ida is a sculptor's dream and just awesome when she got her cookies during anal sex. She then insisted we have an encore, maybe tonight, but right now she has her sights on George. Perhaps he's just what Ruth says he is: very rich, willing and able to party at a moment's notice, especially with new partners, regardless of gender. According to Ruth, it doesn't matter to George.*

Chapter Twelve
Exercise Can Get You Killed

Sergeant Alain Moline was up early for his first morning in Bermuda. He had been to the limousine service again and back to the beach Hotel. Both the driver of the limo, who drove the elderly Argus Trask and his red-headed niece, and the Hotel check-in clerk initially said, "No way these descriptions match the old guy or his niece." However, after further consideration, the check-in clerk said, "But, yeah, put a blonde wig on the red-head and it could be the same woman. Their description is basically the same, but not the elderly dude. If he's a young guy, all I can say is, give him an Oscar 'cause he's one hell-of-an actor."

At his next stop at Bermuda Constabulary headquarters, he was amused to see traditional "London Bobbies" everywhere. Sergeant Moline was shown all the courtesy due a fellow law enforcement officer. The sergeant heard his request to post a description of both Argus Trask and R. Anna Werner, both wanted for questioning, as well as a description of Pelling and his blonde companion who were also wanted for questioning by the Paris Sûreté's Anti-Terrorism Squad. After their meeting was over, Sergeant Moline went back to his Hotel, got into bathing trunks and set out for a long run on the beach.

Immediately after the Bermuda police sergeant finished with Sergeant Moline, he completed the necessary paperwork to comply with the request. When he finished, he picked up the telephone and dialed a number which rang in George Yaro's penthouse apartment.

"Thought you would like to know a Sergeant Moline from the Paris Sûreté just paid me a visit and asked me to circulate the descriptions of an

Argus Trask and his niece, a redheaded looker, name of R. Anna Werner. Also, I'm to post an all-points bulletin from the Sûreté with the description of a blonde muscular young guy name of Teddy Pelling, suspected of terrorist activities, presently using a passport in the name of Rolf Studer. I thought they might be the same two you asked me to be on the lookout for. I just typed up the paper work moments ago. I'll fax it over to you."

"Thank you sergeant. Did our visitor say where he was staying?" George asked.

"Yes sir! He's at the Villas on the Beach. He said he would be leaving for Paris tomorrow."

"Thank you for this," George said and hung up.

* * *

Lieutenant Robert Bizet was at his desk at Paris Sûreté headquarters sorting through his mail when he came across an official Sûreté envelope. These envelopes most often contained good news: pay cheques, promotions, etc. but, before he opened it, he wondered if it could be approval of his proposal to operate his Anti-Terrorism Squad funded mostly by donations from wealthy citizens. He held the letter and tapped it on his desk while remembering the gathering at the Vander Riis Chateau in Utrecht held shortly after Tice's guest Sylvie Bern was shot and injured. He recalled that weekend when he was Tice's guest at the Chateau and how Tice's twin sister, Marta had come on to him. Tice had met and invited flight attendant Sylvie Bern to stay at the Chateau during her lay over. Marta had planned a skeet shooting session for him that weekend, much to his surprise and delight. Both he and Tice had a terrific first day with their partners and looked eagerly toward the rest of their time together.

They were all shocked to hear about the call from Elspeth at her Paris apartment to Tice saying she was taken hostage by the ETA who demanded a million guilders ransom. If it was not paid promptly she would be killed and the twins would follow her to her grave.

Eslpeth said she couriered her cheque for that amount payable to Tice who was to take it to their bank in Amsterdam and cash it for US dollars: about four hundred and thirty thousand. Tice was to wait for her instructions before he left for the bank and was to be driven there by Henk

Veldhoen in their Rolls. Robert organized a game plan at the Chateau while awaiting the arrival of the cheque and Elspeth's instructions. Eslpeth had insisted that Tice not call the authorities and emphasized that she would be turned loose unharmed if the money was paid.

Robert suggested they not alert the Chateau staff just yet and had Tice set up a recorder on the telephone. He advised everyone to stay close to the Chateau until Elspeth called with further instructions. While discussing how Elspeth could have been kidnapped, Marta offered an explanation. She recalled asking her mother if she could fly her to Amsterdam to connect with her Paris flight. Elspeth had refused saying Henk Veldhoen would drive her. Marta had detected her mother was often distracted but very cheerful in the past weeks and asked if she was going to meet a man in Paris. She said her mother blushed but said it was too soon to elaborate on who she was going to meet. Marta said obviously the guy turned out to be her kidnapper. Tice added that she seemed pissed off more than frightened obviously because she knew the guy and knew she would be released unharmed when the money was paid. So they waited.

When Elspeth called days later, she gave Tice instructions to cash the cheque for the US dollar equivalent. He was to go directly to their bank manager in Amsterdam who had the dollar amount waiting to be exchanged for the cheque. Elspeth had called Dirk Visser the manager and arranged the exchange. From the bank, Tice was to have Henk drive him to the Schiphol airport and park in visitor parking. Someone would bring Elspeth in exchange for the money.

Robert suggested that while they would not directly interfere in the ransom delivery they could at least observe it. When the Rolls left the Chateau for the bank in Amsterdam, Marta took off in her Lake A-4 amphibian with Robert in the passenger seat with a pair of binoculars. She followed the Rolls at five thousand feet keeping it in view. She flew circles while it dropped Tice off at the bank and picked it up again heading for the airport. She flew a grid so as not to be seen to be buzzing the Rolls and on her last pass Robert noticed the Rolls pulled off the highway and a motorcycle cop gunning away from it with Tice's briefcase on his handlebars. Marta gained altitude while Robert kept the motorcycle in view as it stopped on a side road by a van. The cop rolled the bike into the van on a plank and headed toward the coast. Marta followed at a higher altitude until the van headed into the road leading to a marina. Marta had landed here many times and radioed for landing instructions. The cop exited the van dressed in overalls, carried the briefcase down the jetty and climbed aboard a pilot house sailboat. Robert told Marta he had been alerted to a missing 44 foot Hans Christian Pilot House sailboat named the SeaOx and the likelihood that the boat and owner, Andre Laurent, were hijacked. When they landed, Marta and the lieutenant went to the marina office and inquired about this particular boat. It was the SeaOx captained by a Teddy Pelling. There were no passengers aboard. While they were questioning the marina manager about what Pelling looked like, he said they had just missed him as he walked by the office with a lady who looked as if she had too much to drink. Lieutenant Robert Bizet showed his credentials and demanded they board the SeaOx. Once onboard, they released a groggy individual tied to the forward berth and found Tice's suitcase containing the ransom money as well as a large brown envelope containing over a hundred thousand dollars and a statement showing a Merrill Lynch cheque for the proceeds of a T-Bill account in the name of Andre Laurent. The boat's log listed the owner as Andre Laurent and showed an entry whereby the ownership had been changed to Teddy Pelling. They took this evidence and Andre Laurent with them after the lieutenant arranged with the local police to have the boat guarded until further notice. Pelling was to be taken into custody if he returned.

Pelling must have seen the guards at the SeaOx after he returned from leaving Elspeth at a booth in a restaurant at the Schiphol airport. She was in a similar state as Andre Laurent, both having been recently drugged. He had called the Chateau and advised where Elspeth could be picked up. Pelling figured Laurent had somehow got free and alerted the police. He chided himself for being so arrogant at not being caught and leaving the money. Laurent was gone and obviously so was the money. Pelling decided he would get Elspeth's attention and more money by killing one of her children. He would put the fear back in her and let her know he kept his promise. He ditched the van and headed to the Chateau on the motorcycle.

When Marta and Robert arrived back at the Chateau with a bewildered Andre Laurent, the family doctor was waiting to examine him. Tice arrived shortly after with his mother in tow. She too would be examined by the doctor.

Robert Bizet remembered the Chateau being a busy place at that time. Even though Andre Laurent had identification on him, nobody connected him with Elspeth. However, the following morning when Elspeth appeared, albeit a bit foggy, she told Robert, Marta, Tice and Sylvie what had happened since she left for Paris to rendezvous with her new love, Andre Laurent.

As she was telling her story, Andre came down the stairway and into the room. When he saw Elspeth he went to her and they hugged both with tears streaming down their faces. Andre said he was relieved she was alive and safe. He asked for water and sat to listen to the rest of Elspeth's story:

She had been looking forward to their rendezvous and was nervously cleaning and primping when the call came. It was Andre who said he would be there in thirty minutes. When her phone rang again, the caller said it was Andre and she buzzed him in. When she heard the elevator stop at her floor and then the knock at her door, she opened the door which was pushed in on her by a brute who pinned her against the wall with a choke hold with his left hand while he held a typed note in front of her face. She was too terrified to read it so he hauled her down the hallway to her bedroom sat her on the side of the bed and let her read it.

She now opened her purse, found the note and read it to the group.

> My Dear Elspeth:
>
> I have sent my partner in my place. His purpose in life is twofold: he likes accumulating large sums of money and satisfying his deviant sexual appetite. I have told him of your abilities under the covers, and while he is anxious to sample you, he will restrain himself if you will follow instructions and arrange to give us the sum of one million guilders in US dollars. About four hundred and thirty five thousand. We suggest you call your home and tell either your son or daughter you have been taken hostage by the Basque ETA and that they mean to kill you if their

ransom is not paid. You will tell them that your personal cheque for one million guilders will arrive by courier tomorrow morning and you will call with further instructions. Either your son or daughter is to be driven to the bank by your driver in your Rolls Royce but they are not to leave until you give them final instructions on where to deliver the money. Impress upon them that if they contact the authorities you will be executed and the ETA will see to it that both of them follow you to the grave.

Andre

Elspeth looked at Andre as she read. His mouth was gaped open and he had an incredulous look on his face while he shook his head side to side. Elspeth explained how the note had 'kicked her in the stomach'. She was shocked and then infuriated at Andre's treachery. She continued by saying she was taken on a car ride and injected with something on the way. She woke up on a sailboat dressed in bra and panties, was given her other clothes and taken to the salon area where she was instructed to call Tice and read him the ransom delivery instructions. She was given something to eat and drugged again and came to in the airport restaurant.

She then told the group that she did not believe that her Andre had written the note nor did she believe he was involved in any way and was actually a victim himself. She and the group then heard Andre's story who was kidnapped and held hostage aboard the SeaOx and continually drugged. He was forced to have the SeaOx transferred to Pelling and forced at knifepoint to call his broker Pierre Turrin to have him cash his T-Bill account and say he and the new owner of the SeaOx would pick up the cheque that morning.

He did tell Elspeth he felt absolutely responsible for her kidnapping because Pelling had found the Polaroid pictures they had taken during their initial get-together at her apartment. Andre was in a terrible place and everything seemed to incriminate him. He went back to his room to sleep. When he woke in the morning, Sylvie Bern had been shot and wounded while playing tennis with Tice on the court beside the Chateau. The staff and family doctor were busy attending to her.

Pelling called the Chateau and spoke with Elspeth saying the ransom would now be one million dollars US and to have it come to the Chateau. He said he would call and tell her how to deliver it to him. He asked did he kill her daughter or did he just wound her? Elspeth said she was badly wounded and she would do as he demanded.

Robert was remembering these events and began to add up Pelling's body count since he came into Elspeth and Andre's lives: The dead highway motorcycle policeman found naked in a ditch. Pelling needed his uniform and motorcycle. Next was the UPS delivery truck lady who was shot and killed after she picked up the suitcase with the new million dollar ransom from the Chateau. Pelling was intentionally stalled in his rental sport car at the entrance to the main highway when the UPS truck pulled up behind him. He shot the lady driver in the face and took the suitcase containing the ransom. Robert wondered aloud: "And how many others we don't know about?"

Robert turned his attention to the official envelope and slit it open. Then, instead of reading it, his mind took him back again to that party at the Vander Riis Chateau:

Elspeth Vander Riis made a rather startling announcement to the three guests - Andre Laurent, myself and Sylvie Bern. Elspeth said she had paid the latest ransom demand of one million US dollars to Pelling and included a note which promised him she would not be a party to his capture and, if he was captured, it wouldn't be because of any help she had given the authorities. She did promise him that, if he ever contacted any of her family again or brought harm to any of us, that she would put a bounty of considerable millions on his head and she would make sure that the newspapers and magazines of the world ran his description continuously. She told us she felt paying Pelling off was what she had to do to keep a bargain she made with him to spare her life. He had threatened to kill her or the twins if the ransom wasn't paid. He had hijacked Andre Laurent's SeaOx and kidnapped her. The ransom was delivered and, while Elspeth was being set free, Marta and Lieutenant Robert Bizet located the SeaOx, set Andre free and recovered the ransom. This set Pelling on a killing mission who lay in ambush at the Chateau and shot Sylvie Bern thinking it was Marta. So, after a number of days of recovery for Elspeth, Andre and Sylvie, the party came to pass. Elspeth told Sylvie Bern that a document was being prepared by her lawyers that would guarantee any medical expenses she may have for the rest of her life. Elspeth went on to explain to the quests that, while the Vander Riis family was wealthy, they always maintained a low profile. She said the events of the past weeks could easily command newspaper headlines. She was grateful that everything had been kept quiet. She said guests of lesser character might sell the story to a newspaper for a considerable amount. She handed envelopes to Andre, Sylvie and myself. Each contained a cheque for $250,000. And every one of us looked at the amount and returned them to Elspeth saying we couldn't accept for various reasons. Andre said, if he had lost the SeaOx, he still would have refused the gift. He said his boat was insured and he didn't think he earned any gift. I told her I couldn't accept the gift because of my job. Sylvie was overwhelmed with the first gift of medical insurance for life and couldn't accept more. Elspeth, Marta and Tice formed a united front and insisted we all sleep on it. Elspeth suggested Robert petition his superiors about setting up a way that his Anti-Terrorism Squad could accept outside funding. He proposed this to his superiors.

Robert finally stopped tapping the official envelope and opened it and read:

> 'Lieutenant Robert Bizet of the Sûreté Anti-Terrorism Squad has been granted permission by the executive committee of the Sûreté to accept outside funding for his work fighting terrorism.'

He was not to solicit funds directly, but was granted much leeway in just how any additional funding could be spent. The executive committee put a cap of two million dollars, which he could accept in any fiscal year. Amounts exceeding this would go into the Sûreté general account. Elspeth Vander Riis and her wealthy circle of friends had brought considerable pressure to bear. The executive committee agreed it was the wealthy who had the most to lose and to fear from terrorist abductions, therefore, they were granted this concession to donate funds to the Anti-Terrorism Squad.

Lieutenant Robert Bizet and his work were becoming known and he was something of a celebrity himself stemming from all the publicity concerning the recent apprehension of Raoul De Vascos, a kingpin in the

Basque ETA hierarchy. In order to become more effective in his work, he had convinced his superiors that he must be allowed more leeway from customary police procedures. Many instances happened in his work, when he or members of his squad would have to be in other parts of the world quickly. He was now authorized to pursue his work without having to go through the regular time consuming request channels to obtain approvals. Personal American Express and Visa Gold cards were issued to him and his squad which were funded by this Special Anti-Terrorism Account. Three people formed the managing group for this account: a Sûreté accountant with the rank of lieutenant, a civilian member of the Police commission responsible for the Sûreté, and Lieutenant Robert Bizet. The SATS funds, at present, consisted of donations from Bizet himself, Andre Laurent, the Vander Riis family, friends of the Vander Riis family plus an annual contribution from the Sûreté. The total of the fund now was very close to the limit set for annual use: $1,800,000. In addition to these funds, and the confiscated 50' Beneteau sailboat, Andre Laurent had recovered four cashier's cheques from Pelling totaling $1,000,000. He had offered it to Bizet, but the Lieutenant asked him to hang onto it for the time being so that he wouldn't have extra paperwork to complete. When they talked about this recovered million dollars, Andre thought that he would return it to Elspeth himself. Robert suggested he wait until Pelling was in custody. Elspeth had given the terrorist this money expecting it would guarantee the Vander Riis' safety. Robert warned Andre he didn't think Elspeth would be pleased about getting the ransom back.

Lieutenant Robert Bizet was delighted with this new funding arrangement, which would allow him to hire and train additional police personnel as squad members. His scope would be much greater from now on, as well as his effectiveness.

He pushed the account particulars to one side and looked again at the information which had arrived in response to Sergeant Moline's passport inquiries of Teddy Pelling and R. Anna Werner. His inquiry brought forth information on Edward Anton Pelling who died twelve years ago in a drowning accident at his cabin in Bremerhaven, Germany. He was survived two days by his widow, Herta, who, distraught with loss, committed suicide by drowning herself in the same river which took her husband.

They were survived by their 17 year old son Teddy. The boy left the area shortly after the funerals with the proceeds of his parents' estate. He was believed to have moved to Greece. The report on R. Anna Werner said she had lived in the Boston area and, at the age of 18, moved to Paris were she enrolled in a business school. She was believed to be living in Paris and working as an independent investment advisor.

Bizet doodled some figures on the report and said to himself, *So, Teddy Pelling, you're now 30 years old and your friend Ruth is 35. Where have you been since Greece, I wonder? And how did you get mixed up with the ETA? Now, those tragic deaths of your parents: first your father accidentally drowns and then your grief-stricken mother drowns herself in the same river days later. This would be enough to twist any youngster's mind into a weird knot. However, a cynical cop like me, will have a closer look at those deaths to see what can be learned about them and* this *young man.*

* * *

The Belmonte Towers Hotel on the beach in Bermuda was less than two kilometers from the Villas on the same beach. When the dinner party guests of George Yaro got ready to leave later that evening, George was certain he was going to get lucky with Ida, but at the last moment, she chose to leave with Ruth and Linus. Linus checked his watch as he bundled his two lady friends into a cab, saying he would be along shortly as he wanted to exercise his knee walking home along the beach. He winked at the two gals and suggested that, when he did get home, he might be up for some more play time. They giggled and told him not to be too long.

As the cab pulled away, Teddy checked his watch again and noted the time was 12:55. He thought he might go back up to the penthouse and interrogate the overly friendly and accommodating George Yaro. Instead, he went back into the lobby lounge and ordered a beer while he collected his thoughts. After a long discussion with himself he finished his beer and was about to leave the lounge when he spotted lovely young Ursula walking toward the bank of elevators. Teddy watched from cover as she stepped into the elevator. When the doors closed, he moved to a better vantage point and watched the elevator indicator stop at the Penthouse floor.

Pelling thought: *Now isn't this interesting? The sexy young schoolgirl showing up at the Penthouse at 1:00 in the morning. Hmm... Ursula what strange habits you have! The only explanation possible is that George Yaro is your guardian. Could be, but more likely you just work for him. I'll definitely need some answers now before I hand over our passports to you, Georgie boy. If you will just send Ursula down soon, I'll get those answers from her.*

Pelling waited until 2:30AM in the Hotel parking lot, near, but out of sight of the Mercedes sports car he recognized as the one Ursula drove away in this afternoon. *She must be staying the night,* he decided. Pelling left for the front of the hotel where he took a cab back to Villa #17. Both Ida and Ruth were sound asleep in the same bed. He stripped and crashed in the other bedroom.

* * *

The following morning Ursula took two full city blocks to catch up with Sergeant Alain Moline, who was jogging a medium pace. She had to shake off a tall guy who she remembered hitting on her the day previous.

"Good morning, would you mind if I run along with you. It will keep the hounds away, if you know what I mean."

"My pleasure, my name's Alain. Yours?"

"Ursula, nice to meet you Alain."

"You live here Ursula or are you a tourist too?"

"I go to college in New York. I'm just visiting my guardian who has a place here. And you?"

"Live in Paris, just here until the red-eye flight leaves at midnight. My run is going to end at the beach hut ahead. Stop with me and we'll visit."

"Sure!"

By 10:00 that morning, Ursula had completely captivated Sergeant Moline. He had always thought he was a nice enough looking fellow but he never imagined anything like this happening to him. When he finally finished his shower and walked back into his bedroom, Ursula was waiting for him stretched out on the bed with just her tiny bikini bottom back on. He stretched out beside her and, as he closed his eyes to kiss her, she withdrew his gun from under his pillow and shot him in the left temple. Ursula rolled over on her side and off the bed away from the dead policeman. She walked around to the other side of the bed, wiped her prints off of the gun with the bed sheet, then placed the gun in his left hand. After removing any trace of her presence she left and resumed her run back toward her Mercedes.

The cleaning crew found Sergeant Alain Moline's body just before noon or 16:55 Paris time. The local police came to investigate the scene, deemed it a suicide, and quickly arranged for an ambulance to remove the body. After the necessary paperwork was filed at the Bermuda police station a fax was sent to the Paris headquarters of the Sûreté advising of the suicide of Sergeant Alain Moline and asking for instructions in the disposal of his remains. This transmission arrived at 23:55 Paris time.

At 23:45 the same evening, at the Vander Riis apartment building, Louis the Doorman was shot and killed when he refused two gunmen entry up to the Vander Riis apartment. The video camera had been damaged by the intruders, but the film clearly indicated who they were after.

Chapter Thirteen
Suicide and Murder

When Lieutenant Robert Bizet telephoned his office the following morning at 07:25 he was told of both deaths. He sat at the telephone desk in his hotel suite holding onto the receiver in a state of shock. When he was finally able to tell Marta of the deaths, he was still holding the receiver in his right hand unaware of the buzzing from the dead line.

"Oh my God, Robert, not the sergeant! He wouldn't take his own life. What in merciful heavens happened?"

"It's true. Sergeant Alain Moline is dead: a suicide they say. And the doorman, Louis, at your mother's apartment building gunned down by unknown assassins," Robert answered.

"Marta, honey... I'm ... I'm... stunned. My premonition was right. Thank God you weren't in the apartment when they got there. Did you bring the fax I sent you?"

"Yes, it's in my handbag," Marta replied.

"Thank God...We can be thankful for that! The ETA gunmen don't know where to look for you, or me for that matter. Ahhhhh... damn it! Not the sergeant!"

Marta tried to comfort him but couldn't find appropriate words, so she just sat close holding his hand in hers.

"What you just said about taking his own life is very true about Alain, you know! He hated suicide as much as I do. It was never a solution with us. Marta, we must get to Bermuda and check this out quickly. You're coming with me. I won't believe you're safe unless you are right beside me. I know who's responsible for the attack on your apartment but, until we check more closely, my guess is Sergeant Moline ran into Teddy Pelling somehow. I'll make the arrangements from here and we'll buy what we need in Bermuda. Agreed?" Robert said.

"Yes, of course! I'll get us packed" Marta replied.

* * *

The last time Raoul de Vascos was allowed a visitor, the visitor, his lawyer, had to be rescued from the cell. Raoul had his hands around the lawyer's neck and had to be bludgeoned off of him. It was thought to be a clear case of, "Don't kill the bearer of bad tidings, he's only the messenger." Raoul was in a foul mood for days.

* * *

George Yaro was as good as his word getting quick clearance to leave Bermuda with his three guests after presenting their passports to the proper authorities. George was known as a high roller who was very generous to the officials he needed to interact with in his travels. He and his guests were free to leave Bermuda one hour after he presented the passports to the very appreciative official who processed them in double-quick time. George thought it wise if his little group left at 2:00PM instead of later. Having received word of the death of Sergeant Alain Moline of the Paris Sûreté from his contact at Bermuda Constabulary Headquarters, George thought it best to be on his way with his valuable human cargo. The Sûreté would send more of their own to this island to investigate the suicide of their sergeant.

Once in the air, George Yaro, ever the congenial host, made sure his passengers were comfortable. After this, he looked in on his pilot and noticed Linus in the right hand seat, flying co-pilot. Well, he wasn't really flying, just observing. George, satisfied everyone was comfortable, was then free to concentrate on Ida, seeing to her every whim, much to the amusement of Ruth, who finally asked him to sit between them and relax.

"I must admit, I'm always a little nervous when we take off. Yes, Cher, it takes me some time to settle down." George said.

George seated himself between the ladies who both wore comfortable travelling clothes. Ida had on a soft cotton halter top and well-worn blue jeans, while Ruth wore a mock turtleneck top which ended at her naval along with khaki battle patch shorts. Ruth said, "I've told Ida about some of our special parties George, especially about what you like. Ida offered to help you relax while the boys are busy flying the plane." Ruth said with a wink.

"What an exceptional suggestion" George said, "but, first I'd like to talk about the passports you gave me."

"What would you like to know about them George?" Ruth asked.

"Well, I've known you for a very long time as Ruth Meikle, but the name on your passport is R. Anna Werner. Are you, perhaps, being sought by the authorities?" George asked.

"Not exactly George. My real name is Ruth Anna Werner, but I've always used Ruth Meikle, sort of like a stage name, I guess. And, Ida Tesh is her real name. She and I have been friends since we were in school together back in the States. Nothing out of the ordinary really."

"Is Linus Svendsen your friend's real name or is he someone else as well?" George asked.

"No, Linus isn't his real name, but it will do for his purposes. He told you as much as he's going to tell you about himself and his activities, George, and I really wouldn't push it for all our sakes," Ruth cautioned.

"No, no! I just want us to be able to pass normally through customs clearance, when necessary, without any problems," George replied.

"I'm quite sure the people Linus works for have given him fool-proof papers and there won't be any trouble," Ruth said.

"I suppose you're right. There wasn't any problem in getting clearance to leave Bermuda, but I do take good care of the officials there and am well known to them. It may not be as easy in South Carolina or the Cayman Islands. Just thought I would bring it up to clear the air. Very well then! I have had my people prepare and stow on board a very interesting meal for us, but now, we should have a little cocktail to kick off our journey, eh?" George suggested.

***

Later, as the sleek little jet was approaching the east coast of the United States on its way to Charleston, South Carolina, an Air France jumbo jet was on final approach into the Bermuda airport. Lieutenant Robert Bizet and Marta Vander Riis spent a good part of their flight discussing the shocking sudden death of Sergeant Alain Moline. The Bermuda authorities labelled it a suicide, but Robert and Marta thought otherwise.

Lieutenant Robert Bizet was taking no more chances trying to keep Marta safe, especially after the near miss at the Vander Riis apartment building. The apartment was broken into two hours after Marta had been whisked away to the Hotel De Lutece by the lieutenant.

Their date at the Hotel De Lutece had been special. Dinner was served in the room, after which they danced together to music on the radio. Their passion sent them under the covers to make love again, then finally, to sleep the safe sleep of the sated. When they awoke in the morning, Robert learned the news of the sergeant's death and the shooting of the doorman at the building where Marta had been staying at her mother's apartment. The lieutenant was told how the gunmen entered the Vander Riis apartment, touched nothing, and left. Robert knew why they had come.

Robert Bizet, although visibly shaken and deeply saddened over his sergeant's death, did not spend much time in self-recrimination. Instead, he put his time to better use and went back to work. As soon as they landed in Bermuda they took a taxi directly to the Villas on the Beach and registered. On the way, Robert told Marta they would work in conjunction with his Paris office. He would not share anything they turned up with the local police, of whom he was very suspicious because of their obvious bungled investigation into Sergeant Moline's death. Suicide was not an option as a cause of death for Sergeant Alain Moline. Robert recalled how he and the sergeant had this discussion every time a policeman had "swallowed his gun" or whenever they investigated a suspected suicide. In their minds it was not an honorable solution to any of life's misfortunes, rather they were in agreement that it was a cowardly act, which was an affront to every living thing. With this in mind, Lieutenant Robert Bizet's mission was to prove the sergeant had been murdered while he was on the trail of a notorious ETA assassin. It was Robert's opinion that, if Pelling wasn't directly responsible for Sergeant Moline's death, he was indirectly involved. Robert couldn't factor anyone else into the sergeant's death; it had to be the ETA who were looking for Pelling or Pelling himself.

Who had the sergeant come in contact with or what information had he turned up to have caused his death? It will take painstaking back-checking of the sergeant's investigation until we turn up the answers to this, Robert thought to himself.

The lieutenant wasted no time once he and Marta were registered at the Villas on the beach. He produced a picture of Sergeant Alain Moline and began at the front desk of their Hotel. The desk clerk recognized the Sergeant as soon as he was shown the picture.

"Yes sir, I checked Sergeant Moline in myself. His death was a real shocker lieutenant and something seems very wrong here sir after the local police were called in and investigated."

"Would you care to explain what you mean?"

"The police didn't bother to ask any questions about the sergeant at all. Just told us it was a suicide and had the body removed" the desk clerk said.

"Yes, it does sound a bit cut and dried doesn't it?"

"Lieutenant, since I've been in the hotel business I've had two heart attack deaths, one death from an overdose of barbiturates and an instance where a body was found in a room occupied by a suspected narcotics dealer. This is my point sir: In each one of those cases the manager had to produce the check-in details and all of the hotel personnel were questioned thoroughly. Why not this time, I ask? Are there some special circumstances in Sergeant Moline's death?" he asked.

"I am here to find out all the circumstances leading up to the sergeant's death and I will want to question the hotel staff, therefore, I am very interested to hear anything at all about the sergeant's movements while he was here," Lieutenant Bizet said.

"Our hotel staff will be only too happy to be of assistance Lieutenant. Just tell me how you wish to proceed and I will make sure the staff are available to you for interviews," the desk clerk said.

Chapter Fourteen
Gulfstream Jet at Your Service

The SeaOx had been tied up to the City Docks in Bordeaux since 10:00 AM and lay swaying gently on the afternoon tide when she was boarded and broken into. The two men, dressed like boating types, conducted a very thorough search of the sailboat. They did not "toss" the inside of the sailboat, rather they put everything back in its place and, with a few exceptions, it would be hard to tell anyone had been aboard.

The locked door to the pilot house had been opened by a "jimmy" and was left closed but in an unlocked position when the intruders left.

When Andre and Ava returned to the SeaOx later that evening, Andre noticed the door wasn't locked. He dropped to his knees, put a finger to his lips as a signal to Ava, and looked closely at the door lock. There were telltale scratches on it, which sent alarm bells ringing in his head. Andre put his key into the lock and re-locked it. Looking at Ava and nodding for her to follow, he stepped off the SeaOx onto the jetty. Ava followed. They went directly to the marina office and reported the SeaOx had been broken into. Andre requested the authorities search the boat in his company as he was not about to step aboard and into some sort of ambush. Ava took him aside, after he made his report, and suggested they stay ashore until after the police investigated.

* * *

George Yaro's Gulfstream V refueled at Charleston Airport and was boarded by a customs officer who looked very briefly at the passports

George handed to him. The pilot accompanied the customs officer back to the terminal to close the flight plan from Bermuda and file another to George Town, Grand Cayman Island. After paying for the fuel with George Yaro's credit card, the pilot, Ramon Atmos, returned to the jet as they were free to go. The pilot cleared with the tower and was given instructions by ground control to taxi out to the active runway. Once at the active runway, the pilot switched his radio to the tower and was instructed he was number two behind an American Airlines jumbo jet. The tower waited until the vortices from the jet had washed over the runway before advising the Gulfstream they were now #1, cleared for take-off. Minutes later they were again at their maximum cruising altitude on their way to the Cayman Islands. The flight from Bermuda to Charleston measured 925 miles and took two and one half hours. The flight from Charleston to Grand Cayman Island was 930 miles and would take almost the same time, depending on the winds aloft, which looked favorable. Pelling had watched the pilot very closely and felt he could fly this jet easily. Settling back in the co-pilot's seat, he went over his plan to recover the money in Ruth's numbered account in George Town. When Ruth mentioned having a stash in a numbered account in George Town, George Yaro had become very attentive and then offered to fly them there. Pelling went over this part of last evening's conversation in his mind very carefully now.

So, how come George Yaro steps up and offers to fly Ruth, Ida and me to the Cayman Islands? He did so immediately after Ruth blabbed she had a stash of money in a numbered account in George Town. Does he know who we are? If he does, is he either ETA connected or is he in league with the authorities? My hunch is he is ETA. Raoul has alerted his network via his lawyers by now and probably has a hefty reward on us. He wants us alive in order to get at Ruth's money as well as the cash I have stashed around Europe. However, Raoul may not be entirely in charge anymore, as his situation grows more hopeless even though he is the nephew of Esau Navarra a member of the ruling council of the Basque ETA. Raoul told me, on more than one occasion, he was heir apparent to the powerful position of "Operations Chairman" for all Basque activities. The ETA will let him continue to operate from his cell as long as he has visitation rights and his lawyers can relay his instructions. According to Ruth, she told Raoul our combined investment account amounted to over six million and he had estimated that I'd stashed another half a million or so in various bank boxes around Europe. He wasn't aware of the million I extracted from Andre Laurent's friend, Elspeth Vander Riis. Doesn't matter anymore because that bloody Laurent, took it off me after he shot me. He has probably given it back to Elspeth by now. I'm sure he won't be getting anymore sex from her for that bit of interference. She will be crazed with fear thinking about my promise that I wouldn't stop until I kill her children. Just thinking about that bloody fiasco makes me itch. First, I make a nice little score of around $500,000 US from the widow and send her home just a little worse for wear. I was positive Laurent was securely bound and drugged, but he gets away, somehow, takes his money and hers. He gives her ransom back to her. That pissed me off big time. So, I shoot her daughter and the widow falls all over herself giving me a $1,000,000. I should have insisted that she seal her promise to keep the authorities out of it with a piece of ass. She would have, I just know it. She pretended she didn't like me watching her, but I could feel her heat. Probably thinking about us together when she was drugged and began playing with herself. Sexy or what? Then, that cowboy Laurent shows up again, in Lisbon for Christ sake, comes on our boat just as Ruth and I are about to bolt, starts blasting away at me like some film hero. Said he was just going to disable me until the cops came to arrest me. He damn well knew I'd spared his life on more than one occasion so he returned the favor. Son-of-a-bitch took a million dollars in cashier's cheques plus about twenty thousand cash, then left me tied but with tourniquets on my leg and wrist. Good thing the drug he injected into Ruth and I was only marginally effective. Ruth came to first and we were able to get loose and into the rental car. Thank God the old man disguise and the red wig Ruth wore were good enough to get us on that flight out of Lisbon. The more I think about it, the more I'm convinced there has to be a big price on Ruth and me, which could be Georgie Yaro's motivation. He'll turn us over to the ETA for a couple million or so. Maybe if Ruth and I give him the impression we can make it more than worth his while to get us in and out of the Caymans, then let us escape in either Argentina or France, we can all benefit. Shouldn't be too difficult to find out what he knows about us. We can slow the plane down a bit and I'll just hang Georgie boy out the door and threaten to drop him in the ocean. I'm willing to bet Georgie is tied in some *way to the ETA. He certainly moves about with impunity. Can't see him just playing the big fiddle for Ruth and Ida just for the sexual perks, even though Ida is promising him everything she has when she dances with him: giving him a good dry hump. Well Georgie boy, whoever the hell you are, if you do score with her, you are in for a treat, my man. And, even if that's all you're about Georgie, I can't say as I blame you, but, how come I'm so lucky? Nope! Too many red flags going up. Paranoia? Nope again! I'm alive today because I don't believe in coincidence or convenient circumstances. Even though there's no doubt about the captivating charms of Ruth and Ida, my take on you Georgie, is you are interested in Ruthie's stash, number one, or you have some other monetary reason to be so obliging. So, Georgie, I think maybe we'll just have you tell us if we have a reception committee waiting down there for us. Don't see how it would help get at Ruth's numbered account if we are intercepted on arrival, though.*

He will have to have assistance bringing us in after we collect the money from the Royal Bank. Ruth and I will have a little chat and then I'll involve Georgie Boy just to measure the size of his greed.

Pelling removed his headphones and tapped the Argentine pilot on the shoulder and said, "Going back to the washroom. See you in a bit."

The pilot smiled at Teddy and gave him the thumbs up signal.

Pelling used the washroom and then seated himself in the vacant chair beside George Yaro, smiled across at the two very attractive ladies and spoke to Ruth.

"Ruth, I need to speak with you privately. George, can we use the tail section bedroom or would you and Ida like to use it and leave us alone in this compartment?"

Ruth thought she understood what Teddy was getting at: sending Ida and George into the bedroom was just his way of getting down to business. Ida spoke next.

"Come on George, show me the bedroom in this fabulous plane of yours." She took him by the hand and he led the way to the back of the jet, closing the compartment behind them.

"Okay Ruth, we have to talk and we don't have much time. We both know how fabulous Ida is at fellatio and Georgie boy won't have much staying power when she gets at him."

"Oh contraire, dear friend. I have first-hand knowledge of George remember, and he is extremely talented in the bedroom. So, I'd say it's Ida who is in for the treat. In other words, lover, they will be more than a little while. What did you want to talk with me about?" Ruth asked.

"About George Yaro who is, as you say, very deceptive. He is either exactly who he says he is: an independent international real estate investor and a loyal friend of yours and others around the world he can play with, or he works for, or has connections to, the ETA. I stayed at the Hotel after I put you and Ida in a taxi last night. I had a beer in the lounge bar. The sexy little school girl, Ursula, came into the lobby and took an elevator up to the Penthouse floor. This was at 1:15 this morning. So, unless Georgie is her guardian, she works for him. I waited until almost 3:00 A.M. and she didn't come back down. My guess is, he sent her to meet and party with us in order to keep us under surveillance. My intuition tells me we need to know what he is up to before we land or we could find a reception waiting. There will have been a substantial reward put on our heads by Tio Esau for turning Raoul in, and, more than likely, the Sûreté has an international warrant for our arrest. Before you object Ruth, I want you to follow my lead and let me get the information we need from him. You've already told him what I'm about, so my interrogation tactics won't seem out of character."

"Are you going to threaten to kill him?" Ruth asked.

"Only if it comes to that. Just stay out of it and let me be the bad guy. I don't want any interference from our friend Ida either. I'll hold you responsible for her."

"Ida won't be a problem. She knows better," Ruth said.

"That's what I thought! Good! I'll start out by asking George questions about offshore banking and see how it develops."

Almost forty-five minutes had gone by when the rear compartment door opened and George Yaro stepped into the main salon area and re-seated himself with Ruth and Linus.

"George, you are aware that we are going to the Caymans in order to better organize a rather large amount of money Ruth and I have moved from France to this offshore Bank?"

"Yes, yes, we discussed this at dinner last night," George answered.

"Just how familiar are you with how these offshore banks do business?"

"Quite familiar, actually! I know there are 45 or so tax havens around the world that are said to hold $5 trillion dollars which, I'm told, is about one third of the international money supply. My own preferences are Bermuda, of course, the Isle of Man and Switzerland where I have both Trading Accounts and Non-Resident Trusts. I've never had any dealings in the Cayman Islands though," George said.

"I see. Well, we are here to set up Non-Resident Trusts in each of our names as our money is all in an International Trading Account and currently invested in a Money Market Mutual Fund," Linus said.

"What would the set-up fees be for the Non-Resident Trusts and is there an annual maintenance fee?" Linus asked.

"Well you have to understand, first of all, who we are dealing with here, right? Bankers, for Christ sake! They are protected by International Banking and Trading Laws and are free to help themselves to our money as they see fit. More precisely, a set-up charge for a Trust is $7,000 to $10,000 and they'll take an annual fee of about $5,000 per account. The Banks will do the legal paperwork for you for free and draw up the trust document as well, as long as they are named as the offshore trustee. These trusts are designed with the highest secrecy. They are not filed with any government agency, allowing the names of the parties involved and the trust's activities to be protected under the tax haven laws. In reality, what actually happens is: the investor usually runs the show and directs the trustee to do whatever he/she wishes. That's how mine all work as a matter of fact," George said.

"That's what I understand. One other thing George, is there any limit to the amount of cash you can take out from an investment trading account?" Linus asked.

"I don't know about the Banks in the Caymans, but I don't think there is any limit to what I could take out in my offshore accounts. They may want to transfer the funds to another one of their branch banks. Just another way to extract more fees as 'Rights of passage' as the money is leaving their hands," George said.

"Ok, that answers my questions. Ruth, do you have anything else you want to ask?" Linus said.

"No, you covered everything I needed to know, however, we still have to decide just how much cash we need to take out and what we will leave in the Trusts," Ruth said.

"We can decide at the bank, but I think it would be wise to have most of the cash shipped to a couple of Royal Banks. We can decide that at the bank as well," Linus said.

George thought to himself: *Well, that's a lot of information but very little detail. They must have a sizeable dollar amount to have arranged an offshore transfer without opening the account in person. I thought only governments could manage that. Hmm! Neither Ruth nor Linus would say what they have in their account or how much they plan to take with them. This Linus is very cagey not admitting to taking any cash, rather having it transferred to Royal Banks in Lord-Knows-Where. This may be more difficult than I figured. Thought for sure they would grab all or most of their stash, which I could help myself to, before turning them over to Navarra's men for a very handsome reward. Faulty thinking though, because Pelling would then have immediately told the ETA and I would have been liquidated. No, I'll just take the reward offered by the ETA and help myself to the perks along the way, like some more of the ultra-erotic Ida and my friend Ruth. Yes indeed, Ida you are a feast in bed. I must report to the ETA when we land or I'll be added to their bloody hit list.* George suddenly noted the tone and manner of the conversation with Linus turn ominous.

"Georgie, I want some straight answers from you before we land in George Town. Do you have anyone waiting for us when we land?" Linus demanded.

"What's the meaning of this question? I resent your tone of voice. Ruth, what the hell is this all about?" George never got to vent the rest of his outrage as the vicious slap across the face caused him to put his own hands in front of his face to protect against further assault.

"Okay Georgie, on your feet. Have it your way. Either you answer my questions and live or I throw you off this airplane," Linus said as he hauled George out of the seat and forced him to the to the cabin door and put his hand on the lever.

"For Christ sake Pelling, don't open that door, the cabin will depressurize," George said as he cowered by the door.

"So, you do know who I am! Answer my question or I'll kill you right here," Pelling said.

"Ok, Ok! Take it easy and relax, Pelling. I don't want to die. I was asked by friends in the ETA to be on the lookout for you and Ruth while I was in Bermuda," George admitted.

"That's what I suspected. Who do you report to in the ETA?" Pelling asked.

"Esau Navarra, now that Raoul is in prison," George answered.

"What's in it for you, Georgie?" Pelling demanded as he let go his grip on George.

"There is a five million US dollar reward for turning you both in to the Basques," George said.

"Now that's what I call incentive," Pelling said.

"Who is Ursula?" Pelling demanded.

"She is my pilot Ramon Atmos' daughter and works for me. When I spoke with you in the restaurant, I wasn't sure you would accept my dinner invitation so I sent Ursula to the beach to keep an eye on you," George said.

"Anything else?" Pelling asked.

"I haven't reported back to Navarra that I intercepted you. That's the truth. I was going to contact him when we landed," George said.

"Is that all of it?" Pelling asked.

"There was a policeman from the Paris Sûreté in Bermuda staying at the Villas on the Beach. Ursula took care of him on my orders this morning and made it look like a suicide. That's the reason we left as soon as we got cleared today," George answered.

"How did you know the policeman was from the Sûreté in Paris? Was his name Robert Bizet, a lieutenant?" Pelling asked.

"No, he was a sergeant. He arrived the day after you did and went straight to the local police station, introduced himself and left a description of you and Ruth. He was interviewed by the Staff Sergeant, a contact of mine, who faxed me all the information. Also, Interpol has an outstanding warrant on both of you. The ETA has a price on your head, and Tio Esau Navarra told me his nephew Raoul de Vascos wanted you alive so they could obtain the whereabouts of your personal fortune along with the money you and Ruth have accumulated. You are being sought on both sides of the law," George offered.

"Alright then Georgie boy, now we can talk some real business. Let's get you and the ladies a good stiff drink first and then we can make some plans," Pelling said as he forced George to his seat.

Ida sat and hugged Ruth. She had been standing in the back bedroom doorway, listening closely to the interrogation then moved back beside Ruth, and snuggled close to her.

Chapter Fifteen
Bidding for a Winery

Raoul de Vascos had not had any further visitors since the "choking incident" of his lawyer. He demanded to see his lawyers again. His agents had bungled both of the assignments they were given. The shooting of the doorman at the Paris apartment of Lieutenant Bizet's girlfriend, Marta Vander Riis, who had disappeared. Bizet, had also dropped from sight. No chance of a kidnapping and exchange of either of these two who, he supposed, were shacked up somewhere together. So far, nothing in the way of sightings of either Pelling or Ruth Meikle from his international network. Nothing had been heard for a couple days now from George Yaro either who had previously been reporting daily. Raoul decided to see what he could learn by telling his guards he was ready to co-operate with the Sûreté.

* * *

Andre Laurent and Ava Haas checked into the Hotel Bell Air, near the City Docks Marina in Bordeaux immediately after they had the SeaOx searched by two detectives from the Bordeaux police station. They concluded nothing was missing, even though it appeared that every drawer and garment had been inspected and replaced, more or less as before. Andre was uneasy after Ava insisted she wouldn't set foot on the SeaOx again until it was leaving. She reiterated her feeling that they would be safest at sea.

Andre had required only part of the day to complete his business at the Winery Estate of Anatole Hubert. Andre had made up his mind he would not take the management position at the winery for two reasons: first of all, he thought the management position was redundant and would only annoy his new friend Dollard Valdene, the residing operator, and second, he wanted to be free to sail the SeaOx. When Andre and Ava had finished their introductions, Andre told Dollard of his decision. Andre explained he would be making a modest investment in the Winery and Chateau on the premise that Dollard continue to run the estate. The only perk of ownership Andre wanted was lodging whenever he was in Bordeaux. Andre and Ava, along with Dollard Valdene, went to see Anatole Hubert in the great house to inform him of this decision.

The crusty old gentleman opened a special bottle of red wine in order to drink a toast to what the old man referred to as "the final obstacle to Dollard's control of the operation." Both Dollard Valdene and Anatole Hubert congratulated Andre Laurent on his non-involvement in the affairs of the winery.

"I can move to Paris now and take up residence in my home near the action," Anatole announced with a wink to his guests, "and when I have moved out, then you and those other two young scallywags from Montreal will be able to stay here whenever it suits you."

When the second bottle of wine was half-empty, Anatole treated his three guests to a ribald tale about an attractive young lady named Ruth, who had tried desperately to buy the Estate from him recently. So desperate, said the old gent, she had offered to have sex with him, then had disrobed and shown him the merchandise. Anatole, giggled when he told them he had declined on the basis of ill health.

Dollard and Ava laughed along with the old man, but not Andre who was deep in thought. Anatole's description of this Ruth woman reminded him of Pelling's blonde friend and his curiosity got the better of him.

"Excuse me Anatole, but did this Ruth show you her card, or how were you to contact her?" Andre asked.

"She left her card. I don't think she's finished with me yet, you know. Thinks she can change my mind about selling to her by getting me into the sack! What in the hell has gotten into young people nowadays? Mind you if I was twenty years younger...eh?" Anatole said over his shoulder as he shuffled out of the room.

He went to a sideboard with a small wicker basket, retrieved the card she had left and handed it to Andre.

Shortly thereafter, Andre and Ava said goodnight and left for their hotel.

When they were in their rental car on the way back to the SeaOx, Andre explained the significance of the card to Ava.

"I was going to ask you about it, Andre. I remember you saying the hijacker was in the company of some Ruth person. I remember after you did your "gangster thing" on his boat in Lisbon, you told me about the blonde he was with. Do you think she is the same person Anatole Hubert was vamped by?" Ava asked.

"Well, when he was describing her, I got a mental flashback of me tying her up, and, yes I'm sure she is one and the same person. We'll run it by the lieutenant when we get back onboard the SeaOx. I don't know whether I mentioned the first time I stopped here at the City Docks Marina, someone boarded the SeaOx," Andre said.

"No, you didn't tell me that," Ava replied.

"It happened all right. I was having an early evening meal in the Marina Fish Shack and was watching the masts around where the SeaOx was tied up, when all of a sudden the mast moved decidedly left and then returned to perpendicular, like it does when someone steps on board. I went and checked at the marina office. I was told there were no messages and nobody from the office had been on the SeaOx. When I checked myself, the door to the pilot house was unlocked, and I know I left it locked. After, I looked real close. There wasn't anything missing so I just forgot about it, until now," Andre said.

"How does this Ruth person tie in with the SeaOx being boarded back then and now?" Ava asked.

"I'm not really sure, but when I forced information out of Pierre Turin, my Merrill Lynch broker, he mentioned his friend Ruth offered to supply the hijacker to relieve me of my T-Bill funds and my boat. If she is the same woman, I don't understand why she would be bidding against us for the Chateau and winery. Unless..."

"Unless what? Andre?"

"Well okay, let's just pick at this knot and see if we can unravel it a bit. We know now, Pelling worked as a hired assassin for the ETA, right? Suppose his girl-friend worked with them too and, together, they have a lot of money to launder or invest. Wouldn't buying a prime estate winery be a great way to place a large sum of money?" Andre asked.

"I suppose so, but why would they be in competition with you over Anatole's property?"

"First of all Ava, there aren't that many choice properties for sale. As you know, I've looked in Germany, Italy and most of France. I'm serious, these Estates with vineyards are just not on the market very often," Andre said.

"I remember looking through the papers for this Chateau back at the Hotel De Lutece after you first spoke with Anatole Hubert on the telephone. The property was never advertised for sale was it?" Ava asked.

"No, not really! Cecil and Giles asked me to find a Chateau/Vineyard for them like Anatole's property and, if unsuccessful, I was to see if he was interested in selling. He did sell to them after my report to them, but you are right, it was never advertised for sale," Andre said.

"Exactly. So how did this Ruth come on the scene and start bidding against you?" Ava asked.

"You remember Anatole telling us how she just appeared at his door the day after I visited and said she liked the layout and would he consider selling to her. I suppose it could be a coincidence but if she is Pelling's girl-friend then it's more likely it was them who went aboard the SeaOx, looked through my papers and found the information on Hubert's Vineyard," Andre suggested.

"Andre, you just sent a chill up my spine. Look, those two are on the loose...you don't suppose they're right here do you? I see it all tied in together, don't you?" Ava said.

"I don't follow," Andre said.

"Pierre Turin, the Merrill Lynch broker and you are acquaintances, he knows Elspeth Vander Riis and he knows this Ruth person. You want Pierre's help in meeting Elspeth. Normal enough guy stuff, I suppose, however Pierre doesn't look at it in this way. He sees both you and Elspeth's son as a threat to his business. I think he then started to plan your kidnapping, figuring it would be easy enough to get your cash from the Merrill account with his help. He needed someone to do the rough stuff though, and that's where his friend Ruth comes in. Pierre and she get together and she tells him she has a friend who could take his sailboat and coerce the sailor into coughing up his cash in exchange for his life. I may be way off line here Andre, but just suppose Pelling did a quick check of the SeaOx and looked through the Hubert Estate acquisition papers. The three of them planned your kidnapping and knew you were going to be dead soon and no longer a factor in the Estate purchase. Ruth and Pelling could have decided to take on this investment as all the preliminaries seemed out of the way. I'm just supposing, but maybe they had ideas of owning an Estate/Vineyard long before you and your Montreal investors came to France?" Ava suggested.

"When you get going Ava, you really get cooking don't you? Mind you, who's to say it didn't happen just that way? You're correct about who is involved though...I did get Turin's confession before Pelling shot him. Turin gave me most of the story, but nothing was said about buying a Vineyard/Estate. That may well have been only Ruth and Pelling's plan. I believed Pelling when he told me he found the Polaroid pictures of Elspeth and me and my notes on the family. He insinuated I was setting her or the whole Vander Riis family up for some kind of blackmail scheme he had caught me at. That's probably when he decided to grab the widow himself for a little "R & R and a cash extraction", which he did, and more, as it turned out.

"Pelling has to be totally pissed at me. First I escape with the ransom and my money. Then we meet again and I shoot him up with bullets and drugs and take cashier's cheques worth a million plus because I figure he owed me for expenses and inconvenience. This leaves him with nothing for his efforts hijacking my boat and kidnapping us, except some bullet holes and a god awful headache," Andre said.

"That's my point Andre, you have to be number one on his list and it scares the hell out of me. We should go to sea and be safe," Ava said.

"First, we ought to go over all this with the lieutenant," Andre said.

Chapter Sixteen
A Person of Interest

Lieutenant Robert Bizet accomplished a great deal since he and Marta Vander Riis arrived in Bermuda that afternoon. He kept Marta by his side everywhere he went, backtracking Sergeant Moline's movements. One of the assistant chefs at the Villas on the Beach he questioned recalled seeing the sergeant running on the beach with a beautiful young girl early on the morning he died. It was the young chef's habit to spend from 6:00 until 8:00, every morning, on the cool sand taking in the early sun until it was time to attend to his kitchen duties. His day off, which had been the day prior to the sergeant's death, he spent all day at the beach at his favorite spot. The reason he mentioned this to the lieutenant was because that was when he had first spotted the brunette beauty. The chef said he made a bee-line for her to chat her up. He was rebuffed, then watched as she put her towel down beside a very muscular type who was doing some stretching exercises. The young chef retreated to his spot, a vantage point not far away, and within minutes was treated to another tall blond bombshell who joined the pretty brunette and the muscled hunk. As if this wasn't enough of a view, he then told the lieutenant the scenery was further enhanced as another gorgeous lady joined them who looked like a twin sister of the other leggy newcomer. The lieutenant got a very good description of the raven haired beauty as well as the twin sisters. He then focused the young witness on the muscled fellow, getting a very up to the minute description of Pelling, right down to his wrist and knee bandages. The lieutenant figured he had all the useful information from the affable witness, but he continued talking about the young brunette.

"As I said lieutenant, every morning I'm in my spot, right over there near the walkway in front of the Hotel. The day after my dream gal rejected me for Mr. Muscles, who do I see run onto the beach right over there in front of me? My brunette. I thought, okay Phil, give her another whirl, so I galloped up beside her and said, "Can I run with you?" She pointed to a guy who was running ahead of us and says she's meeting him. Rejected again? I went back to my spot and watched. The guy she caught up to was your sergeant. When you showed me his picture I knew you would want to hear what I had to say," Phil said.

"Phil, this information has been of considerable help and I have only a few questions left to ask you. First, could the Sûreté count on you to be a material witness, if required? And second, can I ask you to look over some pictures which will help in this murder investigation?"

"Sure, you can count on me, lieutenant. Just let me know when and where," Phil replied.

"Have you seen any of the people you described to me since?" The lieutenant asked.

"No sir and I was "on point" at my regular spot this morning. Nothing."

"Okay Phil, thanks again for your help. Please take my card and call me at my room here at the Villas if you spot any of these four people again. Will you do that for me?"

"Yes sir, absolutely. Just let me know when you want me to look at those pictures. Will there be some kind of reward or something?" Phil asked.

"Perhaps, if your information leads to a conviction. We'll see," the lieutenant answered.

"Who are these people, anyway, sir? They looked like movie actors, to me," Phil asked.

"They are extremely good actors, Phil, and very dangerous as the sergeant found out," the lieutenant replied.

* * *

The lieutenant tasted the tumbler full of ginger ale and scotch and thought: *I've got four suspects all known to each other, two of whom were obviously Teddy Pelling and Ruth Werner. But, this twin sister sighting is something* else and who was the pretty young brunette? My young witness, Phil, said the hunky guy and the three beauties made their way off the beach and into villa #17 where they stayed until about 4:30 in the afternoon when muscles left and walked to Villa #15. He came out of that one shortly thereafter in street clothes and looked to be trailing the brunette who went directly to her car parked nearby and drove off. Muscles then returned to Villa # 15. The very next morning, the lovely young brunette runs onto the beach cutting in front of Phil, snubs him again, and meets up with Sergeant Alain Moline. My further questioning of Phil about what he heard the sergeant and the gal talk about, turned up nothing. Phil said he was out of ear shot. Phil's only comment was, 'If your sergeant and the beauty didn't have a date set up to run, then she hit on him, asking if she could tag along.' Phil then asked, what the hell would you have done, eh, Lieutenant?'

Robert Bizet thought to himself: *So, they took off jogging up the beach and nobody has seen the brunette again and Sergeant Moline is found dead in his villa hours later. This eyewitness information ties the brunette and the look-alike companions of Pelling to the sergeant. The actions of this pretty young brunette seem very deliberate: she puts her towel down beside Pelling and introduces herself then ingratiates herself into his group who retire to Villa #17 for more than three hours. Then, the following morning, she gets right after my sergeant. She's either a plant sent by the ETA to get next to Pelling or she's just a very adventurous young thing looking for action in all the wrong places. Hmmm, but why does she hit on the sergeant the very next morning? The witness, Phil, is a good looking young guy who told me he doesn't get turned down too often. Perhaps she was sent to intercept the sergeant? Who though? The ETA? Pelling? Concentrate on the brunette. Find her and you find the answers.*

Robert Bizet smiled over at Marta who was watching him muddle his drink with his right forefinger and lick it off, when the telephone rang. It was Andre Laurent calling from Bordeaux. Andre had been given Robert Bizet's number by the Sûreté Sergeant on duty at the Paris office. After Andre related news about the mysterious "Ruth", whose name on her card was Ruth Meikle; the lieutenant thought this interesting although somewhat bewildering. Robert had asked Andre to advise the Sûreté Paris office of his whereabouts in case of a quick conclusion to the hunt for Pelling.

***

Robert revisited his notes on the passports of Edward Pelling and R. Anna Werner. After further study he thought Ruth Werner and Ruth Meikle were one and the same person. He wrote a memo to be given to his office in Paris to circulate with customs through Interpol. The memo contained an up-to-date description of both Ruth Werner and Teddy Pelling asking that Ruth Werner be detained for questioning as well as any male she is travelling with, regardless of his name or description. After hanging up with Andre Laurent, Robert had a brief discussion with Marta and then called his office in Paris.

Chapter Seventeen
Gulfstream Takeover

George Yaro had been easily manhandled and badly frightened by Pelling. George tried to stay calm but he could not get past the fear of being murdered by the man. When Pelling threatened to throw him out the door of his Jet, he believed the threat was valid. He told Pelling everything he wanted to know, holding nothing back and, though disinclined to think anything good could result, he began feeling more a part of their plan. He slowly began to think he might still benefit.

George reminded Pelling he would have collected a $5 million dollar reward for turning them both over to the ETA. George also told Pelling about the gossip circulating in the organization that he and Ruth have a nest egg of several million dollars. George admitted this was his motivation in not advising the ETA about locating them. After further conversation he admitted that there had been no trouble with the passports they were using. The heat wasn't noticeable, yet, from customs or Interpol. They agreed that the ETA had spread a net hoping to snag them. They also had to contend with the ramifications of the dead Sûreté Sergeant who had been asking questions about them along the beach, back in Bermuda.

George reiterated how he ordered Ursula to take care of the sergeant and make it look like a suicide. No big stretch, didn't cops shoot themselves all the time? George asked.

"What was the Sûreté after?" Pelling asked.

"The sergeant was looking for an Argus Trask and his niece R. Anna Werner who flew to Bermuda from Lisbon a few days back. This Argus Trask was an old gent in a wheelchair. The niece is an attractive looking red-head. The Bermuda police were also alerted to an Interpol dispatch which listed a description of a Teddy Pelling and a Ruth Meikle and asked the Bermuda Constabulary to watch for them. That's when I took it upon myself to take care of the Sûreté Sergeant in order to give you and my friend Ruth a little more room to maneuver. I hoped you would be grateful for my timely help, getting you quickly to your destination and after, on your way," George said.

"So, you haven't had any contact with the ETA since they sent you looking for us?" Pelling asked.

"That's right Teddy, you don't mind me calling you Teddy now do you?" asked George with a slight smirk, which turned to shock when another back hand blow landed.

"I don't think you have had contact, Georgie, because if you had spoken with the ETA after we met, they would be all over us by now. So let's just cut the bull! We both know what you're after. You hoped to get what you could of our money and then planned to collect the reward from the ETA by turning us in. Between you and me, Georgie, you have more chance in getting a fee for services from us than you have of collecting any reward from the ETA. We've both worked for them long enough to realize this. So, from now on, I'll be in charge of our movements for the rest of this little adventure. One more question, Georgie: is the pilot involved or is he just a hired hand?" asked Pelling.

"He is a friend who works for me. He knows everything about me, but I assure you, he is not involved," George replied.

During Teddy's interrogation of George Yaro, both Ruth and Ida sat motionless, not interfering, fearful of the consequences to themselves or to George. Ida had watched the wealthy man completely crumble when Teddy manhandled him to the cabin's exit door and threatened to throw him out. The sudden violent interrogation of their host was shocking to Ida, who suddenly saw Teddy Pelling in a new light. Ruth, however, didn't seem too upset by the proceedings. Ida had thought she might make some connection with the wealthy George Yaro, but after hearing the amount of money offered for Teddy and Ruth's capture, she knew the two of them had indeed stashed a huge fortune. Ida was excited by the action and looking forward to getting even tighter with Ruth and Teddy. She smiled at herself remembering the ten thousand US cash she had received by courier from them. Ida had looked forward to the sex, the shopping and sun and wondered how much of the money she would be able to keep for herself until she was informed it was all for her. Now it seemed like such small spuds. She was melding right into the adventure and the size of the money being bandied about now was making her moist. She made no further judgments about any of the present company, having made up her mind that Teddy was the prize. She would concentrate on him.

"George, we're in contact with the George Town tower and are number two in the landing pattern. We are fifty miles from touchdown on final approach and will be on the ground in five minutes," the pilot announced.

Teddy Pelling looked across at George Yaro and said in a calm, yet ominous voice, "Do you have weapons on board?"

"Only one, a Berretta pistol," George said.

"Take me to it," Pelling demanded.

George led the way to the aft cabin with Pelling in close pursuit. He claimed the pistol, but knew he wouldn't need it. He just didn't want it pointed at him by George or his pilot. He sent George back to his seat with the ladies and re-hid the gun inside a magazine, which he put back in the rack. Now, only he knew its location.

Pelling returned to sit across from George and asked just what to expect when they landed. He did not like surprises. With this last information, he seemed more at ease and in total control of the situation. Even factoring in the possibility that every damn thing George told him was a bloody lie.

Hell, in the same circumstances, I would have made up a story to keep from getting thrown from a plane at 5,000 feet. My take on George is he doesn't like pain and he'll take his chances with us for a little while yet in order to see what fee for services we'll give him. He has to check in with the ETA with some kind of story, so he should ask to be allowed to do so soon after we land. If he doesn't, I'll know something is up.

* * *

Marta Vander Riis was sitting in her bathing suit reading the notes Robert compiled in the two days they had been on the island. Robert was having a shower after they had taken a break and went for a swim in the ocean and a stroll on the beach near their villa. Marta was concentrating on the description of the brunette, who was the last person to have seen Sergeant Alain Moline alive. She suddenly had an idea and went to join Robert in the shower.

After the shower Robert was still in an amorous mood, but Marta got him to pay attention to her by promising to resume this activity later. She stood and began pacing back and forth reviewing the notes he'd made after interviewing the young chef. She refastened the towel wrapped around her and continued. Marta figured if they had an artist's drawing of this young beauty, they would be able to show it in the hotel beauty salon and the other hotel salons along the beach. Someone that stunning would certainly be remembered. Robert watched her animated pacing, which did nothing to alleviate his level of arousal, but gradually he began listening more intently to her plan. She was right. Someone must know her. Marta suggested a police artist. Robert was adamant about not involving the local police, although he did want to confront the investigating officers to question them about why they concluded Sergeant Moline had killed himself. Every time Robert thought about the dutiful sergeant, he blanched at this cavalier indictment which sullied the sergeant's good name.

"You are absolutely right about this beautiful mystery person. Someone has to know who she is. I'm going to fax all the descriptions I have of her to our Paris headquarters and have the identification artists fax us their sketches of her as well as one of Pelling, Ruth Werner and her look-alike. When the sketches come back, we'll start checking the beauty salons in the Hotels on the beach. Great idea, Marta."

The police sketches that came back over the fax at the hotel office were received by the assistant manager who immediately advised Lieutenant Robert Bizet. The assistant manager confirmed that the sketches of Pelling, Ruth Werner and Ida Tesh all were good likenesses. He had no comment on the sketch marked Ursula as he had never met or seen her. Lieutenant Bizet summoned Phil, the young assistant chef and had him examine the Ursula likeness.

"It sort of looks like her lieutenant, but she really is more... strikingly beautiful in person," Phil said.

"In what way?" The lieutenant asked.

"She reminded me of that Paris model, Gabrielle Thierry, I saw in a magazine I have at home," Phil answered

"Oh really! Well then perhaps I could ask you for a favor. Could you bring me a picture of Gabrielle that you think resembles this Ursula person?" The lieutenant asked.

"Is that her name? Ursula? Well ok, sure…I'm on a break now so I can go home and get you the magazine. I'll be back in ten minutes or so," Phil said.

"This will be a great help in the investigation," the lieutenant replied.

The young chef was back at the hotel lobby in fifteen minutes with the magazine. He opened it to the article about Michael Kors, the young American designer who had taken over the French fashion house of Celine. It went on about how he was the talk of Paris fashion. The young chef pointed to a picture of Gabrielle Thierry modelling one of Kor's creations. It was Marta who, after comparing the sketch with the picture of the model, agreed about the likeness.

"We can show both the sketch and this picture and see what we turn up," Marta said.

Lieutenant Bizet thanked the young man again and he and Marta returned to their Villa room. They clipped the picture from the magazine and put it in a file folder that they would show to the various Hotel beauty salons.

* * *

During that afternoon while Marta Vander Riis and Lieutenant Robert Bizet were making inquiries at the hotels on the beach in Bermuda, Ursula was landing at George Town in the Cayman Islands. She had been instructed by her control, Esau Navarra, to fly to that Island on the first available commercial flight. Tio Esau had called her at midnight the evening of George Yaro's departure. Upon arrival at George Town Airport, her instructions were to check first to see if Yaro's jet was still at that airport and, if so, she was to discreetly look for him on Seven Mile Beach. He advised her that all the better hotels were located on Seven Mile Beach, which was only a short distance to the banking district. He also advised that the Caymans boasted some 700 banks, most of which were located in George Town. However, if the jet was not there, Ursula was to find out if and when it landed and when it left and its destination. She was to follow the Gulfstream by commercial airline until she located it. He counted on her to find and report the jet's whereabouts. Her father, Ramon Atmos the pilot, worked on occasion for her control as well. In fact, it was her father, a worldly sort, who had given her to Esau Navarra when she was fifteen years old. The amount of money at stake now was at least in the millions and her fee would be extraordinary. Ursula could be counted on as she had been in love with Tio Esau ever since that first time.

As soon as she had claimed her two bags from the airport luggage reptile at the Grand Cayman Airport, she hired a cab to take her to the area of the airport where the private airplanes were parked. She entered the hangar of the Cayman Islands Flying Club and passed close by the private jet she knew belonged to George Yaro. Her father had flown this jet all over the world in the past six years while in George Yaro's employ.

"Can you tell me where the owner and passengers of the Gulfstream V are staying?" Ursula asked.

"Yes, they were picked up by the Marriott Inn limo. They are only staying for a few days I understand," the clerk said.

"Thank you very much," Ursula said and headed to her waiting taxi.

Ursula asked her driver for the names of the hotels on either side of the Marriott and was told the Treasure Island Resort was on the south side of the Marriott and nothing was on the north until miles up the beach. She asked to be taken to the Treasure Island Resort.

Chapter Eighteen
Who is Ursula?

At the fourth Bermuda Hotel visited by Lieutenant Bizet and Marta, they were told by the beauty salon proprietor that the picture resembled their client, Ursula Atmos. The proprietor looked up her particulars and provided them with her address. The last time she had been into his establishment was one week ago for a trim and style. As far as he knew she was staying for the summer with her guardian and was attending college in New York. The visit one week earlier was her third. The lieutenant gave the proprietor his card and asked to be called either here at his hotel or at his Paris office if Ursula Atmos made another appointment or he happened to run into her or hear of her whereabouts. The lieutenant took him into his confidence and said the young lady in question was wanted in connection with a suspected homicide. This news was enough to animate the shop owner into a flap of assurances that he would call him if or when Ursula surfaced.

The lieutenant and Marta called at the address they had been given: an apartment hotel. They knocked on suite 114 and got no response. At the apartment manager's suite, Bizet showed his badge and asked to be let into suite #114. The manager said it was most unusual but he would make an exception for the Sûreté.

Further questioning of the manager turned up nothing useful as he had not been advised of this tenant's plans. Her rent was paid up until the end of the month. They made a quick tour of the large suite containing two bedrooms. He looked into the closets and returned to the area around the telephone while Marta looked thoroughly through the closets and dresser drawers. When they completed their search, Robert thanked the manager, gave him his card and explained that Ursula Atmos was wanted for questioning in a police matter. If she returned, he was to call the lieutenant at his hotel or inform the Paris office of the Sûreté. He was not to mention anything of this entry to his tenant. The manager was immediately caught up in the intrigue and agreed to the instructions.

In the rental car on the way back to their Villa apartment, Robert asked that they compare their findings.

"I have a picture of Ursula with two gentleman that I found in her jewel box. Her clothes are very chic and expensive: some from Paris, some from Buenos Aires, London and New York. The Gucci luggage is a set of three, and the middle bag is missing. I know because Mathijs bought the same set for mother some time ago. Ursula is a size five and her shoe size is six double A, her bra size is 36 B. She is a natural brunette and takes no medication. I doubt she is a virgin because I found an empty birth control container. I did find her stash of pot in her medicine cabinet and borrowed a small amount that she will never miss. Let's see, what else…oh yes, I couldn't find the bathing suit she was wearing on the beach the other day. I guess that's it."

"I'm impressed, Marta, would you like to work for me?" asked Robert.

"Darling, I will work for you just to be with you. Now tell me what you found?" Marta said.

"She did not leave in a hurry but she did go somewhere. The manager said her Mercedes has not been in its parking spot since yesterday morning. My bet is it's at the airport. I tore the top pages off of the note pad she had on her telephone table. I took the kitchen knife she left in the sink as well as a utility bill she had opened. Should be able to get prints from those. I'll courier them to Paris this afternoon. I would like to get hold of a record of her telephone calls, but that could be tricky. That's about the extent of it for now."

On the way to their Villa from the parking lot, Robert stopped and purchased a pack of cigarettes and matches. Once in their Villa, Robert lit a couple of the cigarettes and let them burn down in an ashtray while Marta busied herself rolling two joints with the pot she had confiscated from Ursula Atmos' apartment. When the cigarettes had burned down, Robert took the filter ends and flushed them down the toilet and concentrated on the remaining ash in the ash tray.

"I've tried this once before and it really works. Come and watch. This is the note page I took from the apartment. I'll just drop the ash onto the paper and stir it around a bit and Voila! Look what we have here...looks like numbers...phone numbers," Robert said.

"Did they teach you that at the police academy?" Marta asked.

"No, I saw it on a TV detective show, actually...works like a damn too," Robert said.

The first number was that of the Belmonte Towers, a hotel on the beach. The second number was United Airlines. The last number was a commercial flying school that was answered by an audex system that advertised aircraft re-fuelling and parking for various size aircraft.

Their next stop was the Belmonte Towers where the lieutenant and Marta questioned the manager and was shown the picture of Ursula Atmos with the two unknown men. The manager demanded to know the purpose of this inquiry and was told that all three could be in danger from terrorists. This seemed to satisfy the manager who identified George Yaro, his private pilot Ramon Atmos and his daughter Ursula Atmos. He further explained that Mr. Yaro owned the hotel and occupied the Penthouse floor when he was in Bermuda. Mr. Yaro had left two days ago in the early afternoon with his guests and did not say where he was going or when he would return. This was not unusual according to the manager who said Mr Yaro visited Bermuda two and sometimes three times a year. This recent visit was less than a week.

The next stop made by them was the flying club at the local airport where, after speaking with the owner, they learned that George Yaro's Gulfstream V piloted by Ramon Atmos had left at just before 2:00PM two days ago, destination Charleston, South Carolina and on to George Town, Grand Cayman Island. He had three passengers aboard and no, Ursula Atmos was not one of the two women passengers. The manager said that the names of the passengers were required on the flight plan but it was not unusual if they weren't, as it wasn't rigidly enforced. He added that they would have to have proper identification to land in another country anyway. Robert showed the owner of the flight station sketches of Pelling,

Ruth and Ida. The owner almost leered and said, yes, that was definitely them and made a comment about how it was hard not noticing those twin sisters.

"Well, we now have Pelling leaving Bermuda on George Yaro's private jet, piloted by Ramon Atmos the father of Ursula, along with Ruth and her lookalike, headed for the Cayman Islands. But, where is the lovely Ursula do you suppose?" Robert asked and continued, "As well, we know that Pelling and the three women knew each other and we also know that Sergeant Moline met Ursula. Or rather, Ursula met Sergeant Moline. Do you suppose she was sent to check him out and find out about his investigation? Could it be that Ursula was working for Pelling, who decided to end the sergeant's investigation?" Robert speculated.

"Pelling could have learned from almost anyone that the sergeant was making inquiries. The connection with Yaro is not clear...unless it was Ursula who made the arrangements for Pelling and the two women to fly to the Caymans with her father in his boss' jet. Why the Caymans? And why didn't she go with them?" Marta wondered aloud.

"Marta, Pelling has a lot on his plate. He has to contend with both Interpol and the Sûreté looking for him. As well, Raoul will have his whole ETA network of agents looking for him. Pelling isn't in any position to be freely making travel plans like this. He arrived here in disguise and has obviously changed his appearance and his passport once again and he remains on the run. If we backtrack a bit and analyze his actions to date, let's see: he takes by force, he kidnaps for ransom, murders, turns in his boss and provides me with proof enough to hang them both. He has hijacked a sailboat. So, why not a private jet?" Robert asked aloud.

"I see what you mean. We will learn more when we check the airport for Ursula's Mercedes. We can drive around the park and ride area first in case she left it there. After that we can check the United Airline flights for yesterday morning to see where she went!" Marta replied.

The Mercedes 500 SL sports car was located in a parkade three blocks from the United Airlines check-in station. The attendant who checked Ursula Atmos' Mercedes in for a two week period said she paid in advance.

The United Airlines official the lieutenant had been referred to by a check-in clerk recognized Bizet from the recent TV coverage he had received after the arrest of Raoul de Vascos. The official pulled up on his computer screen passenger lists of the morning flights. Ursula Atmos occupied an aisle seat on United 124 to Atlanta, Georgia connecting with United 110 to Miami and finally United 128 to George Town Grand Cayman Island. The United official further advised that the ticket she had purchased was an open ended ticket which meant there was no indication when she planned on returning to Bermuda. Lieutenant Robert Bizet and Marta Vander Riis then booked on the late night flight to New York continuing directly to Grand Cayman Island.

Lieutenant Robert Bizet said, "I have spoken with the chief of the George Town Constabulary who seems very uncooperative. He said he has neither the time nor the resources to run around doing the Sûreté's snooping. He did agree to make a couple of phone calls when he has the time. I'm sure he will have something for us when we get there. We'll go and pack and take a taxi to the airport."

Chapter Nineteen
Money Matters in the Caymans

George Yaro was a little calmer now after the threat to his life. The interrogation by Pelling was over quickly once the vicious judo slaps he took to the face had stopped throbbing. He felt sure Pelling would kill him on the spot if he thought he was lying. George was now at the opposite end of the spectrum: He started out in complete control with a very expensive human cargo, which he hoped to cash in for millions, ending at his present state as a hostage, with only a remote possibility of staying alive. He had no alternative but to help in any way he could in the hope of remaining alive.

The Gulfstream V taxied to the location at the George Town International Airport set aside for incoming traffic. Ground control informed them that they would be boarded by customs officials and were instructed to have their plane's papers and the passengers' passports available for inspection. This wasn't George's concern, figuring the custom's check would be routine. Neither would there be a reception by ETA agents because he hadn't informed them of his destination before leaving Bermuda. Unless Pelling approved, it would be almost impossible to contact the ETA. Pelling was extremely cool under the circumstances, which is what frightened George the most. George Yaro was convinced Pelling would kill him as soon as his usefulness ceased. He also realized he could not count on Ruth as an ally. She was clearly in partnership with Pelling. Ida, who had come onto him in such a flagrant manner, culminating in a delicious romp in the bedroom of the jet, could have been a possible confidant. That possibility ended when Pelling slapped him and easily manhandled him to the cabin door and threatened to throw him off the jet if he didn't answer questions. From that point on Ida looked bewildered and became standoffish. It was evident Ida would follow the power, which, at the moment, rested with Ruth and Pelling.

The two customs officers boarded the jet, collected the passports and reviewed them briefly, asking only where each was born, the purpose of their visit and the duration. It was Pelling who asked how long they could stay in the Caymans legally. He had asked this question in response to the customs officer's question: 'How long do you plan to stay?' The officer answered that they could stay 90 days and then would have to make other arrangements. Pelling replied that they would not be that long this time and would leave when they concluded their banking business. The customs officers then bid them welcome to the Caymans, wished them a pleasant stay, and returned their passports.

After arranging parking and refueling of the Gulfstream, the pilot met them in the waiting area and waited along with the others for the limo from the Marriott on Seven Mile Beach, where Pelling had instructed George to book them a three bedroom suite. The limo arrived shortly and drove them via Shedden Road past George Town and the banking district on Harbor and North Church Street to the Hotel on Seven Mile Beach.

When they had settled in, Pelling assigned the bedrooms: The pilot would occupy one, Ruth and George one and Pelling and Ida the other. Pelling removed the telephones from the living room and the other bedrooms and brought them to his. When the pilot questioned George about these strange arrangements, he was told that they would all be shacked up together from here on out. Pelling was in charge. Pelling held all the passports and the keys to the jet. The pilot was only momentarily upset until Pelling told him he would be included in the party, after which he couldn't stop smiling, having understood he was going to get to sample the two lovely ladies. He didn't ask any more questions.

They would eat out this evening together and spend the morning at the Royal Bank arranging the transfer of the money in Ruth's numbered account.

* * *

After the evening meal at the very luxurious Peninsula dining room in their hotel, Pelling suggested they walk. The five of them wandered out onto the beach, came to a small bar and sat at a table under a blue and white striped canvas canopy. They ordered the Island's famous rum punch high-balls and relaxed. Ruth and Ida became rather outwardly attentive to George and Ramon. The promise of intimacy to come lightened the tension in both George and his pilot. Pelling felt he had control of the group. Earlier, before leaving for their meal, he had announced the sleeping arrangements for a reason. He had instructed both women succinctly while the three were in the privacy of his bedroom, as to who to spend their time with until their business was concluded and they were on their way again. Ruth would keep George busy and Ida the pilot. Any pillow talk would be reported back to him immediately. He also told Ida that for her co-operation she would be very well compensated. Ida thanked Pelling with a kiss that included much tongue. Ida then pulled Ruth close with her arm around her waist and kissed her as well.

"Let's double George tonight Ida, after you look after the pilot," Ruth suggested.

"Why not come in and take care of the pilot after I'm finished and let me be with George alone for a while. Would you mind? He got to me real good on the plane this afternoon and I'm literally itching for an encore," Ida replied.

"You are a little tramp! Aren't you though? That's why I love you so. Great, I'll play with the pilot after you. Something about that guy that I'd like to explore. Teddy honey, aren't you feeling just a little bit left out?" Ruth asked.

"Not at all, just do what you guys are both so good at and things will be very manageable.... otherwise..."

Ruth put her finger to Teddy's lips and shushed him with, "We will see to it that they are well looked after, partner. Don't mind us sweetie, we just really like our work, right Ida?"

"Hmmm...Yes lover and Teddy honey you and I have some unfinished business as well, right?" Ida said.

"Plenty of time for the three of us after we get through here in the Caymans," Pelling replied.

Sitting at the beach bar, Pelling watched the interaction of the pilot and Ida with outward indifference. George and Ruth were talking about banking while she stroked him under the table. When the waiter appeared for their second round order, it was George who suggested they call it a night. Teddy paid the bill and they made their way quickly back to their hotel suite. It was 11:00PM when Ruth took George into his bedroom to relax and calm him down. She had kept him in a state of arousal on the walk back to the room, whispering in his ear, promising him things. The door to the other bedroom was barely closed before the pilot began discarding his clothes while leering at the slow disrobing dance Ida was performing for him.

Teddy locked his bedroom door with the key and left the hotel suite for the front desk to rent a safety box where he stashed the passports, wallets and the keys to the airplane. He went back down the beach and stretched his injured knee. The constant opening and closing of his left hand had gotten rid of the numbness in his wrist, but an aching pain had set in. He sat at a beach bar at the Treasure Island Inn next to theirs and ordered a Pauli Girl beer. He had only licked the stir stick of his rum punch at the previous bar with the others. Now, he took long pulls on the cold beer and thought about what might go wrong between now and tomorrow. All kinds of possibilities ran through his mind about how the four people back at the hotel might discover him gone and take off. *Right! I have all the papers, passports and wallets locked up in the hotel lock box. They will try my door and assume I'm in there asleep. Right! No way Georgie is going to break in. No worries about the pilot either. He's only thinking with his little head, and about as expectant as a high school kid who's getting it for the first time when he found out he was going to be allowed to get at the girls. Can I trust the girls though? Hard to say, but Ruth must have learned her lesson with Raoul, and she should realize that he had a hell of a lot more money and power than Georgie Boy has. No, Ruthie won't bolt. She wants to get her hands on our money and she will remain loyal until she does, but then...I think she would sell me out in a New York minute. Since I got a little rough with Georgie boy on the plane, I notice Ida has stopped doting on him and has shown more interest in me and Ruth once again. I think Ruth's right when she said,' Ida knows better and will remain in line', especially since I* said she would be getting a nice chunk of money for herself after she saw me take charge. Teddy in charge! Yes sir! Trusting Ruth almost got me killed once, even when I knew better. As long as they continue to serve a purpose, I'll keep them alive, otherwise...

* * *

Ruth and George got into bed without any preliminaries. Both had things on their mind.

"Cher, remember you said in the first phone call you made to me at the Belmonte penthouse back in Bermuda, that you may need my help... what did you mean? Anyway, I think we are both in serious danger from Pelling."

"George, I am in no danger whatsoever from Teddy! You however, are. He is a very dangerous guy. So, what do you propose to do about it?" Ruth asked.

"Then you agree that as soon as I am of no more use to him, he will kill me. Is that how you see it?" George asked.

"Yes, that's exactly how I see it," Ruth said.

"You must speak to him on my behalf, Ruth, I beg you," George said.

"But George I'm just a ...."

"Alright! Listen closely to what I have to say. Let's suppose I transferred a large sum of money from one of my offshore accounts to your account here tomorrow, a down payment on a much larger amount from ETA funds. Would that guarantee my safety?" George asked.

"Be specific George. How much money are you talking about?" Ruth asked.

"Two million tomorrow and three million more when I'm safe," George said.

"Is this possible?" Ruth asked.

"Yes, absolutely! I transfer funds from one offshore account to another all the time by wire instructions. It is money from ETA operations. For them, I am known as a financial advisor, but really I am one of their trusted accountants," George said.

"Is this your money or does it belong to the Basques?" Ruth asked.

"Does this matter?" George answered.

"Not to me, but it might to Teddy, and I've learned never to take Teddy Pelling for granted and to never presume to speak for him. He would have to answer you. Why have you suddenly gone 180 degrees? You started out helping us, granted for what you thought would be a big score, and now you want to offer to pay Teddy millions for your safety?" Ruth said.

"Pelling needs both of us to get the money and then to get out of here to somewhere where he is safe. I have made plans for the day that I would have to abandon ship with the Basques. Pelling is right when he says, we have both been in their employ and while they pay top dollar for our services, their retirement plan sucks! I doubt very much that there are any who are alive and enjoying the money they made while working for them," George said.

"George, you must talk with Teddy first thing in the morning and make your deal with him. Just don't piss him off, okay? Now tell me what you and Ida did in the back compartment of your jet. It'll make us both horny and then we can play. As far as the help I mentioned you might be able to give me...you have already done it. I was going to ask you to fly us here, that's all. Now then, aren't Ida's nipples fabulous? You must have done her real good this afternoon because she told me she wanted an encore. C'mon George, show me what you did with her, please?" Ruth teased.

Ruth's "naughty talk" was all that was needed to result in a vigorous coupling in which her experienced movements caused him early release. She knew from past trysts with him that he was better than this effort, but understood his angst in his present situation. Ruth said she would go and see how Ida and the Pilot were getting on. As she was leaving the bedroom, she whispered that she would send Ida in to say a special goodnight.

It was almost an hour later when Pelling returned to the suite and saw Ida peeking in the Pilot's bedroom from which squeaky bed noises were coming. Actually, the bed was squeaking and Ruth was coming. Ida turned to Teddy and walked toward him naked.

"I'm going to have a shower in your room. Care to join me?" Ida asked.

Teddy said nothing as he keyed his bedroom door open allowing Ida to flow past.

Moments later they were in the shower. He was soaping her marvelous appendages and she was busy soaping his. They were both momentarily interrupted when joined by Ruth who busied herself soaping his back.

Chapter Twenty
Ava SailsThe SeaOx to St Jean de Lux

Andre Laurent listened with interest as Ava Haas proposed they sail the SeaOx from Bordeaux back along the French coast down to St. Jean de Lux, a small resort town near the Spanish border. Ava explained to Andre that she had heard about this idyllic area many times from her partner in the Hamburg marina who had vacationed there over the years. She had always known she would one day go and see it for herself. What better time than now? Ava convinced Andre that they both needed to be sailing again and safe. They would leave in the morning. Once Andre had agreed to the trip, he decided to settle with the marina for their tie-up time and services. He would do it now in order that they could leave early in the morning. When he arrived at the marina office there was a message to call a number he did not recognize. No name was left, only the number. Andre inquired of the clerk about the call but the manager had taken the call and was not available. Andre took the phone number to the pay telephone kiosk outside the marina office and made arrangements to bill the call to his telephone number on the SeaOx. He thought it strange that the call came to the Marina office rather than directly to the SeaOx.

Marta Vander Riis answered the phone in their Bermuda Villa suite.

"It's Andre Laurent from Bordeaux, someone called me and left this number. Who am I speaking with please?"

"How are you Andre? It's Marta Vander Riis here. Please, just talk with me for a minute until Robert finishes in the bathroom. He does want to speak with you. So, are you and Ava both still in Bordeaux?"

"Yes, but Ava has just convinced me to sail the SeaOx to St Jean de Lux near the Spanish border. Do you know where that is?" Andre asked.

"I do. It's lovely there. My father used to take us there for summer vacations. We also used to stay at a villa in Biarritz which is the town next door. Oh, excuse me please, Andre. I'll put Robert on the line," Marta said.

"Hello Andre, is Ava with you now?" Robert Bizet asked.

"No, she is back on the SeaOx. Incidentally, why didn't you call direct to the SeaOx?"

"Andre, it is important that I speak with you alone," Robert replied.

"I don't understand..." Andre said.

"Andre, I want you to fly to George Town on Grand Cayman Island. The Sûreté will pay all of your expenses. I need you to make a positive identification of your hijacker, Teddy Pelling and his girlfriend," Robert said.

"Is Pelling dead? Or what?" Andre asked.

"No, he is very much alive! We have traced him to George Town. Marta and I are leaving Bermuda for the Caymans as soon as we can get packed. Our flight leaves in three hours," Robert said.

"Ah...alright Robert, I'll make plane reservations and confirm back to you when my flight will get into George Town. It sounds like you want me to come alone. Any particular reason? And why the secrecy?" Andre asked.

"Yes Andre, I would like this little adventure to be just between you and me. Do not tell Ava or anyone else where you are going, only that you will be gone for four or five days. Nothing else. This is very important Andre," Robert insisted.

"I will do as you wish, and when I arrive I'm sure you will explain further. Do you really think you have a chance at capturing Pelling?" Andre asked.

"Well, we have him located but I need your help before we make any arrests," Robert said.

"I'll help in any way I can Robert. I'll leave as soon as I can get a flight. Ava will be very suspicious. She has absolutely had it with terrorists. She is convinced that we are only safe when on the ocean. Can I say I'm meeting you? Oh, by the way, where will I meet you in George Town?" Andre asked.

"We have a room reserved for you at our hotel on Seven Mile Beach - The Treasure Island Resort. Just come straight to the Resort please Andre.

I don't want anyone to know where you are going. This is very important. If you must, tell Ava you will be away for five days at the most and it's a surprise for her to be revealed upon your return. Women love surprises. Please make your flight arrangements, then call me back at this number. Pack some sports clothes and please make sure you go to the airport yourself," Robert instructed.

"As you wish, Robert. Stay by the phone, I'll book the flight and call you right back with the details," Andre said and hung up.

Ten minutes later Andre called back to tell him he would be leaving in four hours for New York where he would have forty five minutes to make his onward connection to George Town, Grand Cayman Island. He said he would tell Ava he had to fly home to Montreal to settle some business with his friends, Giles Ruel and Cecil Audette. He would have a taxi come to the marina and pick him up and take him alone to the airport.

Back aboard the SeaOx, Andre told Ava he had a message at the marina office to call Montreal. He called and spoke with Giles Ruel and Cecil Audette. He said he could not tell her anymore at this time because all he knew was that he must fly to Montreal immediately on an urgent business matter. They would explain when he arrived and he would call her and tell her why this was so urgent. When she offered to go to the airport with him, he said he had already made arrangements for a taxi to pick him up in an hour and a half. There was simply no need for her to see him off and he would return in a couple of days. If she wanted, she could sail the SeaOx on to St Jean de Lux by herself, and he would meet her there. This was the only part of the dialogue about this sudden change in plans that seemed to arouse Ava's interest and she seemed to become less annoyed at his sudden departure and more like her old self. Andre did not like lying to her, or anyone for that matter, but the lieutenant had been adamant about secrecy. *Why?* Andre wondered, but put it out of his mind and concentrated on packing a few items in a leather overnight bag he could carry on the aircraft. When he had packed, Andre stripped down and began arranging what he would wear while travelling. He was about to begin dressing when Ava appeared with nothing on except her panties. She kissed him and pushed him gently back onto the berth, where she began to fellate him. Andre was near climax when she slipped out of her panties and straddled him. He looked into her eyes while his hands where full of her lovely breasts and saw something in her eyes he hadn't noticed before: Lust!

Andre seemed to be outside of himself watching as he thrust into her as she started her climax. She took her eyes from his, lowered her head on his chest and thrust back down on him until she was completely spent. Andre could not finish but remained rigid inside her until she finally rolled off him.

"There now handsome, you just remember who loves you, and you come back to me as quick as you can," Ava ordered.

While Ava was in the head, Andre put his credit cards and a sizeable amount of cash in his money belt as well as the four cashiers' cheques totaling one million dollars. He finished dressing in grey slacks, grey socks, penny loafers and a long sleeved dark blue sport shirt. He would go again to the marina office and pay the bill this time as Ava had decided she would sail the SeaOx to St. Jean de Lux after all. When he returned from the marina office Ava had prepared a quick meal but the taxi arrived before they could finish. They kissed passionately and he left.

* * *

George Town, Grand Cayman Island

Ursula Atmos unpacked her bag and put on the bathing suit that displayed her figure in such a flagrant manner because there was little left to the imagination. It was the same suit she wore on the beach back in Bermuda. She referred to it as her 'hunting outfit'.

In the first store she came to, in the hallway of shops in the lobby, she purchased a straw hat that seemed the "in" headgear worn by so many tourists. To complete her ensemble, she bought dark sunglasses and a straw shopping bag. She left to find a taxi to take her to the Marriot.

* * *

Teddy and Ruth sat in their suite and discussed with Ida how they would move their money located in Ruth's Royal Bank of Canada numbered account. Ruth would ask for five cashiers' cheques for one hundred thousand each. She would wire transfer three million to a Royal Bank in Panama City, Panama. She would transfer five hundred thousand to Ida Tesh's account in Atlanta, Georgia. She would transfer the remaining two million to the Royal Bank in The Hague, The Netherlands. Teddy would take ten one hundred thousand cashiers' cheques and have Ruth wire transfer two and one half million to the same Royal Bank in Panama City in the name of Linus Svendsen. He would also transfer five hundred thousand to Ida Tesh's account making the wire transfer to her one million dollars. These arrangements were made in the open while George Yaro sat and listened and the pilot, Ramon Atmos, ironed his sports slacks.

"George we need your help here. You've heard what we intend to do this morning. Do you see any problems in what we are going to do?" Pelling asked.

"No, it won't be a problem to pay you the cashiers' cheques. Ruth is in charge of the account and can make cheques out to whoever she likes. Wire transferring money is easy to a branch of the same bank in another country also. If the Royal doesn't have a branch in Ida's city, then the bank will want you to open an account for her at one of their other affiliates. It won't be a problem. It should only take a short time to do all this banking," George said.

"Ok then, we can get going now," Pelling announced.

"Pelling, could I have a word with you in the hallway outside?" George asked.

"Why not. We will be ready to leave in a minute, so get dressed Ramon." Ramon smiled at Pelling and nodded. In the hallway George got right to the point.

"Just as soon as you have the Panama City account opened, I will transfer two million to this account from one of the offshore accounts I manage for Esau Navarra of the ETA," George said.

"Wait a minute here Georgie boy...why the sudden outpouring of generosity?" Pelling asked.

"I do not wish to die, Señor Pelling. This is a down payment for you to guarantee my safety," George said.

"What do you mean a down payment?" Pelling asked.

"If you will shake hands to seal a gentleman's agreement with me to guarantee my safety, I will deposit another three million to this account when I and the plane are free to go, once we drop you off in Panama City. You must know that I also will be hunted by the ETA when they find out I have given you five million of their money. I would say we both have about two days' head start on them at the most," George said.

"Well now Georgie boy, I certainly will shake with you on that, but tell me, how much money have you pocketed of theirs on the side?" Pelling asked.

"Fifteen million after I give you five million; more than enough to disappear into retirement," George answered. "Well, well…good luck with that. Yeah, I figure we'll both need some luck in that regard," Pelling said.

When the group gathered at the entrance of the Marriot and entered a limo to take them to the banking district in George Town, they were being watched by Ursula, who sat at an outdoor bar table under a canopy. Even if they took the time to look at her very closely, she doubted they would recognize her, the floppy straw and tourist glasses concealing her face. As soon as the limo left, Ursula left money for her drink and hailed the taxi she had arrived in. She had tipped the driver handsomely and arranged that he accept only her as a passenger. He was to wait until she hailed him. Back in the taxi, the driver was asked to follow the limo up ahead at a safe distance. When she handed him a $CI 50.00 bill he smiled at her and nodded. Ursula was conflicted watching her father, George Yaro, Pelling, Ruth and Ida waiting for the limo at the hotel entrance, all looking bright and cheerful as if they were off on a shopping spree. Her taxi slowed as the limo came to a stop in front of the Royal Bank of Canada. Ursula had her driver wait until the occupants of the limo had dismissed it and they all had entered the bank.

She wondered: *Is this where it gets interesting? Is George going to take money from one of his banks and give it to Pelling? What is happening here and what will George do next? I've followed instructions to the letter: I trailed him here. I've located his plane. I've got them all in sight and they seem to me to be just a happy group of shoppers. I should report in, but I don't want to let them out of my sight. I have to stay close so as not to lose them. Stay on the ball and do this job, remember Tio Esau has a short memory and I haven't been paid for the Sûreté Sergeant yet.*

Chapter Twenty One
Ursula's Assignment

When Andre Laurent left the SeaOx for the taxi cab waiting to take him to the airport, he made himself comfortable in the back seat and wondered at the way Ava had said goodbye. She had hung on to him after they had kissed as he babbled instructions to her about the SeaOx and the provisions that hadn't been put on board yet. She looked deep into his eyes through her tears and did not smile. Andre wondered if Ava believed him when he said he was off to Montreal to sign some important papers needed by his friends Giles Ruel and Cecil Audette. He must call them as soon as he arrives at the airport and warn them not to call the SeaOx until further notice. He would not have to ask them to lie for him in case Ava called for him because he was sure she didn't know how to get in touch with them in any event. He thought back to the moment he had told her to take the SeaOx on to St. Jean de Lux by herself. She had not looked either happy or sad at the suggestion, but had simply replied that she would probably do that. Because she loved the SeaOx as her own and was happiest when she was sailing the big pilot house cutter, he thought she would be ecstatic at his generous offer. He certainly didn't have any worries about her competence as she was a more experienced sailor than he. Why all the secrecy from Ava by the Lieutenant? What's that all about? He made his call to Montreal and left word with Giles and Cecil not to call him at the SeaOx until he advised them. By noon tomorrow he would be in George Town and Robert would give him the answers to his questions concerning Ava.

* * *

Back at the marina, Ava Haas walked to the office and spoke with the clerk. She was told that Mr. Laurent had paid for the SeaOx and it was free to go or remain, as Mr. Laurent had left his credit card imprint in case she decided to stay. Ava asked if the clerk had a copy of the message given to Mr. Laurent. The clerk had only come on duty when the manager had left for the evening. There was no evidence of any message, only the telephone number she had given to Mr. Laurent. No, she did not remember the number but, perhaps when the manager came on duty in the morning, he could help her. Ava made change with the clerk exchanging small bills for coins for the pay phone outside the office. At the phone booth outside the Marina office, Ava placed a call to the airport and asked flight information for Montreal, Canada. She was told the flights to Montreal and Toronto left the Bordeaux airport at noon local time. The only flight leaving this evening was to New York City which was due to leave in thirty-five minutes. The next flight was to Miami leaving at 8:00AM. Ava hung up and dialed another number and gave all the details of the evening's happenings to the person on the other end of the line. She asked should she stay put or make the voyage to St. Jean de Lux. She was told to make the voyage and to leave in the morning. She hung up the receiver and made her way back to the SeaOx.

* * *

In George Town, on Grand Cayman Island, Pelling posing as Linus Svendsen, along with Ruth Werner and Ida Tesh, were occupied at the Royal Bank opening accounts in Panama City, The Hague, and Atlanta, wire transferring large amounts of clean money to new accounts at these branches of the Royal, much to the delight of the assistant manager who was helping them. As well, George had transferred two million to Ruth Werner's account at this bank and instructed her on how to send it on to her newly established account in Panama City. George did the transfer this way in order to show Pelling that he could. George was as good as his word and within fifteen minutes the assistant manager that was looking after their business confirmed that the money had arrived at her new account at the Royal Bank in Panama City. Pelling was not easily impressed but a smile crossed his face when he thought: *This is the first time I've been paid money for not killing someone.*

While documents were being signed, the pilot Ramon Atmos sat in a comfortable waiting area and read magazines. He was about to begin re-reading one of the magazines when George beckoned him that the limo had arrived and they were ready to leave.

Sitting across from the Royal Bank at an outside bagel and coffee shop sipping an iced coffee, sat Ursula. She watched the limo pull up to the Bank and the five get in and drive away. Ursula rose quickly, catching her large hat on the edge of the table knocking it from her head just as the limo drove by and she didn't notice Pelling watching her. She was in a hurry to get to the taxi she had waiting for her return.

Pelling, looking out the window of the limo, thought to himself: *Well, isn't this interesting? Who shows up in George Town but the lovely young Ursula? What a coincidence, right? Last time I saw her, she took an elevator up to Georgie Boy's penthouse and didn't come down. So Georgie has her trailing us. Interesting! I wonder if Georgie really did order her to kill the Sûreté Sergeant in Bermuda. Well we won't be leaving until early morning, so I'll see if I can intercept her and have a chat because there's no doubt she's following us.*

Ursula had her taxi driver follow the limo back to the Marriot where George et al climbed out and made their way into the lobby. Ursula then instructed her driver to take her next door to her hotel, the Treasure Island Resort Inn.

In the lobby of the Marriot, the two women, George and the pilot Ramon all left for the suite to change into their swim suits and spend some time on the magnificent beach. Pelling had given his blessing and said he was going to check out the shops in the hotel. As soon as the four had entered the elevator, Pelling left the Marriot and strolled over to the Treasure Island Hotel next door. Ursula wasn't registered at the Marriot but Teddy figured she would be close by.

Pelling spotted Ursula waiting at the elevator and ducked behind a pillar. When he looked again, he saw four people leave the elevator and Ursula get on. He watched the floor levels light up as the elevator lifted to the 7th floor and stopped. The elevator began a descent, stopped at the

4th floor, resumed it's descent to the lobby where two young men in swim trunks got off.

Pelling made his way to the 7th floor, went immediately to the two native ladies who were making up rooms and flashed a $CI 100.00 bill at them. He asked in which room was the dark haired Señorita that had just got off of the elevator. The younger of the two, with a knowing smile, pointed to room 709. Teddy motioned to the older maid to open the door for him and put his finger to his lips to shush them into silence. She keyed the door open for him as he put his forefinger to his lips again stifling their giggles as he handed over the 100.00 bill and slid past them into the room. He heard water running and he closed the door as quietly as possible, but was unable to avoid the clank of the catch. He then slid the knob of the bolt closed, which could only be opened from the inside. Pelling slipped off his loafers as he peered around the corner of the bathroom and saw the shadowy figure of Ursula through the opaque glass of the shower doors. Teddy removed his shirt and dropped his trousers and underwear to the floor. He walked the five paces to the shower enclosure and slid the glass door open, stepped into the loud tepid shower and encircled Ursula in his muscular arms. Ursula was startled, but only for a moment.

"Ursula, try and enjoy what I'm going to do to you before you die. Let's go to the bed." He pulled her, helpless, toward the queen sized bed. She lay on her back, knees wide arching up to him. He played with her breasts and nipples and slipped his hand around her neck and held her in a choke hold while he dipped his chin into the triangle of wet jet black pubic hair. His tongue began a frenzy of thrusting. He looked up at her face when she started to come, her moans and the orgasmic mewling coming from her constricted throat he remembered from their orgy the other day, but the terror in her eyes was new. It excited him. He licked her into another shuddering orgasm. Pelling knelt between her spread legs and positioned himself for entry. He liked this part the best, when they thought they were spent. He entered her and waited until her involuntary shuddering resumed before he began to thrust into her. She went to another place in her head while he got her off again. Then she began to plead with him for her life in the only way she knew how: she began to beg him to come in her. No one he ever had sex with before had ever talked to him during sex like this. Ida, to some extent, and also Ruth, but not like this. Ursula wanted to feel his release inside her. She said even when he didn't come inside her the other day she still had a tremendous off of her own. She asked him to allow her to hold it while he thrust into her. She said she wanted to feel when he surged into her.

"You did me real good with your tongue. I'm still so hot I just might shatter when you come inside me."

Pelling lost it and Ursula experienced her third orgasm. She held him tightly by the penis as he thrust through her hand into her. Ursula was again shuddering as she counted. "Six, seven... ooh, wow! It's starting to run out of me. God, I can't believe how much you came. You certainly can rattle a girl's brains. Honey, I need a strong drink!"

Pelling pinned her to the bed in a death grip with his left hand and reached for a pillow to cover her face. The look of terror was back in her eyes. She was going to die. He held her under the pillow for a minute. Long enough that panic consumed her. He removed the pillow and loosened his death grip.

"Who sent you here?" Pelling asked.

"Esau Navarra, he's my benefactor. Please don't kill me Teddy, I can help you, honest."

"Did you kill the Sûreté policeman?"

"Yes, he was getting very close to you and my orders were to eliminate him. The ETA want you very badly. Raoul is in prison and his uncle Esau has all agents alerted. I reported to him just as I returned to the suite. I'm supposed to keep an eye on all of you until help arrives from Miami at noon tomorrow," Ursula said.

"Does George Yaro think you are working for him?"

"Well yes, my father has flown his jet for the past six years and George does give me little jobs to do for him. He pays me real good, sure, I work for him too, I guess. It's funny in a way, he tells the story often to new friends about how he deflowered me and put me out of my misery at being a very horny virgin. I was 15. He still thinks he was the first man to have me. What he doesn't know is, I chose Esau for my first, the day I met him. We were visiting his villa, my father, George and me. I was a very precocious 15 year old but I knew what I wanted. Esau was captivating and when I had a chance to get up close to him, I whispered in his ear that I was a virgin and picked him to fuck me first. He asked if he could show me his house, took me on a tour upstairs and into a maid's room. He took off his clothes and I mine. He started jerking himself but then let me do it for him. I tasted him and put it in my mouth and sucked him. He sucked my nipples and my pussy and made me come. Then we had sex. He got into me and it hurt a bit until he got me real juicy. I remember, it was starting to feel awfully good when my stomach started to feel strange, Esau was very excited, getting his hard cock into me. So deep on some strokes I could feel his balls slap against my butt. He paid me 100 bucks and asked that I listen closely and call and tell him what George and Dad talked about on the way back. I called a number he had me memorize. He thanked me for the mundane information I gave him and then introduced me to phone sex. He paid me well and dropped in on us unexpected or found an excuse to call George to fly to his villa and bring me along. It was six months later that Esau asked me to seduce George Yaro and make it look like he was the first. I wanted to screw him anyway and was pleasantly surprised when I seduced him.

George really knows how to take care of a woman. He taught me so much, mostly how to suck and enjoy anal sex. So at the tender age of 15, I was looking after two very active men both old enough to be my Dad or even Grandfather. And, honey, I just loved it, literally getting my brains fucked out for a solid year until it began to taper off to only an occasional happening. I've had sex with Esau four times in the last six months. I'm sure you won't mention I report to both Esau and to George. Esau pays me very well because I'm one of his favorite young ladies, and you should also know that my father is not in any way involved. My father is George's private pilot and parties with him sometime but that's all. I knew they were coming to the Caymans and then probably on to Argentina. I told them I might meet them here and continue on with them. George mentioned you and the girls had banking business here in George Town."

"Why aren't you staying at their hotel? Why are you incognito and following us today?"

"According to Esau, George Yaro's usefulness to the ETA has come to an end and I'm quite sure he will never leave this Island alive. Esau knows that you and your friend Ruth are with George and because he didn't report back to Esau when he was supposed to, Tio Esau suspects collusion between you. So George has become a liability."

"Have you been ordered to kill him?"

"Not him. Just the Sûreté Sergeant, but I do know that Esau's men are on their way here."

"When are you to call Esau again?"

"Tomorrow, after six in the evening."

"Tell me the number!"

"011-49-56-223 3345"

He put the left hand choke hold on her throat again and put the phone closer to himself on the bed. Pelling dialed the number from memory.

"Yes?"

"This is Pelling the Corporal calling Tio Esau. I plan to keep in touch with you. Ursula was kind enough to give me this number before I killed her."

"Great news! I would have killed her myself for this indiscretion. Thank you for your service in this regard. Enjoy your final few days here on earth before we sanction you, Corporal," Tio Esau said.

Pelling hung up the phone and arranged the terrified Ursula on top of him, backwards. With her legs outside him, she kept her balance as he thrust into her. The familiar action stirred her innards to involuntary feelings that took over making her a more than an obliging partner. She obliged him like it was her last sex on earth. Pelling increased the pressure on her throat when she started to come, cutting off her ability to breathe. She thrashed about while he continued. Her death throes really turned him on, and he climaxed, enjoying the last shuddering twitches of her spent body. He rolled her off of him and covered her in her own bed covers. After he toweled himself off from his quick shower, he got dressed, wiped the phone receiver and anyplace else he thought he may have touched. A glance at his watch told him it was 2:30. They wouldn't discover her body until they made up the room in the morning. He left the 'do not disturb' sign on the outside doorknob, wiped it clean of his prints and pulled it closed.

As Pelling walked out of the lobby, he was observed by Lieutenant Robert Bizet, Marta Vander Riis and newly arrived, Andre Laurent.

To Andre's surprise on his arrival, Marta and Robert had made some purchases and left the clothes on Andre's bed with a note, 'compliments of the Sûreté.' As a result, they were all dressed in new touristy island outfits, sitting at a table at the edge of the lounge, nursing drinks with umbrellas. Andre put his hand on Robert's and let him and Marta find his eyes and then focus on who he was looking at: It was Teddy Pelling walking with just the hint of a limp, crossing the foyer from the elevator to the revolving doors, out into the afternoon heat.

Chapter Twenty Two
Pelling in Control

"That's Pelling or whatever the hell his name is. I thought you said he was at the Marriot next door?" Andre said.

"He is! Must be visiting someone. Wonder who?" Robert answered.

"Robert, I'm sorry I don't have a gun. I could save us all a bunch of trouble," Andre said.

"Easy, Andre, be calm. This is good! We have him now that you can positively identify him. Now we close in on him, but not without some help. This Ursula, who was the last person to see Sergeant Moline alive, is registered at this hotel and is in room 709. I think that's our first stop," Robert suggested.

The three of them took the elevator to the seventh floor and saw the Do Not Disturb sign on her door. Robert was suspicious and went for help. The other two were to wait until he returned. The Bell Captain knocked loudly on the door three times and then keyed the door open. They discovered the occupant, Ursula Atmos, wrapped in her bedclothes, staring at the ceiling with a perplexing look in her dead eyes.

"I would like this kept very quiet until I have a chance to speak with your management. Is that clear?" Robert ordered.

The Bell Captain agreed, saw them out, replaced the DND sign and locked the door.

When Pelling arrived back at their suite at the Marriot, he was told by Ruth about their antics while he was gone. After the sex, they all went to the beach, Ramon and Ida were still down there, but she and George decided to come back to the room and initiate round two. Teddy thought to himself that Ruth and Ida were definitely doing a job on Ramon and George, keeping them occupied.

Pelling listened to this blow by blow account of their activities and then said matter of factly, "The ETA are due here tomorrow noon Georgie boy, but we will be long gone."

"How do you have this information?" asked George.

"I ran into Ursula who used to work for you but was on an assignment to follow you and us. I persuaded her to tell me all about her interesting but short life after which she gave me Esau Navarra's private phone number. I called him and let him listen to her die while I choked her to death," Pelling said.

"Jesus! Pelling they will be all over this island tomorrow," George said, the fear in his voice nearing panic levels.

"Ruth, go down and bring Ramon and Ida back up to the suite," Pelling ordered.

"Sure, need anything else anybody?" Ruth asked.

"Just bring the others up!" Pelling said.

Ruth Werner returned to the suite with Ramon and Ida in tow and listened to the directions given by Teddy Pelling. George and Ramon would schedule a five AM flight to Panama City, Panama. George called the hangar where his jet was parked and alerted the manager of their early departure. He was assured that the jet was flight ready when they were, as it was pre-cleared to leave at any time. Ramon would do the weights and balance math prior to takeoff. Everyone seemed nervously anxious about their departure. Teddy looked around at his group and wondered what Esau Navarra and Ursula had planned for this group. Or, was it Ursula and George and her father, Ramon Atmos who had something in store for them? He noticed Ruth was a bit jumpy and had been since he had advised George that he had snuffed the life from Ursula Atmos while on the phone with Esau. Neither George nor Ruth would tattle this tale to the pilot. Why risk being thrown from the jet on the way to Panama City?

Chapter Twenty Three
Murder at Sea and the Pompous Cayman Cop

Lieutenant Robert Bizet was going over a list of coincidences concerning Andre's relationship with Ava Haas. He was pointing out to Andre that he was quite possibly set-up by her and unknown parties. The last straw was when Ava suggested they sail the SeaOx to Lisbon, Portugal. Too many coincidences to suit the shrewd police officer. He had asked for a deep background check on Ava Haas and had been given a thick folder on her. She was a very radical college student in her day. She belonged to Red October and was trained in the deserts of Libya in terrorist tactics. Her real name was Ella Meyer. She married a Basque cell leader of the ETA who was liquidated eight months later by the ETA for insubordination. Ella had reported his disobedience to his control, which lead to his death days later. She then dropped out of sight for about a year after making an investment in a marina operation in Hamburg. Her partners are suspected Basque sympathizers.

As the damning weight of the evidence of who Ava Haas really was gradually got through to Andre, he began to feel the sadness of loss creeping inside his gut. He realized that she had planned to hijack the boat from him from the day she sold it to him. How in the hell had he managed to get himself into this bloody jackpot anyway! His mind flashed back to the original 'learning voyage' they had taken from Hamburg to Oostend across the channel to London and back across to LeHavre. Then, the quick excursion into Paris to shop, the idyllic stay at the De Lutece. It all reeled past his mind's screen and everywhere he saw Ava smiling at him.

He felt sick to his stomach and left for the washroom and soaked his face with cold water. He toweled his face dry and looked into the mirror at his blank expression, then returned to the table occupied by Robert Bizet and Marta Vander Riis. Marta did not say much while Robert and Andre went over the facts of this evidence. Robert said, "I made up my mind in Bermuda that it would be relatively easy to locate a stolen boat but practically impossible to find a missing sailor. That's why I got you here alone as quickly as possible."

"Robert, I want you to have these four cashier's cheques that I took from Pelling. Judging by what has happened I should have taken a few more to compensate for the SeaOx which I'll probably never see again. Andre unzipped the long pocket of his money belt and picked out the four cheques totalling one million US dollars and handed them to the Lieutenant.

"I'm going to hold these in safekeeping but will not log them into evidence because, if we try and return this money to Elspeth, she will know we have been meddling with the ransom and that goes against our promise to her. I'll find an unofficial place for them for now. This amount of money would be a very big inducement for a hijacking. Did Ava know you had this kind of money on the boat?" Robert asked.

"Yes, I told her everything, up until last night that is," Andre said.

"My guess is that she has scoured the SeaOx by now looking for this money, probably with some help," Robert said.

"The SeaOx has been boarded two different times that I know of, both times it was when we were at the City Docks Marina in Bordeaux. I didn't think much of it after I reported the first incident but I had the local police investigate the latest boarding just this week. Nothing was taken but everything was looked over very thoroughly and then replaced. Strange. Ava said she didn't want to know anything about my money and how I got it, but she was happy that I had some. She kept our relationship all tied up in seamanship and the sailing. I told her that I owed her my life for looking for me when I was hijacked. She evidently was more concerned with the recovery of the SeaOx. This information about her is difficult for me and really hard to relate to. Should we put an alarm out for the SeaOx and have her taken into custody?" Andre asked.

"I have alerted the sergeants at the Paris office to keep your boat under surveillance as it moves down the French coast toward St. Jean de Lux," Robert replied.

* * *

Ava Haas knew she was having company when the helicopter dropped out of the sky and deposited an agent into the mildly pitching cockpit of the SeaOx while underway. He entered the doghouse and said he was ETA working for her control with instructions to search the boat thoroughly. She went back to the steering position and left him to go over the boat in a very systematic search. His search was very efficient taking about forty minutes. The agent didn't find what he was looking for and told her so while producing a nasty looking knife. Ava faced the agent, crossed her arms in front of her and lifted her sweater over her head, showing him what she would willingly offer for her life when his lightening-like slash cut her throat. She slumped to the deck as her life gurgled out of her once vibrant body. He searched her before he turned the sailboat's engine off. When he heard the wuffing of rotor blades, he moved back out to the cockpit to be lifted up off the SeaOx by the returning helicopter.

Maritime Patrol had been keeping tabs on the SeaOx by means of a fly-over four times each day. Ava Haas was on her way to St.Jean de Lux on the Southern French coast. It was easy to track the SeaOx as the helicopter's radar screen would show a blip, every ten seconds, emitted from the electronic device epoxied under the SeaOx's bowsprit. The Maritime Air Patrol had been warned of a possible attack on the private sailboat and, on their third routine fly-over, the crew of the helicopter noticed the sailboat was adrift and no one at the helm. The crew, hovering above the gently pitching vessel, immediately notified the Sûreté who gave instructions to board the SeaOx, investigate and report. The lifeless body of Ava Haas was lifted off the SeaOx by the helicopter a half hour later and two Maritime Patrol Crewmen stayed onboard in order to sail the boat back to the City Docks Marina in Bordeaux. This turn of events was reported, immediately, to Lieutenant Bizet at his hotel in George Town, Grand Cayman Islands.

***

"Lieutenant, Sergeant Debois here. Ava Haas was found dead in the doghouse of the SeaOx this morning on a surveillance flyover. Her throat had been slit. The boat had been thoroughly searched judging by the condition of the main salon area, sir. The body was taken off by the helicopter crew and flown to Bordeaux. Two Maritime Patrol crewmen are on board the SeaOx and have it under control. Is there anything you wish me to do sir?"

As the lieutenant hung up the receiver, he faced Andre Laurent and Marta Vander Riis and said, "Ava Haas has been murdered on the SeaOx while en route. The helicopter crew of the Maritime Patrol that we requested keep a watch on your boat noticed the SeaOx was adrift. They boarded your boat and found Ava Haas dead on the deck of the doghouse. Her throat had been slit. Andre, her body was taken off the SeaOx and flown back to Bordeaux."

"Good God, Robert! Ava...aaah! But...?" Andre gasped.

Andre's face was ashen as he looked at Robert who continued, "The SeaOx is on its way back to the Bordeaux City Docks Marina. It is being sailed by two experienced Maritime Special Crewmen. Andre. This changes a few things for us and how we should proceed from here. If Ava was working for the ETA, it's possible she made arrangements for a hit on you and your boat at sea. They, undoubtedly, were after the money she told them you had on board. I'm only guessing, but her motive may have been to have them kill you at sea for the money, leaving her with your sailboat. Ava was connected to the ETA, so this may be a possible scenario. The report also mentioned how the SeaOx was ransacked. Looking for those cashiers' cheques, no doubt, and when they didn't find the money they eliminated her. I don't think we'll ever know, short of a full confession from whoever ordered her death. One thing for certain: we know Pelling didn't kill her!" Robert said.

Both Marta and Robert noted the intake of breath from Andre Laurent and waited for his response to this tragic news about Ava Haas.

"I'm really freaked over this news, Robert...Good Lord...Ava! What in hell were you into and who are the murdering bastards you were involved with?" Andre turned away from Marta and the Lieutenant and took a couple of deep breaths before he turned to face them once more.

"Look, don't think me a callous son of a bitch if I don't appear too broken up about Ava, but...to die like that! I just want you to know that ever since your evidence convinced me that Ava wasn't who she represented herself to be, I've been mentally backing out of the relationship. This news of her murder puts an end to it for me. Now I'll quit thinking up scenarios about why she wasn't a part of my kidnapping or involved in anyway. Christ, she had to be, but an ending like that I wouldn't wish on my worst enemy. She obviously was involved with some very heavy people. Robert, I'm grateful to you for calling me here when you did, otherwise I might have been the one murdered at sea. Her killers came up empty. They have to think I still have the million dollars, so they'll be watching the SeaOx for my return. Don't you agree?" Andre asked.

"I've asked my two sergeants in Paris to check for a Ruth Werner or Ruth Miekle who could be a stock broker or a financial planner in Paris and if they find her, to run down her finances as well as any connection with Pierre Turin. If she was working in the financial industry, she would have had to be registered. I've asked them to check anyone with the first name Ruth matching the description we have of Pelling's companion. We'll just have to wait until we hear back from Paris," Robert said.

"I think it's time we visit the local Grand Cayman Constabulary for some assistance in bringing Pelling and the others into custody," Robert suggested.

"Sergeant Debois informs me that he's getting repeated requests from Raoul de Vascos asking to speak with me. Raoul may not be 'in the ETA loop' anymore and getting more than a little nervous about his situation."

"Well, when this puzzle is finally put together, we'll all be wiser and safer. However, we have to wait another couple of hours to hear back from Paris, to see what Sergeant Debois can tell us about the Gulfstream V. Why else would he have stopped in these offshore bank havens since Lisbon?" Robert said.

"I think it's time to ask the Cayman Constabulary for assistance in seizing the Gulfstream and taking Pelling and his girl-friends into custody," Robert added.

***

The inspector of the Grand Cayman Constabulary who received Lieutenant Robert Bizet, MartaVander Riis and Andre Laurent at his office in the George Town Station, was Granby Pennington aged 65 on his next birthday, October 15. Pennington had come up through military police ranks and had been in his present command for the past three years. He was looking forward to his retirement in four months. This posting had been a blessing for the career policeman who planned on living out his retirement doing the things he loved: socializing and golfing at his private club and fishing off the many reefs around the Caymans. His tour of duty so far had been strictly by the book. The inspector took no chances at all, hoping that the next four months would play out as mundane as the past three years. However, as he listened carefully to this Bizet chap who insisted that he was in charge of an anti-terrorist crew operating out of the Paris, France offices of the Sûreté, the Inspector was immediately on alert. It wouldn't do to get in the middle of some sort of shoot-up donnybrook on his docile Island. He would have to divert the Sûreté and stall any sort of intervention from his end. After all, he was entrusted with keeping the peace and couldn't be involved in any terrorism business. Granby Pennington was a careful man and while this Sûreté chap's identification confirmed who he was, he didn't hold any sway on this Island, unless the inspector had some directive from the fellow's superior officer in writing on official Sûreté letterhead. Lieutenant Bizet went patiently over the request again for a swat type team to lead in the capture of a very dangerous terrorist who was located on 7 Mile beach. He could leave George Town at any time as he was thought to have commandeered a private jet located at the local airport. Another important matter was a young woman named Ursula Atmos wanted for questioning in the murder of Sergeant Alain Moline of the Paris Sûreté. The lieutenant pointed out to the inspector that he had trailed Ursula Atmos to this Island and she is registered at the Treasure Island Hotel on 7 Mile Beach. She is suspected to be working with Pelling who was observed entering her hotel room earlier today. She hasn't been seen since then. The lieutenant requested that she be arrested and held for questioning. However, judging from the stern disapproving stare he saw on the inspector's face, he knew he wasn't convinced and they might not receive any help whatsoever without some official directive from his superiors in Paris. So, Bizet asked for pen and paper and wrote out a fax requesting his Paris office to call and then fax Inspector Pennington with authorizing paperwork so that he could lend assistance in the arrest of Ursula Atmos and the capture of Teddy Pelling. What Bizet didn't know was that the inspector wouldn't be too crazy about assisting in this international terrorist's business even if the proper paperwork should arrive. If this Sûreté fellow wasn't setting him on some wild goose chase and this preposterous story was true, he figured he had better at least go through the motions, so as to be seen to be complying with a request for assistance. He would have Detective Captain Lewis check into this Ursula Atmos person at the Treasure Island Hotel in the morning.

When the lieutenant, Marta and Andre finally left the police station, they decided they might as well have dinner somewhere while awaiting some response from the Paris office. The Inspector had promised to send his Detective Captain over to the Treasure Island Inn to arrest Ursula Atmos. It was nearly 6:00 in the evening, so they hailed a cab and asked to be taken to the Treasure Island Inn. They would eat in their hotel dining room and get ready for the evening's activities as the inspector would get more interested, and hopefully involved, once his Detective reported that he had found Ursula Atmos dead. By that time the Sûreté would have called the inspector and provided the George Town Constabulary with an official request to lend assistance in the arrest of Teddy Pelling.

They finished their meal by 8:30 at which time the lieutenant called the Constabulary and asked for the inspector. The Staff Sergeant on duty said they hadn't received any communication from Paris and the inspector had gone to his club at 7:00PM. Bizet hung up the receiver, trying not to indicate his displeasure. He relayed the information to Marta and Andre who became even more incredulous. It was Andre who said, "To hell with them Robert! Does the US Drug Enforcement Agency have a presence here in the Caymans?"

"I'm not sure. Damn, I may have to locate the private jet and arrest it myself. I thought locals in Lisbon, Portugal were slow off the mark. I wonder if the inspector even sent my fax to the Sûreté office. He certainly didn't appear to want to get involved at all, did he?" Robert said.

"You can count on my help Robert," Andre said.

"And mine as well!" Marta echoed.

Chapter Twenty Four
Death on Departure

After the very sumptuous dining experience at the Sugar Mill Restaurant, Teddy Pelling announced that they would take the limo to the jet and settle in for the night. They left for the private airfield at 8:45. It was a thirty minute drive. The others all boarded the jet in the hangar and awaited Ramon's return from the hangar office. Ramon Atmos settled with the on-duty clerk and checked the local weather and asked for assistance in flagging him out of the hangar safely while he taxied the jet out onto the runway. Ramon took the pilot's seat and Teddy sat in the co-pilot's seat while they taxied out into a takeoff position. George Yaro wanted a magazine to read while in the washroom and couldn't believe his eyes when the gun he had given to Pelling fell out of the book back into the magazine rack. He put the gun in his trouser pocket and closed the washroom door behind him. George had heard Ramon say, upon his return to the jet, that they were cleared to leave at any time except between 10:00 and 10:15 when an inter-island flight was due to land. George checked his wristwatch: 9:45. He wondered why Pelling was taking his time?

George would have to make a move against Pelling or put the gun back in the magazine rack and take a chance that Pelling was greedy enough to want the other three million US dollars promised in order to guarantee his safety when they arrived in Panama City. The arrangement was that they would all go to the Royal bank together to arrange the transfer from one of George's offshore Banks to Pelling in Panama City. Ruth and Pelling would then decide where they would wire this money. He left the washroom, but instead of putting the magazine containing the gun back in the rack, he walked toward the cockpit, nodding, and smiling to Ida and Ruth as he passed them. He knocked on the cabin door announcing his entry. He stepped into the compact cabin and withdrew the gun from his pocket so that both his pilot and Pelling could see it and asked, "What are we waiting for Pelling? Why don't we leave?"

Pelling never took his eyes off the gun, which was hanging limp in George's right hand, but gradually turned the copilot's seat inward toward the exit position. In a snake-like motion Teddy's left hand grabbed George's right hand and twisted it all in one motion. George shrieked in pain startling Ramon and the two women. Teddy got to his feet keeping George's wrist bent into his groin area which caused his right hand to lock tightly around the gun. Teddy's strength backed George out into the main cabin.

"Jesus...Pelling for God sake you are breaking my wrist..!" George made a clumsy attempt to extract the gun from his locked right hand by digging at it with his left but succeeded only in discharging the weapon. The sound of the gun was followed by the guttural death wheeze of George Yaro as he slid to the floor. Ida was holding Ruth who was slumped over dead in her arms; the bullet exited George's gut and hit Ruth in the neck. Teddy Pelling picked up the gun and aimed it at George's head, saying nothing. George, looking up at Ida rocking Ruth, who was soaked in her own gore, grimaced at Pelling, "You paranoid son of a bitch, Pelling. I was going to give you the gun which fell out of a magazine I took to the washroom. You've killed Ruth you crazy bastard, and me...Jesus, now you won't get a cent of the money I wired to her account because you have no way to retrieve it without her," George taunted.

The next shot startled both Ramon and Ida. George lay looking up at them with a hole in the middle of his forehead.

"Get back into the cockpit and take off Ramon," Pelling ordered, as Ramon scurried to the pilot's seat, buckled in, began his pre-flight check list and looked at his watch: 9:57. He looked up at Pelling and tapped his watch.

"You have time! Do your run up here and roll onto the active. I'll watch for incoming. Go! Get on with it!" Pelling yelled.

Ramon ran the engines up and began his roll onto the active runway. He rolled back up the active to the button and swung around into the wind just as Robert Bizet, Marta and Andre Laurent turned into the flight center parking lot and spotted the Gulfstream ready to take off. Robert, who was driving the Lincoln rental, pulled onto the active in a cavalier attempt to cut off the departing jet. They met at the halfway point on the runway. The rented Lincoln angled sideways effectively blocking the little jet. Ramon had no alternative at the controls of the jet but to brake to a stop. He looked down at the Lincoln and a blinding light dropped out of the sky onto the runway ahead. Ramon knew a crash was imminent and gunned the throttles of the Gulfstream, pulling a sharp right turn off the tarmac onto the infield grass, completed the 180 and raced back toward the button staying on the infield grass leaving the active for the landing aircraft.

The arriving Inter-Island commuter flight braked at touchdown but had too much speed to avoid the retreating Lincoln as it reversed back across the runway. The incoming 737's nose wheel missed the retreating car but the starboard main wheel assembly struck the front of the rental sending it skidding to the side of the runway as the blown wheel assembly sheared off, sending a spark shower as the struts dug into the tarmac. The 737 pivoted and spun to the right side finally coming to a stop, facing in the opposite direction. Seconds later, the crippled airliner burst into flames.

Ramon, arriving at the button, circled onto the active, pushed the throttles full forward, sped down the runway, lifted off abruptly, clearing the burning airliner, and rocketed into the twinkling darkness.

Teddy Pelling took the dead body of Ruth Werner from Ida's arms and placed her on her back beside the dead body of George Yaro. He then went through Ruth's purse and found the five one hundred thousand dollar US cashier's cheques and put them in his pocket. He handed the purse to Ida Tesh and said, "From now on you will become Ruth Werner, at least until we transfer the money in her accounts into our hands. By the way Ida, you are now a very wealthy woman. What do you say to that?" Pelling asked.

"Ah...how? Oh, you mean the million dollars you guys gave me. Right?"

"I'll need you to pose as Ruth in order to withdraw money and transfer the remainder to The Hague accounts. I'd like you to start practicing Ruth's signature. It's a simple signature. I'll be transferring another two million to your Atlanta account," Pelling said.

"Are you serious Teddy? Can we do that? Wow! I'm sorry but I'm still just fractured by Ruth's death and George too. God what a waste...please don't be concerned, I'm just shook up a lot, but I'll be ok!" Ida assured him.

"Look Ida, George was warned by me and Ruth to just do as he was told, nothing else. He caused what happened to him. As far as Ruth goes... that was an unfortunate accident, but we have to get on with our lives. Now, while you practice Ruth's signature, I'm going to do a little passport doctoring, which will make you into Ruth and me into George Yaro. So please don't fret. You and I are going to be very wealthy friends. C'mon now, start learning her signature, Okay?" Pelling asked.

"Okay, but would you mind if I had a drink?" Ida asked.

"Sure, go fix us both a strong one and then when I finish up here we can go have a little lie down if you feel like it," Pelling said.

"Yeah, sure, I guess. I have to change this outfit. It's got Ruth's blood on it. I'll change, make the drinks and wait for you in the bedroom," Ida replied.

"Alright then! I'll be with you in a bit," Pelling said.

Teddy went forward into the cockpit and seated himself in the co-pilot's seat while he counted the five cashier's cheques and then slapped them into his palm in order to get Ramon's attention.

"Set a course for Panama City, Ramon. We will stop there only long enough to do our banking, then take off again for The Hague. That was very quick thinking getting us out of there like you did. This is for your co-operation Ramon," as he handed the five cheques to the pilot who now showed a trace of a smile on his face.

"Have you flown into Panama City before?" Pelling asked.

"Three times in the past 18 months, Señor Linus."

"Good, good! Will you have any problems with the landing?" Pelling asked.

"We have two dead persons in the plane, Señor Linus, and customs will board us when we land to check the passports and the airplane's papers," Ramon answered.

"I'll dispose of the bodies over the ocean. When it's time, slow the jet down to its slowest safe speed at five thousand feet and I'll open the cabin door and push them out. Just blink the seat belt indicators and I'll know you are down to five thousand feet and ready for me to off-load them."

"Of course, Señor Linus."

"I plan to become George Yaro by changing my photo from my passport onto his. Is George Yaro known to any of the officials at the Panama City airport that you know of?" Pelling wanted to know.

"No sir! Always a different customs agent boarded the jet when we visited, but I could land at the smaller airport which is also closer to the City," Ramon suggested.

"Sure. Why not! Good idea. Let me do most of the talking when we are boarded. We'll only be passing through, so I want you to arrange fuel and anything else you think we'll need for our flight to The Hague. Do not file a flight plan and do not mention to anyone where we are bound. Is that clear Ramon?" Pelling instructed.

"Yes, Señor Linus. I will do as you say."

"That's fine Ramon, because when we are safely back in the air after our stop, I'm going to give you another five of these cheques for your cooperation," Pelling said.

"Gracias, Señor Linus, or I should say Señor Yaro."

"That's the spirit Ramon! Now I have some cleaning up to do in the cabin. I'll check with you when I'm finished. Anything you need up here?" Pelling asked.

"Si Señor George, a double scotch, but I'll wait until we land," grinned Ramon.

Ramon Atmos aged 47 was trying not to think about the five cashier's cheques tucked inside his flight maps, but after Pelling had left the cockpit, Ramon had read each one separately. They were in proper sequence and "pay to the bearer" US cash money, no questions asked. Ramon thought: *Just show your ID and deposit or cash them for that matter. I can do anything I want from now on. Although George was a good boss and let me party with some of the women at some of the stops we made, he really didn't pay me that well. He said many times he could get experienced pilots to fly for him for $30,000 US. So, I should be happy with $3,000 per month, all expenses paid and a cash bonus at holiday time. He never failed to bring up the perks that he allowed me with the girls in his life and indeed some of them were girls,* much younger than Ursula even. I knew that the only reason he kept me on was that he sleeps with my daughter whenever he can, but, what George never knew was my little darling was also sleeping with Esau Navarra and was in his pay as well. I will not mourn you, George Yaro. I imagine I can fly this Gulfstream until the gold card gets filled, then neglected, which it will be without George to pay the bills. Should be good from here to the Netherlands and back to Argentina before trouble happens. When we get to The Hague, I will put all but some cash, maybe $10,000 into the bank and transfer the rest to my bank in Argentina. If Pelling, or whatever his name is, decides to take back this money, he won't be able to. I won't get out of his sight in Panama City or The Hague and I should test his sincerity by asking can I transfer some of this money from Panama City to Argentina. I wonder if that would be taking a chance at offending him. I think I will ask if it would be possible to be with Ida again! He will either claim her all for himself or share her. Yes, that might appeal to him. He is supposed to be the fugitive soldier of fortune with no real attachments. We'll see.

Ida never did dress in the outfit she took from Ruth's bag, figuring that Teddy would come back for his drink and want sex. How did he put it? Oh yeah: 'In case you want to have a 'little lie down.' Well now, Teddy if you only knew. With everything that's happened today, I still can't believe I'm so calm. Hey girl, you came on this junket because you wanted some first class sex. And boy you got that in spades: three guys and two absolutely fabulous ladies. Hell, and I was worried that they would want that ten grand back or what was I supposed to do to earn it? Now, my bank account has over a million in it and another two million is promised. Wow! My head is spinning and I can't believe it. I'm hornier than I was when I first got to Bermuda. It must be all this money, either that or I really need my noodle examined.

Here comes Teddy. I wonder if he really knows just how sexy he really is!

Chapter Twenty Five
Dereliction of Duty

The airport on Grand Cayman Island was awhirl with activity since the incoming Inter Island 737 had landed and collided with an automobile on the active runway. When the airliner finally came to rest just off the active runway on the infield grass, the right side wing tank had exploded. Fortunately, this flight had only 42 passengers, but by the time they were off-loaded, two had been slightly injured as they slid down the canvas escape chutes. The driver of the Lincoln, Lieutenant Robert Bizet, only suffered seatbelt strain while his passengers Marta and Andre had minor cuts and bruises. The Lincoln rental was a write-off.

When the accident at the airport occurred, the only on-duty people were the staff of Inter Island Air: two stewards at the luggage retrieval area, two baggage handlers and one person to operate the refueling tanker. As well, the night attendant and the grounds man at the flying school were working this shift. All of these employees were pressed into service to help the disabled airliner and distinguish the fire. By the time ambulances from George Town arrived, the local Constabulary put in an appearance. Inspector Pennington was called from his club and headed up the investigation. His first official act, after a brief interview of the airline pilots, was to arrest and take into custody the occupants of the rental Lincoln who, in his estimation, had been on the runway illegally, causing the crash. He would not be returning himself to the Station House this evening delegating his Detective Captain to take statements which he would review when he arrived in the morning. He told the Detective Captain that 'in light of the events of the evening' he should make the arrest of this Ursula Atmos person this evening rather than in the morning, as previously ordered. The Inspector ordered the occupants of the rental car to be held overnight.

Robert Bizet, Marta Vander Riis and Andre Laurent were treated for their abrasions, minor cuts and bruises at the George Town Hospital under the scrutiny of Detective Captain Lewis, then escorted to the Station House to make their statements. Lieutenant Bizet was adamant that the Sûreté, Interpol and the DEA be alerted and put on the trail of the Gulfstream that they had stopped on the runway in order to arrest Teddy Pelling, a terrorist wanted for murder, kidnapping and who was believed to have hijacked the departed Gulfstream.

"In fact, I hold your boss Inspector Pennington totally responsible for this whole mess. I pleaded with him to lend us a team to intercept and arrest Pelling and stop this jet from leaving. As you are well aware, he refused, giving the excuse that his hands were tied until the proper authorizing paperwork arrived. We will give our statements and be on our way, Captain."

"I'm afraid that is not possible sir. After you give your statements, you will remain overnight in our custody. These are the specific instructions of Inspector Pennington who will attend to the investigation in the morning. Now if you will fill out these forms and tell in your own words exactly what happened this evening and the events leading up until the crash of the Inter Island 737, I will be back in one hour to look at your statements."

Detective Captain Lewis went directly to the Treasure Island Inn, contacted the bell Captain and had him accompany him to the room occupied by Ursula Atmos. The Bell Captain knew exactly what the policeman would find.

After Robert, Andre and Marta had written out their statements of the evening's events, Robert began a mild tirade at this joke of a police department which seemed to him to operate in a semi-conscious manner as long as it did not disturb the Inspector's social life. Marta put her hand on his arm and looked him in the eyes and smiled. He took a deep breath and said, "Where do these people come from anyway?"

Marta asked how many people were hurt on the airliner and was given the last count by the duty officer: just the two injured in the escape procedure. All three of the accused looked at one another and shook their heads.

When Detective Captain Lewis returned to the station, he told them that he had found Ursula Atmos dead in her room and would await the findings of the forensic group he had dispatched to the crime scene. It was his observation that the young woman was strangled to death. Robert asked the Captain to get him a copy of his request for assistance and a copy of the fax to Sûreté headquarters that Inspector Pennington was to send. The Captain simply nodded and got up to retrieve these forms. He returned in ten minutes time with the form the lieutenant had filled out requesting help in arresting a known terrorist and the fax he had asked to be sent to the Sûreté authorizing his activities. The Detective Captain also handed a typed request asking the inspector to arrest Ursula Atmos as a suspect in the murder of Sûreté Sergeant Alain Moline. Time of these requests 5:10 this afternoon. It was now nearing midnight.

"Here you are sir. I believe these are the forms you requested," the Captain said.

"Thank you Captain. Can you show me some proof that my fax was actually sent? You might just print out the fax log for me if you don't mind. Say, from five o'clock this afternoon until the present."

"As you wish sir. I will be back in a jig."

The Captain was back promptly with another sheet of paper showing the fax log from five o'clock until the latest fax was sent over two hours ago. The fax he had requested the Inspector send to the Sûreté in Paris was not on the log. It had never been sent.

"Captain, I would like you to send this fax again for me, as well as this new one I have just written out. Would you please also print me out a fax log after they go, showing me that they were sent?" Robert requested.

"I'll see to it immediately sir," The Captain said.

As the Captain went to the office area once again, Marta said to Andre and Robert, "It appears that the Inspector has been neglecting his police responsibilities and I get the impression that the Captain is quite enjoying the fact his boss has been caught in the act."

"The Inspector is a pompous ass who could have given us instant assistance and we wouldn't have this bloody mess to contend with. Two people injured because he wouldn't get off his ass. I certainly hope the airline has insurance, for their sake anyway, and the Sûreté can expect law suits for damages for sure. Not sending my fax after demanding authorization from my superiors is a deliberate act of dereliction of duty. The Inspector better have friends in high places because in any other police organization, his cowardly refusal to give assistance is grounds for dismissal," Robert said.

The Captain handed the page print-out showing confirmation that both faxes had been transmitted to Paris.

"Thank you Captain. Can you shed any light on the Inspector's behavior this afternoon?" Robert asked.

"No sir, my rank and training will not allow me to comment on the behavior of a Senior officer," the Captain said.

"We hear you loud and clear Captain. Do you have an Interpol file with their warrant postings?" Robert asked.

"Yes sir, I believe it is still on the Inspector's desk. He requested it shortly after you three left earlier today."

"Well now, your boss must have at least thought about my request if he checked to see if there was an Interpol warrant out for a Teddy Pelling. Can't understand him not sending the fax after stating to me that he couldn't lift a finger until he had proper authorization. Thank you Captain. By the way are you the 2IC here?" Robert asked.

"Yes, I am sir and will be only too happy to assist in any way I can."

"Thanks for that Captain. Could you arrange for a telephone for me to call my Paris office?" Robert asked.

"Come with me Lieutenant. You can use my office," the Captain said.

On the way into the Captain's office Lieutenant Bizet looked at his watch: 12:15AM and 7:15AM in Paris.

"Captain, do you have a wall map of this area? I need to check something before I phone," Robert asked.

"Follow me sir."

The Captain marched into the duty staging room which had a large map of the Caribbean on the front wall. Bizet stood in front of it and made some notes, thanked the Captain and followed him back to his office. The lieutenant sat at the desk, lifted the receiver and telephoned his headquarters in Paris.

"Sergeant Debois, it's Lieutenant Bizet calling from George Town, Cayman Islands. I need you to do a few things for me."

"Yes sir, we have your two faxes and a reply is being sent to the return address as we speak."

"Good, that was the first job I needed done in order that we can get on with the investigation. Pelling has slipped through our hands. We had him located at the local airport. He arrived in a private jet. Actually, it's a Gulfstream V with the following markings: AG112299. It landed here two days ago, back from Bermuda. It took off from the George Town Flying Club this evening at about ten minutes past ten local time, destination unknown. I want everything you can get on the owner, George Yaro. Also, check the places he could land and alert those possibilities to report in to the Sûreté or Interpol if it does land. The jet and occupants should be held until further notice. Did you get all this down sergeant?"

"Yes sir, but give me those alphanumeric markings on the Gulfstream again please."

'AG112299' and Sergeant, start with the manufacturer's records in case it was purchased new. The locals are trying to hold us overnight because of an involvement with a rental car and an airliner that ran into us while we tried to delay the Gulfstream. The airliner collided with our car and then the jet burst into flame. Thank heaven no one was killed, but two passengers were injured as a result of the explosion and fire. We may be on the hook for damages, heaven forbid! Had this silly, asinine Inspector Pennington responded to our request for help in the first place, none of this would have happened. Our release from custody is top priority, so please get on it," Bizet ordered.

The captain re-entered his office where Robert Bizet was making notes in a notepad he always carried with him.

"I have just received a fax from the Paris office of the Sûreté demanding your immediate release in order that you can continue your pursuit of the ETA terrorist Teddy Pelling. They also want a full report from Inspector Pennington demanding to know why he refused to offer you assistance in delaying the private jet Pelling was suspected of hijacking. I am going to release you lieutenant and trust that you will return to face any consequences as a result of the collision with the Inter Island airliner and your rental car. Do I have your word on that, sir?" The captain asked.

"You do, Captain Lewis, and thank you for this courtesy. We are staying at the Treasure Island Inn until further notice," Bizet said.

Chapter Twenty Six
Basque Banking

Ida Tesh had mixed herself and Teddy Pelling a double scotch and soda. She took a long slug, the burning sensation felt good down her throat and into her stomach. Standing beside the bed, she drew Ruth's small leather over-night bag toward her and then hoisted it onto the bed. They were the same size and, what the hell, poor Ruth wouldn't need them anymore. She pulled a suitable outfit from the bag and set it aside, closed the bag and put it back where it lay. She walked out to the area where Teddy had stripped the clothing from both bodies, disrobed and returned to the bedroom. Teddy returned from speaking with the pilot and could feel the jet descending and slowing down. He stood at the ready when the plane levelled off and the 'fasten seat belt' signs blinked. Teddy braced himself and opened the door and forced the bodies out the door. He tied the clothing in a ball and kicked it out as well. The final resting place for his long-time pal Ruth Werner and George Yaro was the Caribbean Ocean about 300 miles from Grand Cayman Island 200 miles from the coast of Honduras. Teddy levered the door closed and made his way to the cockpit area. Moments later, the jet was back up at altitude and cruising speed. They had about 410 miles remaining and would be arriving in one and one-half hours. Teddy consulted with Ramon, after which it was agreed they should be arriving at close to midnight local time. Teddy had some work to do in order to be ready before Ramon advised customs and the tower in Panama City Airport.

Ida's passport photo was substituted for Ruth Werner's and 'presto' Ida became Ruth. Normally, this substitution might be detected, but such was Teddy Pelling's expertise that these photo transfers would easily pass inspection. Teddy had extra pictures of his new look taken in Bermuda and used one of these photos to replace that of George Yaro's. Ruth and Ida were often taken for twins and their descriptions were almost identical. George Yaro was heavier and older than Teddy but it wasn't enough of a difference for any concern. He had studied border guards, customs officials and various authority types over the years when he had handed them his many phony passports. Teddy noticed that they all focused first on the picture then on the traveler's face. Back and forth until they were convinced that the photo was of the person. They very seldom, if ever, read any of the text in the passport. Most of these guards would not be able to read the languages that the passports were written in anyhow. Teddy had a special stamp that left the official looking markings on any picture he needed to use on his passports. This certified that the picture was put on when the passport was issued legally to the owner. When he finished, he left both open in order to properly dry the special glue on the back of the photos. He put all the special components of his passport kit back in the fold-up leather case, zipped it shut and made his way to the rear of the jet.

**

When the Gulfstream landed at the Panama City airport, the Customs officer who came on board signed off on both the arrival document and the departure clearance at the same time, then returned the passports to Mr. Yaro and thought to himself:

Señor Yaro must be a very important man who knows how to get things done, judging from the opened envelope containing US money inside his passport. When I handed the passport containing the envelope back to him, Señor Yaro took the envelope of money out and said, "This must be yours."

"Ah, yes Señor, Gracias."

Teddy Pelling put all the passports into his portfolio and asked Ramon to make sure he took the customs official for lunch after he had taken care of the pre-departure routine.

The Panama City Real Hotel, which was close to the Royal Bank, sent their limo to the airport to pick up Señor Yaro and Ms Werner who had advised they would be staying only as long as it took to conduct their banking business.

Ramon figured Pelling would clean out George Yaro's accounts using the information contained in the small black portfolio he had given the terrorist prior to their landing. He explained to Pelling how George always had this leather case with him when he did his banking. Pelling remembered seeing it under George's arm when they visited the George Town Royal Bank.

In the Hotel limo, Pelling examined the contents of the folder again, carefully, while he went over his plan. If there was a way he could get at any of the ETA money managed by George Yaro, he might just risk it. He found George's bank book from the Citizen's Trust of Douglas, Isle of Man. It showed a balance of thirteen million US dollars after a transfer of two million to the Royal Bank in Panama City. This was part of the five million George promised him to guarantee his safety. It was like winning the lottery, Pelling thought, forcing himself to stay calm. He studied the two other bank books: one for a Bermuda numbered account and another for a numbered account in Nevis in the Caribbean. The balance in the Bermuda account was twenty-nine million US. The Nevis account showed a balance of nineteen million US. Pelling was sure that these accounts were operation accounts of the ETA. Pelling went into deep thought, then smiled suddenly, sat upright and concentrated on the role he would play for the bankers.

He checked into the Panama City Real Hotel as George Yaro, paid cash in advance for one day while advising the clerk that they would be gone in a few hours. He requested the limo be available to take them to the Royal Bank and then back to the airport. Once they were in the safety of their hotel suite, Pelling explained to Ida what they would do at the Bank. While she listened to Teddy's plan, Ida compulsively practiced Ruth Werner's signature. Pelling removed the papers from Ruth's attaché case given her by the assistant manager of the Royal Bank in George Town. He laid them on the desk, produced a yellow legal sized pad and began a list of the money in Ruth's name and in his own. When he was finished he said, "Ida have a look at this, will you please."

Ida put her pen down, walked over and put her arms around his shoulders, leaned in close to him and looked at what he had written.

"Teddy, dearest, that's quite a list you have there!"

"This is what we'll do at the Bank. We will ask to see a manager to assist us. I'll order some cashiers' cheques and then we'll wire transfer money to the Royal Bank in The Hague,"

Pelling went on to explain the transactions to her.

"These transfers will clean out Ruth's account here in Panama City. *You getting all this Ida?* Let's just focus on who we are pretending to be and what we will be doing, Okay?" Pelling said in an angry voice.

"Really Teddy, don't treat me like some air-head. I'm just as smart as Ruth and for your information, probably a better actor. I'll do just fine and to help me be a little more distracting at the bank, I'll wear something special. I'll go get dressed," Ida said.

"Good, I don't want to spend any more time here than we have to. After we get Ruth's funds transferred to you in Atlanta and to me in The Hague, I want to try something with George's accounts, but not until our business is confirmed," Pelling said.

While Ida was changing into a very conservative grey business suit, cut exceptionally low in the chest area, and very short in the skirt, she thought to herself: *I'll bet this outfit got a few new clients for Ruth. I can't believe the money this guy has in his possession. Every time we go banking, I get richer. So, I'll just do as he says. I'm going to be a fucking millionaire, twice over.*

Teddy Pelling looked at his reflection in the mirror and was satisfied he was a passable impersonation of George Yaro. He didn't have to worry much about being recognized by anyone anyway. He only had to be himself as the picture on George Yaro's passport was his, or at least, that of Linus Svendsen. He had role-played with Ida, what they would say and do, once inside the bank. He was sure Ida would pass for Ruth and he would just have to play it by the moment as far as impersonating George Yaro.

As soon as they were seated in the comfortable back seat of the limo, Teddy focused on becoming George Yaro once again. The Gucci bag with the two hundred and fifty thousand in cashiers' cheques and cash was at his feet. Back at the room he had covered up the cash with hotel stationery. The other Gucci bag, on the seat between them, contained one million, eight hundred and seventy-five thousand in cashiers' cheques and cash. Teddy's money belt held one million, three hundred and fifty thousand dollars of cheques and cash. He wasn't worried, being totally preoccupied with the job at hand. Pelling could not imagine a reception of either ETA agents or the authorities waiting for them at this Bank. There was no indication in any of George Yaro's records that George or the ETA had ever used this bank. He knew ETA agents would be looking for him in George Town by now, and figured he still had a half-day head start. The Gulfstream wouldn't be very hard for anyone to trace if it stayed in one place for any length of time. He thought he might need at least one more stop after this one. Pelling decided he would pay off George Yaro's credit card and give it to Ramon to fly the jet all the way to Argentina if he cared to. It would also indicate to those in pursuit that George Yaro was still alive. The limo driver was asked to return in thirty-five minutes and drive them directly to the airport.

* * *

Teddy Pelling and Ida Tesh walked into the bank up to the customer service counter and asked to see a manager. Teddy put both Gucci bags down at his feet and watched as a smiling young banker came hurrying to the counter. After introductions, the ruddy faced young assistant manager-who had been transferred here two months ago from Red Deer, Alberta, Canada-asked how he could be of assistance! Pelling informed the eager young banker that his associate wished to transfer the money in her account at this branch to Royal accounts in The Hague and Atlanta, Georgia. The banker escorted them to a small office and took his place behind the large desk trying desperately not to look down Ida's cleavage while he listened to the details of her request.

The banker focused, reluctantly, and began typing at his computer keyboard. He quickly realized that this was going to be formidable business. It took only twenty minutes to get the transfers confirmed: two million to an Ida Tesh in Atlanta, three million to a Linus Svendsen in The Hague. *Nothing out of the ordinary. Two very easy transactions - the money going in-house- to Royal Banks in both places. Straight-forward business*, he thought as he held the bank book out to her, making her lean forward giving him a good look down her front. *Wow, she's a knockout. Wouldn't it be...C'mon, focus on what you are supposed to be doing my man!*

Teddy sat very stiff through the whole charade and, while Ida was putting her bank book in her purse, he offered the banker his passport and asked him to open an account at this bank because he planned to start a business in Panama City. Yaro asked to wire transfer all thirteen million in his account at the Citizen's Trust in Douglas, Isle of Man. He asked the banker if it would make any difference if the money came through the Panama City branch first, and was then transferred to his associate at The Hague.

"Do you wish us to pay you any of the funds from here, Mr. Yaro?"

"Well, yes as a matter of fact! I would like to take cashiers' cheques with me now for three million," Pelling said.

"I see, will you be leaving any funds on deposit at this branch, sir?"

"No, not at this time, but have the balance in the Citizen's Trust account come here first, then I can transfer the remaining balance of ten million to my associate, Linus Svendsen's account at the Royal in The Hague. I would have transferred everything to The Hague, but I won't be back there for some time and, as I said, I have business to do in Panama City. This transfer to my partner's account will allow Svendsen to proceed with our plans at The Hague. Transferring the money this way should compensate this branch for its services. Am I right about that young man?" Pelling asked.

"That's what I was getting at, Mr. Yaro. You obviously are aware of the bank's handling fees in these matters, right sir?"

"Oh Yes, indeed, over the years I've paid my share of fees to the banks. Discretion does have its price, doesn't it?" Pelling smiled.

"What denominations did you want in cashiers' cheques, Mr. Yaro?"

* * *

Thirty eight minutes after entering the bank, they stepped back into the waiting limo and headed toward the airport. The Gucci bag with the US cash now contained the newly acquired three million in US cashiers' cheques,(eight two hundred and fifty thousand dollar cheques and ten one hundred thousand dollar cheques). Ida was buzzing with excitement, but kept purposely calm as she watched the limo driver's eyes on her cleavage. She slipped her right hand between Teddy's legs and began a very blatant massage of his member. The driver's eyes where lust-filled as she removed her suit jacket and gave him a real show. Teddy enjoyed Ida's playful attention and smiled at her marvelous superstructure. She wore a white cotton tank top with a very low scooped neckline. Her nipples where prominently displayed, unrestrained by a bra, delighting Teddy and the driver, who had to get back to watching the road, occasionally.

Ida looked into Teddy's eyes and smiled saying, "They need some attention...It would feel real nice if you would just pinch them a little, lover."

The limo swerved, then quickly straightened out, as the driver's eyes returned to the road. Pelling grinned at her and obliged.

Ramon was standing with the Customs officer by the little jet when he spotted the limo pulling onto the tarmac and heading in their direction. He quickly shook the officer's hand and climbed the steps to the cabin of the Gulfstream.

The customs official watched the limo pull along-side to off-load Señor Yaro and his sexy looking lady. The limo driver eased the big car away from the jet whose engines began warming up. The jet began rolling onto the active runway the moment the two were aboard. Reaching take-off speed after what seemed a short distance, the Gulfstream V climbed into the sky at a very steep angle.

Reaching into his pocket where he had put the envelope, the customs officer withdrew it and looked inside once again to confirm the five thousand Yankee dollars were still there.

* * *

Pelling put the two Gucci bags onto the passenger seat nearest the flight cabin, opened one, withdrew five of the $100,000 cashier's cheques and then buckled himself into the seat beside Ida. When the jet reached altitude and levelled off, he unbuckled and stepped into the flight cabin. He nodded to Ramon, who was concentrating on the instrument panel. After settling into the co-pilot's seat, Pelling buckled up and put his headset on, then reached over and placed the five $100,000 cheques on the console between them. Ramon looked down at them and then across to Teddy whose eyes were waiting for his. Ramon pointed at the cheques and then at himself and watched Pelling's eyes as he slowly nodded yes. Ramon smiled at the terrorist and gave him the thank you thumbs-up sign.

The steepness of the climb out had forced Ida's body back into her seat giving her an exhilarating rush. After Pelling left for the flight cabin, she loosened her seat belt, somewhat. She knew the Gucci bags, across from her, contained at least the three million in cashiers' cheques just issued from this bank, plus a whole hell of a lot more. She was trying to remember what amounts were in the various accounts on that list Teddy had shown her in the hotel room.

She wondered: *Can it really be that easy? Assume a rich man's identity and help yourself to his fortune? Damn! It was almost funny watching that young banker fall all over himself getting the transfers done and issuing those cheques, then his manager got into the act as well, stopping by to shake hands, bringing the cheques over himself to get a close-up look down my front while thanking us for the business and the opportunity to be of service.* She grinned remembering.

Ida examined just what she had done back at the Bank an hour ago: *Okay, so, what am I guilty of, actually? After all, aren't I in the clutches of an international terrorist who forced me, on pain of death, to impersonate Ruth Werner? Not to mention the psychological terror I endured never knowing when he would rape me, again? Well, no, actually, it wasn't quite like that. Teddy told me how we would go about getting the money and just assumed I would play along, and I did. Hell, I was still trying to figure out how I was supposed to earn that first million I received from him and Ruth. At this bank, I hardly opened my mouth, not even to introduce myself. Teddy even did that: "Ruth Werner is an associate of mine, who wishes to wire-transfer funds, as do I". So smooth and so bloody cool. I handed over the account passbook with the piece of paper listing the transfers I wanted done and the nice young banker was pleased to comply. He filled in the necessary forms and then typed furiously at his computer and printed out the confirming transfers. It was a very simple, quickly carried out procedure. I signed off the bottom of the forms and caught the banker quickly eye-checking the passport signature with mine. I smiled at him and leaned further forward redirecting* his scrutiny. I would have loved to take my suit jacket off at that moment and given him a real show, but he seemed satisfied just peering down my cleavage at every opportunity. I leaned forward often. His focus turned to the business of getting the transfers completed quickly, so as to impress us with his efficiency.

Ida looked out the porthole window of the Gulfstream, smiled, realizing how easily Teddy could take back the money given to her whenever he wanted to. *He may yet trot me into the Royal in The Hague and say, 'Transfer the two million in your Atlanta account to the account of Linus Svendsen', and what the hell could I do about it? Nothing. So relax! Hell, I was thrilled being a week-end escort when I found out I could keep the ten grand. This, however, is the big time girl and he still needs me. Ruth has two million in The Hague, which Teddy will want to get his hands on. So, I won't be spending any of this fortune just yet."*

* * *

Pelling and Ramon were discussing their destination possibilities while Pelling studied the airport maps of the area.

"Have you ever landed in Nassau in the Bahamas?" Pelling asked.

"No, not Nassau. Is that our destination?" Ramon replied.

"Yep! Let's head for the Bahamas. I'm a bit leery about Charleston, because we were just there a few days ago, but we should be okay in and out of Nassau. Then, after we top up, we can make a destination decision," Pelling said.

Ramon wondered at Pelling's reason for stopping in Nassau and decided he would query him, but not just yet.

"Let me see that book of airport maps, please." Ramon asked. Pelling handed him the fat little book of indexed airports of the world. Ramon put the Gulfstream on autopilot and located the airport info on the Nassau airport. He studied it, then turned his Radio Direction Finder knob to that of the main outbound beacon at Nassau airport and witnessed the jet correct its course toward Nassau, 1200 miles away.

"Is it necessary that we stop in Nassau?" Ramon asked.

"Not really, why do you ask?" Pelling said.

"We have a full fuel load which will give us a range of 6,500 nautical miles with reserves.

We could make Leningrad from here non-stop." Ramon said.

"What distance is it to Amsterdam?" Teddy asked, knowing it was about 5,500 nautical miles by his rough calculations.

"5,600 nautical miles," answered Ramon.

"So, if we fly right over the Bahamas and keep on going, we can set her up for long-distance cruise at, say .80 Mach, and get there in good time with plenty of reserves, right?" Pelling said.

"You are just about dead on, we will get 5,700 nautical miles at long distance cruise at .80 Mach. You have been studying the manual, I see," Ramon said.

"Hmm, well, keep this heading to Nassau and we'll decide our destination just before we get there. I'm going back into the cabin for a while. I'll be back in a half-hour when we'll decide," Pelling said as he left the cabin.

Ramon smiled and thought: *Señor Pelling gives the impression he is making a shared decision, but he is definitely the one calling the shots. Checking the range and everything to see what I would tell him. Yes indeed, he's definitely in charge, but very generous the way he pays for co-operation by peeling off those hundred thousand dollar cheques. He has given me ten, but I am under no illusions at all that he would shoot me dead in a second and take back all of them, but not while we are in the air. Even though, he could probably land this plane by himself, but why should he? He's getting my full attention and co-operation. I had my chance to get away in Panama City with a half million dollars if I really wanted to leave. Pelling must have reasoned: if I was still there waiting, ready to go when they returned from the bank, I would be along for the adventure and a bigger payday. Pelling has a very cool way about him. Wonder how much money he took off poor George back there in Panama City. He will be keeping Miss Ida all to himself now that the other one is gone. Strange though, how Ida shows so little remorse about her friend's death. She's probably also getting well paid for her services. Pelling is very quick with his wallet and doesn't lay down a bunch of rules. He just expects you will be onside with him and then he shares the wealth. Hell of a deal, hell of a guy. Yeah right! I remember how he grabbed George's hand which held the pistol and gut shot the poor bastard. Quick as a Cobra and just as deadly. Ruth just happened to be in the way of the exiting bullet. Such a waste. I think he knows exactly where we are heading and I'll bet he changes the destination a few times before we get there. He doesn't want any reception waiting for him from either the ETA or the authorities. Even though he expects cooperation, he doesn't trust anyone. It's probably how he's managed to stay alive this long. I wonder what else he has up his sleeve!*

Chapter Twenty Seven
A Heart To Heart Talk

The Pan Am flight from George Town, Cayman Islands was on its final leg: Atlanta to Paris. Marta Vander Riis and Andre Laurent were calculating their arrival time at Orly. Robert Bizet withdrew a stenographer pad and a pen from his leather portfolio stowed under his seat. Andre occupied the aisle seat, in the three seat row, as it allowed him to stretch his long legs. Marta sat in the middle and Robert had the window seat. Robert flipped open the note pad and wrote, "We need to talk about a few things, so let's use this note pad in order to keep the conversation private." He passed the pen and pad to Marta, who wrote "OKay" then passed them to her left to Andre, who turned to face his companions, and mouthed 'fine,' while handing both back to Robert. Andre and Marta were alert, waiting for the message Robert was writing amidst the humming engines and muffled sounds of the crowded jetliner. Robert sensed they were all beginning to feel the effects of the cramped conditions they had endured for the past five hours: A two-hour flight from George Town to Atlanta, plus the last three hours of this flight. He checked his wrist watch and wrote, "It's 10:00 P.M. here and 4:00 tomorrow morning in Paris. Arrival time at Orly, is 9:00 A.M. Andre, what are your immediate plans? Marta?" He passed the pen and pad to Marta who read what Robert had written and gave them to Andre. Andre read the note and began tapping the pen on the pad while he thought, then wrote, "I would like to get back to the SeaOx as soon as I get in. Why?" Andre handed the pad and pen to Marta who wrote, "I would like to check on my plane at the flying club, freshen up there, then have a big breakfast. After that, it all depends."She tucked her chin

140

into her chest, glanced sideways to watch Robert's facial expression as he read both answers to his question. He turned to his left to face Marta and Andre, who had both caught his troubled look. Robert wrote: "The SeaOx is under continuous surveillance, as is Elspeth's Paris apartment. Because Pelling is still at large, my concern is the ETA, who will be following any lead in order to turn him up. You are both prime targets, as am I. Any one of us would be a good trade for Raoul in the eyes of the ETA.

Therefore, we should not resume our old habits. I suggest, upon arrival, I visit the Bastille where I can question Raoul de Vascos again, then come back to the flying club. I propose we fly to your Chateau in your plane, Marta. Nobody will be looking for us in Utrecht. I can continue the investigation from there. Marta, would it be all right with you and your mother if Andre and I were guests for a while? Andre, do you have any objections to this?"

Marta held onto the pen while resting the note pad on her left knee in order that she and Andre could both read the message. When they finished reading they looked at each other and Marta smiled at Andre. She began to write, "A great idea! Mother will be delighted with the company. I'll take Andre with me to the Flying Club where we can both freshen up and have breakfast. After you finish with Raoul, come to the club and we'll take off for the Chateau. I'm excited!" She handed the pad to Andre who wrote, "Okay, I'll tag along. I've thought about the ransom money and I'd like to give it back to Elspeth and explain how I recovered it. I don't like holding anything back from her." He passed the note pad over to Marta who had been reading as he wrote. She smiled at him and squeezed his arm while she handed the pad and pen to Robert. Robert read both notes, tapped the pad a few times, reached under the seat for his leather portfolio, withdrew the four cashiers' cheques and handed them across to Andre. Andre undid his seat belt, stood in the aisle to stretch while he slid his wallet from his trouser pocket. He put the folded cheques into the wallet and returned it to his trouser pocket as he made his way up the aisle in search of a vacant washroom. Anybody watching him would never have guessed he had just tucked away a million dollars in cash.

Robert rolled the page over and wrote, "Ok, we'll leave for Utrecht as soon as I return. I'll have my sergeants meet me at the Bastille. I only need about forty-five minutes with Raoul, then I'll have the sergeants drop me off at a taxi stand in case they're being followed now as well. Thank you for this last minute hospitality, Marta. Andre, I agree with you about telling Elspeth everything. She should know exactly what has gone on since we saw her last. I'm not quite sure she'll understand about the return of the ransom. Nevertheless, if there isn't anything else we need to discuss, I'm going to get some sleep."

When Andre returned to his seat, he stood in the aisle until Marta returned from her washroom visit. Once reseated, they read the message Robert just wrote and they both said, "Goodnight." Marta passed the pen and pad back to Robert who put them away in his portfolio and stowed it under his seat. Robert buzzed for the flight attendant and requested a pillow. She found one in the overhead compartment for him. He placed it next to the window and lay his head against it. Marta patted his left arm causing his eyes to open and find her. She mouthed a goodnight, then winked at him, causing him to grin as the oncoming sleep wave washed him away.

Marta was not at all sleepy. She wanted to talk with Andre and turned in his direction. He was waiting for her and began, "Marta, we haven't really had much of a chance to talk. Could we do that now?"

"Absolutely!" Marta responded quietly. "I've wanted to ask you your side of the story ever since I grilled mother about why you two aren't together."

Andre looked into Marta's dark eyes searching her face for some time before he asked, "When did you speak with your mother last?"

Good start, thought Marta, no excuses, just concern. "Two days ago, just before I went to bed. It was early morning in Utrecht. She had been to New York since we left Paris and seemed in good form. Mother does like to travel, as you are aware, but confessed it was wonderful to be home. After that, it was just girl talk mostly."

"I'm pleased to hear she's well. I'm looking forward to seeing her again and, nothing really happened to us Marta. Just the circumstances we found ourselves in. We were so thankful to be alive after that terrifying week and agreed that we both needed some time to ourselves. I had to see Ava Haas because I felt such a compelling obligation to her for insisting the police search for me and the SeaOx. I had to thank her personally. Now, after hearing Robert's evidence, I realize she really just wanted the SeaOx found. Then when she found out how much money I had on me, she had a bargaining lever to have her contacts in the ETA take me out and leave her with my boat. She probably planned to assume title by some bogus will she would present to the authorities. Digesting her background information as well as the news of her death threw me for a loop, again. Because, ever since I forced a confession out of that arrogant little broker, Pierre Turin, my self-esteem has been on the rise. I was finally able to prove to Robert that I was innocent of any involvement with Pelling. Even though it was my carelessness that planted the idea in Pelling's head to kidnap Elspeth."

"Well, I told mother you were with us in the Caymans and had identified Teddy Pelling as the same person who hijacked your sailboat and took you both captive. Mother listened without comment, then asked how you looked and how you were doing."

"What was your reply?" Andre asked.

"I said you looked well, but troubled, and then I told her about Ava Haas and her murder," Marta said.

"How did your mother react to this news?"

"She began to cry, and said, 'What a horrible way to die' then added, 'No wonder Andre appears troubled …so many near misses.' That's when I asked her, "Can I ask Andre to call you?"

"What was her answer?"

"She said, 'Now Marta, just let things unfold as they will. Don't interfere. If and when Andre decides to call, he will.' You may say hello to him from me, but that's all."

"Marta, Elspeth and I did promise to keep in touch, but I've been so consumed by this Pelling stuff that I haven't been a very good friend to her. I'm pleased to hear she asked about me. Aside from that, I only have one regret concerning the events of the past few weeks which is: I didn't let Pelling bleed to death when I had him tied up and his life was seeping out of his gunshot wounds. Did I tell you and Robert, that Pelling said he had planned to kill me two or three times but spared my life and I owed him the same mercy? I was about to leave him bleeding and if the police didn't arrive in time to save him, so what, good riddance, but I couldn't stop his arrogant demand for mercy from playing over and over in my head and it literally forced me to put tourniquets on his wounds. It was like I'd been hypnotized and given post-hypnotic suggestion to stop his bleeding. I figured he'd be arrested within the hour, thrown in jail and eventually hung, but the slippery bastard got away somehow. When Robert told me later, I could not believe it. And the suspicions of my involvement with Pelling were revisited all over again. The worst of it is, since his escape, he's caused the death of two people we know of and probably more. I have this on my conscience.

Not so long ago, Marta, I led what was considered a rather carefree life. I got to know my share of women, but after meeting Elspeth, well, without a doubt, I thought she was the most exciting woman I'd ever met…very special. Elspeth told me she was attracted as well. The chemistry between us was intoxicating. Perhaps, a bit too intense! So, we parted and went back to our lives for a breather, both looking forward to our rendezvous in Paris a month later. Then this bloody nightmare happened, skewed our plans and damn near destroyed our relationship. Pelling saw a profitable opportunity by kidnapping her. He figured he could get to her easily by pretending to be me. His plan was to implicate me as his partner with that typed letter purporting to be from me. That was so deviously clever it could have sealed my fate. Elspeth told me she felt devastated and betrayed by me when she read the intimate details he included. The evil bastard knew how those words would be like a sledge-hammer blow to her stomach, turning her into an easily handled victim. Well, no need to rehash it. You heard your mother's response at the Chateau. At the time you and Robert rescued me, I was so out of it, so weak I didn't realize until later just how fortunate I was that you found me. I was glad to be alive and relieved, more than I can express, that Elspeth was home safe. However, when the questioning began at your Chateau and I heard how Pelling had involved me, I began to realize the mess I was in, and how every stammering attempt to prove my innocence just appeared to be the ravings of a cornered criminal. I was ashamed to be alive, Marta. I was angry at myself but more so at Pelling who put me in this position. I have never felt hate like that toward any living thing, and believe me, Marta, I would have shot the bastard on sight. I had to quickly rethink that as well, because doing so would really have quieted suspicion wouldn't it? Silencing my alleged partner. Christ! I couldn't escape the web around me. The time spent at your Chateau enabled me to regain my physical health, but my mental state was in the crapper. I thought my life was destroyed. Then, Sylvie Bern gets shot. My God! I could see Elspeth was frightened to the core, convinced that this evil son of a bitch would kill you or Tice. That's the reason your mother made the bargain with him. It was a bargain for all of our lives and, for some reason that none of us can fathom, she thinks he'll honor it. Then, when Ava and I came across Pelling at the marina in Lisbon, I got carried away. I saw it as my chance to square things with Elspeth if I could have him arrested. I reported Pelling's sighting to Robert and he assured me he would arrange for his capture that evening. Back in the safety of our hotel room, I got thinking about how he might slip away, so I decided to go to his boat and stand watch. Well, you know the rest. Later that same night, I began to shake in my bed covers over the earlier confrontation with him and began to worry that if he bled to death, even with the tourniquets, I'd be held responsible and would have put myself on his level. I'd have been back under suspicion, big time. When I relieved him of the ransom plus the extra, I was telling Pelling that we were all even now. I'd taken back only what he took from us and left him the worst off for coming into our lives with evil intent. I figured he'd be arrested and hung for his crimes. I feel giving your mother back her ransom money would be far less invasive of her privacy than claiming the money back through proper channels with all the resulting publicity. I didn't sleep that evening, as I said. I panicked myself with thoughts of Pelling being found by the police, shot and trussed up like a hog. A mobster-like execution. It was beyond my comprehension that he could escape. It still is! It really put me in a bad place, more questioning, more damned suspicions. I was boiling with anger. Marta, I know you understand this: As long as he is out there, he's a threat to all of us. Your mother had the best of intentions buying him off, but I believe, as Robert does, that he can't be trusted. I realize now, letting him live was a mistake but, as I said before, if I had killed him, it would just look like I was silencing a partner. My only hope now is that Robert catches him and the truth comes out, which will exonerate me once and for all."

"Andre, I'm happy that you and mother met and I'm hoping your friendship continues. By the way, Tice and Sylvie said to say hello to you," Marta said.

"Are they at the Chateau now?" Andre asked.

"Yes, and they left most of their purchases from their tour of The Netherlands. I think they're going somewhere warm and private where they won't have to wear much of anything."

"Sounds delightful," Andre said.

"Robert is sound asleep. The poor guy was exhausted. I'd love to snuggle up to him, but he needs his sleep. He just becomes a log when he crashes. Hardly moves at all. I've watched him while he sleeps, but I'm in love," Marta said.

"This is not news, Marta," Andre smiled.

"Hmm, don't tease, Andre. By the way, did you know Mother's birthday is this coming Saturday?" Marta asked.

"That's right, it is! I've been thinking about her so much lately, but had completely forgotten her birthday," Andre replied.

"Not to worry, you will be the perfect birthday surprise for her. Damn, it just occurred to me that Tice and Sylvie won't be home for her birthday and birthdays are big deals in our family. Brother, dear, this is really not like you at all!" Marta said.

The dinging bell and flashing seat belt signs preceded the airline captain's announcement to fasten up as they were about to experience some turbulence for the next while.

Marta and Andre snugged their seat belts and enjoyed the bumpy ride for the next ten minutes. She watched Robert's head slide back and forth on the pillow but the turbulence never woke him. After the last of the bumpy air, Andre looked at Marta and said, "Moguls!"

Marta smiled at his comment then both retreated into their own thoughts.

Chapter Twenty Eight
Destination Undecided

The Gulfstream V flew over Nassau at 3:00 P.M. Pelling had instructed Ramon to forget about getting a time and altimeter check from the tower in Nassau, no need to bring any undue attention to themselves. Their fuel would allow them to cruise nonstop to Stockholm and land with adequate reserves, should they decide. Pelling hadn't given their destination yet. When they were a half hour past Nassau, he instructed Ramon to correct his course to Lisbon, Portugal. Ramon looked up the relevant information in the thick little book "Airports of the World" which contained: One page for each airport showing diagrams of the landing strips along with other pertinent data. Ramon studied the main airport in Lisbon, selected the outer beacon and changed the Automatic Direction Finder to that frequency and noticed the automatic pilot make a slight correction to the Northwest. He then busied himself with the fuel consumption and distance math for the next half hour while Teddy Pelling went back to keep Ida company.

Ramon imagined what was happening in the bedroom of the executive jet, uncomfortable as he was, sitting buckled up with a hard on. When his calculations were completed, he checked his watch. Twenty minutes had gone by since Pelling left the co-pilot's seat. At that exact instant, the door to the cockpit opened and Ida stepped in wearing only her panties and bra.

"I've come to keep you company while Teddy gets some shut eye. I tried to interest him in some sex, but he crashed dead to the world on me and I'm all worked up, Ramon. Couldn't you just play with me a little, huh Ramon? You have to help me out, please Ramon. I know Teddy won't mind. Hell, he loves to share. You should know that by now." Ida coaxed.

Ramon wasn't sure, but as he turned his head toward his guest he was facing Ida's panties which looked inviting, indeed. Ramon reached the lever on his seat and swung as far to the aisle as it would allow. Ida stepped over the chair arms and buried her panties in his face. They both tried to pull her panties lower but her spread legs would not allow their descent. It didn't matter, as Ida got off quickly on Ramon's enthusiastic tongue. He needed more, so she got off of his face and helped him up as he dropped his pants and shorts.

Ida had all of him in her mouth before he straightened up. She worked him to that level of "almost," then squeezed him hard with her fingers as she withdrew him from her mouth. She stood, dropped her panties, turned her behind to him and lifted his hands to her breasts. His hands cupped them, then slid to her back and unfastened her bra. Ida arched her back to protrude her unleashed breasts and brought his hands to her nipples. She got him positioned at her rear and literally backed onto him. She bent over forward spreading her legs wider to let him enter. Ramon was too excited about what he was experiencing to enjoy it for very long. He had only just started, when he lost it. Ida tensed up, got off, announcing it with her own special sounds. They untangled and dressed quickly. The aroma in the cockpit left nothing to the imagination. Ramon sat back in his pilot seat as Ida left the cockpit.

She went directly to the airplane's bedroom where Teddy was lying on his side in just his underwear. She lay down beside him and said, "Ramon has just had some yummy sex and is back flying the plane. He's probably worried you will find out and I didn't want to spoil the excitement by telling him that you sent me to him to "relieve his tensions."

"Fine! I'll tell him that I'll share you until we land and he drops us off, then he is on his own. Now, if I know you, you are just warmed up and ready for more. Hmm feels like you are ready all right," Pelling said.

"I had to convince him to do me, so I gave him a panty rub all over his face and he got me off with his tongue. It's all your fault, you made me so horny before you sent me into him. Just let me rub myself all over it until you want in. Sweetie, it makes me so hot to slide on it like this. . . oohhh .

. . lover, you can't wait, huh? Oh! Teddy you feel so good inside me you're getting me so close, yes…yes, lover!!

Pelling soon followed her to his own relief, experiencing with her again a type of bonding, talking with him, explaining her pleasure at how he was loving her. He was learning to like the way she involved him personally in her intense pleasure. She didn't cry, she didn't call out anybody else's name like Ruth always did. Ida was involved entirely with him when they had sex. This was new for him, however, he wondered if he really wanted this close of an attachment. Perhaps, but likely not. He rolled Ida off of him and covered her, he ran the palm of his hand down her flat hard tummy to feel the quivering of her subsiding orgasm. She was sound asleep. Pelling wondered whether she ever thought past the pleasure of the moment. Didn't matter, really.

He began to plan his arrival in Antwerp, Belgium. He thought to himself: *A good choice, as it was only 100 kilometers to The Hague and from there a short 65 kilometers to Utrecht. He would do his final money transfers in The Hague and then see to some unfinished business before he moved on. His passports of George Yaro and Linus Svendsen would have to do him until he could arrange another identity. He would need to travel fast and alone. He would land as George Yaro, do the banking he planned to do in that name and then become someone else. He would take some of that money out in cashiers' cheques but transfer most of it to Zurich, Switzerland. Ida would become Ruth Werner for the last time in order to take out one million in ten cashier's cheques of one hundred thousand US dollars each. The remaining one million she would transfer to the account of Ida Tesh in Atlanta, Georgia. Teddy smiled when he realized that neither Ramon nor Ida had mentioned the money he had given them. He reasoned that, as he had complete control over the airplane and their lives, they probably figured, because he could, he may snatch back what he had given them whenever the mood took him. No wonder they didn't mention the money if they were thinking he had just parked it on them temporarily and won't they be surprised, when they realize they can keep the money I gave them? I can afford to seem magnanimous, as I have over twenty million dollars. Half in offshore banks and half in cash and cashiers cheques. I believe in greed rather than loyalty, so giving a million to Ramon and three million to Ida is only good business. If only Ruth could have purchased that winery estate in Bordeaux I would be able to change my looks and hide safely under the noses of the ETA and the authorities.*

Pelling now had more than five times the amount of money he had set as his goal, but in order to make good his escape, he needed Ramon to keep on flying the Gulfstream as long as he could to keep the authorities and particularly the ETA in pursuit. Ramon would be well paid for this action. Pelling would suggest to Ramon that he should courier some or all of this money to himself at whatever hotel he planned to book. A precaution, so that he wouldn't have to explain the money if he was ever stopped and searched. Pelling would have the pilot refuel and leave for either Rome or Tunis as soon as possible then abandon the Gulfstream and make his way to his money. Pelling didn't care where the jet ended up as long as it was away from where he was. He knew the ETA would be looking for it, as would the authorities. He would give Ramon the money to pay George Yaro's Credit Card, which would show any trackers that George was alive and on the run.

Pelling considered his involvement with Ida who would be an exciting companion to have along, but he reasoned that if he sent her home, she would feel free enough that she could go to her money and actually get to feel and enjoy her new wealth. Used to travelling alone, he needed to travel light and fast and get set up somewhere quickly. He could find Ida if he decided to, and, he reasoned, she may even want to come and play with him again. However, if she was to be a special friend of his, he had to let her go, then just wait and see what happened after that. Who the hell knows? He wasn't good at predicting the future.

When Pelling returned to the cockpit, he told Ramon to go freshen up in the washroom while he took over the flight deck. Ramon rose and was about to leave when Teddy said, "Oh, let Ida get some shut eye. She said you and I wore her out completely."

Ramon blushed and said, "Roger that, boss."

* * *

Ramon washed himself clean of the scent of Ida and wondered about this Pelling character who was so generous with his money and his lady friends. He thought: *This was a trip to beat all previous ones, for sure. We're heading for Lisbon, Portugal but we will probably land in France somewhere. Pelling looked over the past Gold Credit Card bills and might be considering paying it up to date in order to keep the Gulfstream in the air. Off the top of my head I'd say we have just about exhausted the credit on Yaro's gold card. It would take a good chunk of cash to put it in usable order. If we pay it off, it will be good for some time. I could set a course and file a flight plan to Tunis and change it half way there to anywhere. I get the impression that Pelling and Ida will be gone when we stop this time. He says to a holiday in Sweden, right? Judging by how often he changed our destination since we left Panama City. If he leaves me with the impression they are off to Sweden, he probably figures if I'm intercepted by the authorities, I can send them on a goose chase to Sweden while he is probably skiing in the Alps.*

Ramon Atmos made his way back to the cockpit and stood beside Pelling, watched out the cockpit windows for a few minutes, then resumed his seat. Pelling looked over at Ramon from the co-pilot's seat and asked, "What's our ETA in Lisbon, Captain?"

"We should land in another five hours which will be 5:15 tomorrow morning. We're on Bermuda time now which is to our left about 300 miles. Its 8:15 there and 15 past midnight in Lisbon," Ramon answered.

"Good! When we land, I want you to clear us through customs as George Yaro and Ruth Werner. We will be leaving you at this landing and ask that you fly to either Rome or Tunis from there. You can refuel and pay off the Gold Card. I'll give you another $100,000. Cashier's cheque. I'll also give you an additional $500,000 in cashiers' cheques for your cooperation. I'd suggest that you get rid of the money before you leave so that they won't be found on you if you are stopped and searched. If the money was found on you, you could just say I gave you the money for your cooperation but then you would have a hell of time claiming the money from the authorities. I doubt you would ever see any of it again. It's up to you, it's your money. As I told you before, Ida and I are going on a little holiday together to Sweden. Any questions about what I want you to do after we leave?" Pelling asked.

"I'm to have the jet refueled and then pay the Gold Card by depositing a $100,000 cashier's cheque to the account. After that I'm to fly to Rome or Tunis, my choice. You suggest that I do something with the cashier's cheques so that I don't get caught with them by the authorities and have to explain them. I will do as you suggest. What should I do with the Gulfstream after I land in Rome?"

"Ramon, I don't care if you fly it to Argentina. The plane is yours to do with as you will. But, personally, I would abandon it in Rome or Tunis, because it will soon be a hot tamale."

"I will leave it at a Flying Club I know of in Rome," Ramon said.

Pelling said nothing in response to this because he was deep in thought. He left the cockpit and quickly returned with six cashiers' cheques. He peeled the $100,000 cheques into a pile on the console as Ramon watched him.

"Five hundred thousand for your cooperation and one hundred thousand to be paid on the credit card account. It has been an interesting few days, hasn't it? Now, if you wish to go and stretch out for a couple of hours before we land, I'll watch the flight deck for you," Pelling suggested.

Ramon said he would go and catnap for an hour or so. He scooped up the six cheques and put them in the breast pocket of his tailored uniform shirt.

Pelling, alone in the cockpit of the sleek executive jet, watched the automatic pilot adjusting the steering wheel in front of him slowly one way a few degrees and then back to the course for Lisbon. He was convinced that he could fly and land this marvelous piece of modern technology if he really had to.

Chapter Twenty Nine
The Rome Diversion

Ramon Atmos smiled to himself on final approach into Antwerp Airport. Pelling had changed destinations again from Lisbon to Antwerp. Ramon had just asked the tower for landing instructions and was given runway 27, number two behind a British Overseas Airlines Corporation 727 arriving from London. Ramon looked over to Teddy Pelling who was paying close attention to the landing procedure. Immediately upon touchdown, the tower welcomed them to Antwerp, gave them the local weather and instructed them to switch radio channels to ground control. Ground control instructed the Gulfstream toward the re-fuelling pumps in the parking area and advised that Customs would be along shortly.

Once they were parked by the pumps and refueling was underway, Pelling asked Ramon to bring the jet's papers along with his passport to the main cabin where Ida Tesh sat patiently waiting for them. Pelling went over the plan on how they would handle the people from Customs. Pelling would present the George Yaro passport as owner of the Gulfstream and Ida would present her Ruth Werner passport. Pelling looked over the passports and handed them to Ramon to hand to the people from Customs. He went over the story once again until he was convinced that they all knew their parts.

Ramon opened the door to the Gulfstream and lowered the stairway when he saw the Customs van approach the jet. Only one officer came aboard and asked for their passports. He compared the faces to the passport pictures as all of these minor officials are trained to do and, without reading, began his routine questions: where had the flight originated, their last stop, how long did they plan on staying, was the purpose of their visit business or pleasure?

"We will stay in Antwerp for only a few days. Madam has a very sore throat and has lost her voice, so after we register at a hotel, we must take her to a Doctor for an examination. Our length of stay will be determined by the Doctor's diagnosis," Pelling said.

"I see. What is your next destination Mr. Yaro?" Customs asked.

"I have real estate business in Stockholm, Berlin and Prague, after which, I plan on a few weeks of relaxation on the French Riviera," Pelling answered.

"Very well then, enjoy your stay in Belgium and I hope that you are feeling better soon, Madam," with that he handed the passports and airplane's documents back to Ramon and left the Gulfstream.

"That was almost too easy! Ramon, I'm going to make hotel reservations for Ida and myself using Yaro's credit card. You will come along with us while we deposit a cashier's cheque to his American Express Credit Card account. You should get rid of the money I gave you, Ramon. I'd do that first off. I have to dispose of my cash as well. I would like you to stay on the Gulfstream overnight and leave for Rome or Tunis in the morning at 8:00. Do you have any questions about what you are to do?" Pelling asked.

"Get rid of the money, get back here to the Gulfstream and leave for Rome or Tunis at 8:00AM. One question: will you be giving me George Yaro's credit card?" Ramon asked.

"Of course, of course! You will need it to pay for the fuel. As far as I'm concerned, you can fly this damn thing all the way back to Argentina, but I've already told you that I think that would be unwise as both the authorities and the bad guys will be looking for this plane. You're better off to ditch it when you land and then make your way to your money," Pelling said.

"How would you suggest I get rid of these cashier's cheques you gave me? Other than sending them by courier or mail to myself," Ramon asked.

"Well, I'd phone to your next stop and make a hotel reservation, then I would courier a letter to myself at that Hotel. You should arrive in plenty of time prior to the delivery. Otherwise, send it by special delivery to a relative or friend somewhere. I just don't think you should take the chance of getting caught with all that cash," Pelling replied.

"All right then, I'll ride with you to your hotel and after you check in with the card we'll go pay it up. After you're finished using it, I'll need it to pay for the jet fuel," Ramon said.

"Let's be on our way then! Ida are you ready to leave this fancy get-about?" Pelling asked.

"I'm just bringing Ruth's over-nighter. I've stuffed a few of my things and some of hers into it. I'll bring her portfolio along and I guess that's it. Teddy, I think you ought to take us shopping for some new clothes," Ida suggested.

"Hmm, okay then! We're outta here!" Pelling said.

The three left the jet and walked toward the office of the fuelling depot. Teddy had asked Ramon to have the service office book a suite at the Sint Erasmus Gasthuis and refuel the Gulfstream. He did this on the radio as he brought the jet to the fuel pumps. Ramon turned to wave to the service person on the fuel truck who was busy filling the Gulfstream's tanks. They had only a fifteen minute wait until the limo from the Sint Erasmus Gasthuis arrived and took them back to register. Pelling had stayed at this elegant hotel the last time he passed through Belgium. He recalled it having a banking centre and a mall with a variety of shops and, very convenient, only a two kilometer drive from the Airport where they had landed. Better still, it was located just off the Rl on N184. Pelling planned to leave Antwerp for The Hague on the RIO and the Rl ran right into it. Once they had registered as George Yaro and Ruth Werner, Pelling checked the Gucci bag with the most cash with security and sent Ida to the room with the other Gucci and her bag. He and Ramon walked to the banking centre. They paid the credit card balance of $67,000 US by depositing a $100,000 US cashier's cheque onto the card. The cashier gave the card back to Mr. Yaro smiling at him while she stamped the signed off cheque. He asked for thirty thousand in hundreds and fifties in US currency. She did some calculations on a form and signaled to a clerk, who came, took the form, read it and went down the circular staircase to the lower level of the bank. The teller assured Mr. Yaro that the clerk would return with his cash momentarily as she pushed a cheque-like withdrawal slip toward him to sign. He signed. She wrote the credit card number on the slip, smiled again, as the returning clerk handed her the bundle of US bills. She counted it out for him, as he watched her closely. He then put the money in his leather portfolio, thanked her, turned and left the bank with Ramon in tow. The next stop was at the front desk of the hotel where he asked for the bell captain and spoke briefly with him. He then returned to where the pilot was waiting and said, "Come, I'd like to buy you a drink before the taxi I ordered for you arrives." They walked into the lounge, where Ramon ordered a scotch and soda and Pelling ordered a Beck's beer.

"Well, I guess we part company here, Ramon. Here's George's Credit card which you'll need for servicing the Gulfstream. And here is some cash you'll need until you meet up with your money again." Pelling handed the pilot five thousand dollars in US currency.

"At least let me buy these drinks Señor Yaro. It has been an incredibly interesting trip," Ramon said.

"Well, it's not quite over with yet Ramon, you still have to get rid of the Gulfstream." Pelling reminded him.

"Yes, I intend to ditch it in Rome in the morning. I'll take your advice and send the US cashier's cheques to myself at the Hotel. Can you suggest one for me?" Ramon asked.

"Hmm, there's the Focene right at the Leonardo Da Vinci Airport in Rome, but I'd take a cab to the Villa Tre Colli north of the airport on the circle. It's a little more inconspicuous," Pelling suggested.

"Here comes the Bell captain, your taxi is outside. Go do your business and then get back to the Gulfstream. Good luck the rest of the way and thanks for the flight instruction," Pelling said.

Pelling thought it was pointless to tell the pilot to forget about the events of the past week and relied on his observation that Ramon was motivated to do as he was told by all the money he received. It would be foolish for him to go immediately to the authorities and tell all he knew because he would risk the loss of the money he was given, not to mention the wrath of the ETA. The pilot certainly wouldn't contact the ETA, because their tactics at extracting information would be hazardous to his health.

Pelling reasoned that Ramon would fly the Gulfstream somewhere, ditch it quickly, and find someplace where he could enjoy his new found wealth. Surely Ramon wouldn't try to sell the jet. He couldn't be that stupid. That would almost guarantee that the ETA would pay the pilot a visit. Pelling figured the Jet was on too many lists and much too hot to be useful any more. Ramon should understand this and would get rid of it as instructed.

"Señor Yaro, it has been a journey to remember," Ramon said.

Their eyes met briefly. Pelling, staring coldly, could see the fear behind the pilot's eyes as he shook hands.

Ramon left with the Bell Captain for his taxi. When the cab pulled away from the hotel, Ramon asked to be taken to a shopping area, where he could send a package by courier and make hotel reservations. The driver said there was another shopping area with those services, up ahead on the Rl, about three kilometers. Ramon looked out the rear window, still not convinced he was really away from the terrorist. He was sweating profusely from his dealings with Pelling. He shook his head in disbelief at the terrorist. He had expected Pelling to take the ten cashier's cheques back from him at the last minute. *Instead, he suggested how I could make it safe by sending it to myself, and then, I couldn't believe it, he gave me more money: $5,000 in US bills. It has to be vitally important to Pelling to get the Gulfstream on the move and as far away from him as possible. But, why does he want me to wait until morning to leave? And then it struck him!*

Ramon had a frightening thought, then a recollection, deciding in the next instant, he would book himself into a hotel he had stayed at nine years ago, while stationed in Rome for a two week stretch while serving in the Argentine Air force. He remembered the young married lady who had danced with him at the Officer's Mess. She was on the loose she said, her husband was a medical officer, stationed in the north, and was most certainly getting all he could handle from the nurses in his outfit. Ramon and Ciccilia had spent five lusty days together at the Casa Kolbe before he had to return to Argentina. She made him promise to call her if ever he returned to Rome. But, he hadn't been back to the Eternal City, until now. He would book a suite at the Casa Kolbe.

The taxi dropped him at the entrance to the indoor shopping complex, where he quickly found a directory, located a DHL office. On the way, he stopped at a telephone kiosk, pulled his wallet from his rear trouser pocket, stepped into the booth and lay the billfold open on the little metal shelf. He found what he was looking for in behind a photograph; a small folded piece of paper on which he had written Ciccilia and a phone number. On the back of the paper he had written: Casa Kolbe, 44 Via Di San Teodoro, Roma, telephono number 0667949740. Ramon dialed the number and was relieved when the receptionist announced, "Casa Kolbe". He reserved a suite for one week stay and asked to confirm their mailing address. The receptionist confirmed the address and added a postal region. He thanked the reservations clerk and hung up. Ramon went directly to the DHL office and made up a delivery letter containing an envelope which held the ten cashier's cheques. He addressed it to himself at the Casa Kolbe and asked that it be delivered in the early afternoon of the following day. He paid for the service in cash. Next, he went shopping and bought a number of items, returned to the telephone and tried his daughter Ursula's apartment in Bermuda. He listened to the message on the answering machine saying she would be out of town for a week and would return all calls upon her return. He hung up without leaving a message.

After spending nearly an hour in the indoor shopping complex and feeling relieved that he was no longer carrying the million dollars, Ramon, feeling an increasing urgency, went in search of a taxi to take him back to the Airport and the Gulfstream. He had left the fueling station manager the keys to the Gulfstream so that they could park it out of the way of the pumps after they filled the tanks. The taxi dropped him at the office where he used George Yaro's credit card to pay for the fuel and signed George Yaro's name, as he had done every other time when servicing the Gulfstream. Ramon took the foil and card back and put them both away in his wallet. The attendant handed him the keys to the jet and asked if he wished to file a flight plan. Ramon filled out the form, stating Tunis as his destination and no passengers aboard, handed the form to the attendant, thanked him and then left for the plane.

Ramon had no intention of sitting on the tarmac, waiting for 8:00AM to arrive, before he took off. Especially if the generous Teddy Pelling had called the authorities or the ETA to tell them were the plane was. When he thought more about it, he couldn't imagine Pelling bringing additional heat on to him. It could be that Pelling might return to the Gulfstream as an alternate escape route if he was trapped somehow. After a quick check of the interior of the craft brought on by a mild attack of paranoia, Ramon, satisfied that he was indeed alone, quickly went through his preflight check-off and began rolling onto the service runway while asking the tower for clearance to take off. Ground control directed him to the active runway number 95, then gave him back to the tower, who cleared him for take-off. Ramon ran the engines to a screaming pitch, rocketed down the runway and lifted off feeling the power of the jet as it climbed steeply up to cruising altitude. He located the airport map of Tunis International in the thick little ring-binder "Airports of the World", studied it for a minute, tuned his ADF to the outer beacon at Tunis and set the Gulfstream up for automatic pilot. He watched as the jet corrected slightly and aimed at its destination. Once he had flown three quarters of the way along his route he planned to change course into Leonardo Da Vinci Aeroporto in Rome.

Chapter Thirty
Rendezvous at the Utrecht Chateau

Lieutenant Robert Bizet watched Orly airport getting smaller and further in the distance as Marta flew her Lake Renegade to cruising altitude and adjusted her course for the Vander Riis Chateau in Utrecht, Holland. Their other passenger, Andre Laurent, sitting in the rear seat, finally spoke, "What did Raoul de Vascos have to offer in the way of information?"

"He's willing to make a deal with us. In exchange for clemency, he will tell us everything he knows about the ETA," Robert answered.

"And?" questioned Andre.

"I said I would have to think about it...and, I would need some strong indication in the way of useful information to take to my superiors in order to make a plea on his behalf. He said he would tell me all I wanted to know about George Yaro who is one of the ETA's accountants," Robert said.

"Why the sudden panic on his part?" Andre asked.

"He has been threatened by his own people...his Uncle no less," Robert said.

"George Yaro is the registered owner of the Gulfstream jet we lost track of in George Town, right?" Andre asked.

"Yes and we have since learned, it stopped for a few hours in Panama City and left for God knows where...nothing on it since. Our information seems rather confused because this jet left George Town with five people aboard, but landed and took off with only three people in Panama City," Robert said.

"Doesn't customs check things like that?" Andre asked.

"Apparently not, remember what I said about the lesser developed and how easy it is to bribe officials. When wealthy individuals want to come and go without formalities, it is easy enough to do," Robert replied.

Marta had been intent on flying and setting the Lake A-4 on the course to Utrecht. She had missed her favorite toy but satisfied that everything was functioning properly, she removed her radio headset letting it settle around her neck, turned to Robert and asked, "What information did Raoul give you about Pelling?"

"Raoul said that Pelling has ten million US dollars stashed somewhere and probably a large chunk of ETA money as well," Robert replied.

"Terrific! The fact that he has millions of dollars at his disposal will make him that much harder to capture, won't it?" asked Marta.

"Raoul wouldn't answer any specific questions until I offer him a deal, but he has continued to relate his own history with the ETA and what he knows of George Yaro and Teddy Pelling. He still insists he is in danger from the ETA but feels safer now that he is away from the prison population," Robert said.

Andre said, "Isn't Raoul sort of an "untouchable" because his uncle is one of the leaders in the ETA? Why would he be in danger?"

"Raoul said his Uncle sent him a message saying that nothing could be done for him and for the sake of the movement, he should be a good example and take his own life." Robert answered.

"Lovely people aren't they?" observed Marta.

"Raoul was very sure of himself when I first interviewed him, but he is a changed man now…told me that when you are asked to kill yourself, it's just an option, because if you don't tidy up the mess you've caused them, they will find a way to do it for you. That's why I had to chance moving him to a safer place until I get all the information he has. The sergeants have him dictating constantly while they compile a file of the workings of the ETA which they will fax to me at your Chateau," Robert said.

"That's Brussels over to our left. We're making good time, the winds aloft are in our favor. We have less than 150 kilometers left to fly," Marta offered and then added, "I thought the Bastille was the safest place to keep Raoul."

"It was, up until now. While the ETA worked on trying to free him, he was an 'untouchable.' When they issued Raoul's death sentence, he immediately became a target for anyone who might do a favor for the ETA for profit. The more I thought about it the more paranoid I got. The ETA could easily pay someone to poison his food. So, I instructed the sergeants to bring him his food until we decide where we will take him for interrogation. They are the only visitors he is to have. Absolutely no one else. I have an idea that I'm working on…I'll tell you what it is when we get to the Chateau," Robert said.

After more conversation on the topic of Pelling and Raoul, his former control, Marta announced that they would be landing on the lake at the back of the Chateau in ten minutes and they should fasten up. She brought the Lake A-4 skimming across the lake, touching down gently, with only the sound of the throttled back engine and the water rushing past the hull. Marta lowered the wheels and throttled the amphibian up onto the concrete launching pad on the beach, revved the engine and swung the plane back toward the water and began her shut down.

Elspeth heard the Lake coming in for a landing, spotted it, and headed for the landing area driving the VW "Thing."

As she pulled up to the plane, she saw Robert Bizet and Marta standing beside it and suddenly blushed as she saw who the third passenger was. Eslpeth hugged her daughter tightly, then Robert and smiled at Andre Laurent as she stepped into his space. While Robert and Marta looked on, Andre encircled Elspeth and drew her to him in a very passionate hug. She stayed in his embrace long enough to feel his genitalia join in the welcome. She had her head pressed into his chest and her arms around his neck until she untwined them to hold his face in her hands. Elspeth looked in his eyes and saw his unspoken words and heard Marta say, "OK you two break it up!" Marta dug her elbow into Robert's side as an exclamation to the "yes" she said under her breath.

The ride to the Chateau was quiet and quick. Elspeth drove with Andre sitting alongside of her. Marta sat to the right of Robert in the back seat so that she could speak with her mother, but after a question or two about Tice and Sylvie, they arrived at the circular driveway in front of the entrance to the Chateau and were met by the staff, who said their hellos and then loaded the luggage into the front hallway. Robert needed an office and was shown into the library. He gave his jacket to Marta while he dialed his Paris office. He spoke with his sergeants who put him on their speaker phone while he instructed them on exactly what he wanted done with Raoul de Vascos. He would fax further instructions within the hour. During the investigation into Elspeth's kidnapping, Robert had used this same library as his office. The fax machine, telephone and tape recorder were still there. Robert busied himself writing out the instructions he would fax to his sergeants concerning the special treatment of Raoul de Vascos. He was interrupted by Marta who suggested he go up to her suite of rooms and shower while she brought him a brandy. Marta whispered in his ear that Elspeth and Andre were having a swim before retiring. She had an I-told-you-so smirk on her face as she took two snifters and a bottle of Chateau Brandy from a sideboard, put them on a tray and left the library. Robert finished his writing and sent it to his sergeants at a fax machine located in a little known area deep inside the Bastille. One of his sergeants was waiting for the transmission of instructions. After reading them, he started sending the file they had compiled so far from the information taken from Raoul de Vascos.

> Lieutenant Bizet, this file is transcribed from the information dictated by Raoul de Vascos. (He tended to ramble on but I didn't edit any of it):

> "My uncle Esau Navarra operates his armed separatist network from the twenty-first floor of a luxurious high-rise office building in downtown Bilbao, running both the ETA or Euskadi Ta Askatasuna (Basque acronym for Fatherland and Liberty) and their vast business interests. Since 1894, this Nationalist group has been campaigning for an independent state by violent means. Recently they have turned to political means to attain their goal of statehood. The United Nations have proposed a meeting of the Basque leadership and governments of France and Spain to begin talks in the near future. Esau Navarra, known

throughout his network as Tio Esau, told me that the ETA offshore banks held about seventy million US dollars which will help them in their political goals. His network includes 121 bars or "people's taverns" spread across the four Spanish and three French provinces, located in the westernmost part of the Pyrenees Mountains, which is the 'Basque Homeland'. These taverns are the main fundraising and recruitment points for the ETA. They also serve as 'listening posts' providing timely intelligence to the Ruling Council of the ETA.

Tio Esau told me he had run out of ways to free me, as the Sûreté had provided enough evidence to convict me and it would be in the interest of the ETA's political ambitions if I were to take my own life for the good of the movement. Tio Esau told me he could do no more for me and went on to say he had much on his mind as a Spanish high court judge was heading a movement to outlaw the ETA and their political party the Batasuna. The judge's report listed 836 killings and 2,367 injuries in 3,391 terrorist actions, as well as numerous bank robberies and kidnappings which he described as 'systematically directed against specific sectors of the population, sometimes in indiscriminate terms.' These incidents took place since 1968. During this same period, worldwide terrorism was said to account for less than 10,000 lives.

During the past three years, the ETA geared up their bombing, assassinations, kidnapping and robbery in both Spain and France. The cost in innocent lives was nearing one hundred, yet the authorities in Spain and France had managed to capture and jail less than two dozen ETA extremists." My first assignment for Tio Esau, when I wired a bomb to an ETA agent's car. The marked agent was guilty of colluding with a banker to rob his bank.

The banker had contracted the ETA to rob his bank three years before. His split, was an amount which would have kept any reasonable person financially secure for the rest of his life, but this banker was a compulsive gambler who went through the money in two and a half years, losing it all at the baccarat tables in Monaco. Six months ago, he began using his bank's money to fund his compulsion. A chance meeting in a Monaco casino between the banker and the ETA agent who had participated in the original robbery (the agent was also a loser at the tables), got the plan for this robbery underway. Except, this time, the proceeds of the robbery would be split between the two of them.

Using a very sophisticated zoom camera lens and the latest technology in listening devices, I obtained photographs and a tape recording of the ETA agent and the banker planning the latest robbery of his bank. When I reported this evidence to Tio Esau, his instructions were: Intercept the stolen money when the robbery goes down and eliminate the banker and the ETA agent.

Tio Esau said that his organization would be linked to the holdup, regardless. This time, though, the bag they were usually left holding, would be full of money.

The local papers carried the news of the robbery, which earned the single masked gunman the equivalent of one million dollars.

The following day's headline story covered a car bombing which took the life of the driver. Eye witnesses told reporters: the late model silver Peugeot looked like the car used in the bank robbery the day before. No money was recovered from the explosion, but a partially burned bank money sack was the implicating evidence. Speculation was rampant on the third day after the robbery when the same newspapers reported the shocking news that the manager of the robbed bank had hanged himself in his study.

"I was congratulated by Tio Esau for this expert bit of wet-work. I received a fee of one hundred thousand dollars plus a bonus of fifty thousand after I turned over the one million taken from the bank robber.

My duties included routine surveillance of ETA agents after they completed their training in the Libyan desert. The organization holds their newest agents in high regard after they had completed their first assignment. Tio Esau's motto was: 'Trust but verify'. Then, once they have 'killed for the cause,' they belonged to a select group who enjoyed a rather lucrative lifestyle."

It seemed to be customary for ETA agents that they live life to the fullest, spending their money freely. A few, like Pelling were the exception. He didn't like the bright lights or the cabaret scene and preferred a much quieter life. Tio Esau was kept informed of what his agents did with their free time through the very wide ranging network of informers located throughout France and Spain. I also provided monthly reports of the activities of the "circled" agents which Tio Esau, or the council, placed under suspicion.

"Since that first double sanction of the ETA agent and the Banker, my main duty was as an 'understudy' to Tio Esau. I was paid handsomely: One hundred and fifty thousand each for assignments. It was Tio Esau's habit to pay fifty thousand up front and provide a file containing pictures and information about the target. The hundred thousand dollar balance was always paid when an agent reported, in person, with proof of the completed contract. Proof had to consist of photographs.

Tio Esau considered that I was now 'responsible' with a knack for this type of work. It was not always so, as I had some trouble as a womanizer when I first got back from training in Libya. I got drunk and killed a girl I was romancing. The girl turned out to be the daughter of the local mayor. Tio Esau enlisted me in the French Foreign Legion for a five year hitch. I was instructed to learn all I could about munitions and armament. During this hitch I attained the rank of sergeant and met young Teddy Pelling who, after his term was up, went to work with the ETA under me. Although it was my job to keep informed about the people who worked for us, I kept a close watch on Pelling. I even hooked up with his call girl friend Ruth Meikle and learned through her about how she and Pelling were on the verge of becoming financially independent. The Corporal's (Agent Pelling's) lifestyle was laid back. He never womanized, preferring call girls. His only passion was a fascination with metal work and working on cars. I knew about Pelling working with agent, Reo Racicot, who had a workshop in Bilbao where he spent all of his spare time. I assumed the cars probably consumed most of Racicot's income. I did some checking and found out that Racicot acquired six vintage cars at reasonable prices, then spent judiciously for the parts required to restore them. He saved thousands in the restoration process by doing most of the work himself. I reasoned the cars could be sold at auction for a small fortune. I figured if Tio Esau thought Racicot squandered all his earnings on these cars, so much the better as I planned to take over ownership of these cars when the time came. Most agents didn't live long. These highly paid agents spent their money like the supply would never end. Inevitably, some of them would resort to robberies or kidnapping when they got overextended. When this occurred, their names would appear on either Tio Esau's list or mine, thus marking them for elimination. Those who lost favor, for whatever reason, became expendable and were eliminated. Tio Esau and those in charge of the organization, remained firmly in control, undoubtedly, because they never trusted anyone.

My uncle Esau is totally preoccupied with the possible political arrangement between the ETA, France and Spain. This sudden thievery by their trusted accountant George Yaro and agent Pelling has my uncle enraged so he's assigned Reo Racicot to clear this mess. This assignment of Racicot's consists of three targets, prioritized at $250,000 each, an unheard of amount. Extra expenses were deemed necessary to uncover what actually happened to the missing ETA accountant, George Yaro, the renegade agent, Teddy Pelling and his girlfriend, Ruth Meikle. For this special assignment, Racicot was given $400,000 up-front money. The balance, $350,000, will be paid when he reports, in person, with proof that these targets have been eliminated."

"My lawyers showed me the report from the two ETA agents who sanctioned George Yaro's pilot in Rome, after interrogating him. They stated Ramon Atmos told them how George Yaro and Ruth Meikle were both killed during the flight in Yaro's Gulfstream jet when it left George Town in the Cayman Islands to Panama City. Pelling then dumped their bodies into the Sea. The report stated Pelling was using the name, Linus Svendsen, and Ruth Meikle was using her real name, Ruth Anna Werner prior to her death. The other passenger was Ida Tesh, whom the pilot stated, looked so much like Ruth Werner, she could have been her twin. My uncle Esau told Racicot 'If you are successful in finding Pelling and learn the location of his money, (rumored to be in the millions) you will have earned both the $400,000 and the bonus of $350,000. The ruling council members are extremely pissed because fifteen million is missing from our offshore bank in Douglas, Isle of Man, which was last accessed by George Yaro. 'Force Pelling to tell you what actually happened to George Yaro and this Ruth woman,' he ordered Racicot.

My Uncle is so concerned, he got Racicot's attention by advising him that the council authorized a special $100,000 bonus for every million recovered of the money missing from this offshore bank.'

As I am no longer permitted visitors from my lawyers, I will await your offer of clemency for all this information."

Signed Raoul de Vascos.

Chapter Thirty One
ETA Issues Sanctions

When agent Reo Racicot left Tio Esau's office, he was retired from the ETA in his mind. Racicot wouldn't allow himself to consider how all this bonus money he might earn could impact his future. He wasn't greedy. With the $400,000 up-front money, $600,000 from the sale of his cars, his bank balance in Liechtenstein and his mutual fund account, he was well over his goal of three million. Racicot figured he could simply disappear as Pelling had and take his chances but this wasn't the option he preferred. Nevertheless, he would concentrate on finding Pelling, because it was necessary to have his cooperation in what he had in mind. As he strolled away from ETA headquarters, Racicot couldn't think of any reason Pelling could have not to go along with his plan. It would set them both free of the organization.

He and Pelling had worked an assignment together their first year with the organization. Pelling, or 'The Corporal' (his agent name), had set a bomb in a Sûreté detective's car parked outside his apartment then waited with Racicot whose job was to take the confirmation photos for Raoul, Pelling's control.

Racicot was about to take a picture of the side of the apartment building where the Sûreté detective lived. He framed the shot to include the car Pelling had wired when the policeman appeared on his balcony, wearing a towel around his waist and shaving soap on his face. An attractive young woman waved up at him, then entered his car. Racicot snapped the picture catching both in the frame. He couldn't believe Pelling detonated the bomb as the car burst into a thunderous fireball. He took another picture of the scene showing the policeman gripping the balcony railing, screaming in horror, at the fire ball caused by the explosion.

Pelling's comment later was chilling: 'The death of the girlfriend will serve as an even greater warning to the detective to back off his pursuit of the ETA.'

When the two agents split up that morning, Pelling took Racicot's camera with him. Since that time they had never been on sanctions together, but they had worked on Racicot's classic cars on a few occasions. Racicot remembered how Pelling was skilled at working with metal and was an inventive mechanic. They'd spoken at times over the years and enjoyed duty together as bodyguards for Tio Esau and his nephew, Raoul de Vascos when they attended the Cannes Film Festival the last three years.

Racicot had heard of some of 'The Corporal's' assignments since then, but nothing much until recently when the buzz about 'the Corporal' became continuous with daily rumors of his whereabouts and the millions he'd somehow stolen from the organization. Pelling had worked exclusively for Raoul de Vascos. The rumors indicated Pelling went on the suspicion list when he became tardy in his latest call back to Raoul. The gossip also concerned Pelling's girlfriend, Ruth Meikle, who was not only a knockout but some sort of financial wizard as well. She, apparently, had invested the Corporal's money over the years and amassed a fortune.

When the ETA network heard Pelling had made Raoul's death list, the consensus was: Pelling, if captured, would make a deal with Raoul to exchange his stash of money for his life. The rumor mill ground out updates on a daily basis, making Pelling out to be some sort of magical phantom who had, somehow, turned the tables on Raoul.

The headlines of the newspapers in the Basque Provinces shouted about the capture of the ETA council member, Raoul de Vascos by Lieutenant Robert Bizet of the Sûreté's special anti-terrorism squad. The rumblings in the ETA organization suggested many reasons for this dramatic turn of events, but the bottom line remained: Pelling was at large with millions of ETA money, while Raoul de Vascos was behind bars.

Ordinarily, it wouldn't have been that difficult for the ETA network to extricate Raoul from jail. By bribing the right insiders with a substantial amount of money, guards would look the other way when Raoul was exercising in the yard, allowing him to walk out the main gate, which would be left ajar. An ETA car would be waiting to whisk him into hiding. The ETA had managed this at other lesser prisons with other agents. Any number of scenarios could have been arranged to get him out of prison. Not this time though, because Pelling had provided evidence of Raoul's involvement in a murder. The Sûreté made sure this particular ETA bigshot was kept under close guard. Raoul de Vascos' confinement at the Bastille in Paris was supervised, personally, by Lieutenant Bizet, whose fiancé was killed in the car bombing ordered by Raoul years before. This evidence was confirmed by voice prints on an audio taped telephone conversation between Raoul and Pelling, along with the photographs provided taken at the scene of that crime.

The story was carried by Spanish and French papers and TV. Robert Bizet became a celebrity, which made the approaches by the ETA impossible to get cooperation from any of the police forces.

Robert Bizet went over the file of information obtained from Raoul de Vascos. It was informative and filled in many of the gaps he had in his own compilation of the workings of the ETA, nevertheless, he needed to learn more detail of their operations before he offered Raoul anything.

Chapter Thirty Two
Ruth's Millions

Pelling and Ida Tesh took possession of the Mercedes sport coupe at their Hotel and loaded the two Gucci bags into the trunk along with the two other bags containing their belongings. Ida had arranged for the Mercedes using Ruth Werner's credit card and driver's license. The car was taken out for one week. Pelling hadn't checked out of the hotel, telling the front desk manager that they would return after a short trip around Belgium and Holland. Ida swung behind the wheel, adjusted the seat and the mirrors, buckled up and drove off as she concentrated on following Pelling's instructions onto the Rl. Minutes later, they were travelling northwest on the RIO which would take them to The Hague.

"There is a good shopping area close to the banking section of The Hague. We can get some new clothes there if you like," he said to Ida.

"I like!" Ida answered and pulled off at a rest stop in order to let Pelling take the wheel. Ida contented herself with surfing her hand in the airflow past her open window as Pelling accelerated the Mercedes up to cruising speed.

He smiled at her and thought: *She looks like she hasn't got a care in the world. She doesn't act like she has millions in her bank account. She's just along for the ride and having a wonderful time. She's far less complicated than Ruth, but I wonder...what the hell's going through her mind sometimes. The way she follows instructions is very refreshing. She never asks why or what's next. Doesn't want to burden herself with too much information I guess. And what a package she comes in and every bit of it available, at any time. Don't want to think about that right now, got to concentrate on the plan to empty The Hague account of George Yaro by transferring that money to another identity. Linus Svendsen is about to become someone else as is George Yaro. But first, I need to pick up a few items in order to make myself over and then have some new pictures taken. After Ida poses as Ruth Werner and transfers Ruth's money to one of my new identities, I will put her on a plane back to Atlanta and insist that she move her money once more to maybe Nassau or the Cook Islands and then maybe disappear for a time. I don't think she will put up a fuss once I tell her the adventure is over for now. I am torn between getting her to transfer some of the three million back to one of my identities leaving her with a million or so, or having her transfer all of it back to me and snuffing her. I haven't really decided on what course of action to take. I don't think it would be in my best interests to just kiss her goodbye put her on a plane for Atlanta and hope she won't cause me any problems. Ramon couldn't believe his good fortune at me giving him that extra cash and wishing him luck. I'll bet he has already taken off in the Gulfstream. He seemed to be getting very antsy about having to wait until the morning to leave.*

The drive from Antwerp, Belgium to The Hague, Holland was 118 kilometers. The border station into Holland located two kilometers past the Belgium town of Essen is where they presented their rental papers for the car, the passports of George Yaro and Ruth Werner. After the usual questions asked of tourists, their papers were returned and they were waved on through. The first sign after the border crossing announced it was 52 kilometers to The Hague. They would arrive before noon. Ida grew bored and, with her hand surfing, moved over close to Pelling and found something more interesting to do with her hands.

Chapter Thirty Three
Andre and Elspeth Reunited

Andre Laurent swam a few lengths, mostly underwater, in the Vander Riis' indoor pool and felt the effects of the cramped airplane rides leave his body. He surfaced immediately in front of Elspeth who was sitting on the poolside dangling her legs in the water watching him. She was smiling down at him and it took him back to a time when he was totally consumed with their approaching rendezvous. The horrendous events of the past month, which prevented that very personal get-together, seemed to have disappeared. Andre realized the cloud of suspicion had been lifted from him and that he had finally begun to resume his life again. He drew himself up to his full height to stand in front of her in the waist-high water at the shallow end. He kissed the inside of her hand as it brushed by his face and entangled in his wet hair, getting a gentle grip, while her other arm encircled his back and brought him closer, between her opened knees. Elspeth looked deep into his eyes and kissed his lips setting off a very passionate session. Andre lifted her off the poolside and holding her tight to him, slid into the water. They hugged each other until Andre finally said, "I've been thinking of you constantly over the past week or so...there's something I must tell you."

"Andre, I have been trying to forget you ever since you left here. I've been forgetting you every hour. It was such a surprise to see you that I blushed like a schoolgirl...and when you hugged me tight to you and I felt your arousal...well, I was shameless Andre...I must have embarrassed you as well as Robert and Marta."

"No, you misread the moment. I was thrilled at your greeting and excited, as you know. I am looking forward to bedtime tonight though," Andre replied.

"You must be beat! It's been such a long day for all three of you and I think what's best is that you and I go up to my suite immediately, get into bed together and pretend it's tonight .....agree?" she said.

That's the way he remembered her from their romp in Paris. Exciting! And exactly how he had hoped it might be when they met again. She was not one to play coquettish games; just very matter-of-fact in her special way of being right up front. Elspeth left no doubt that she wanted him, now! They left the pool in their bulky terry-towel robes and made their way up the big staircase to Elspeth's suite. They took their bathing suits off, showered together, and toweled dry before they got into her bed. Andre could feel her warm breath immediately as she attacked him, kissing him furiously from his chest downward to her prize. He tried to relax thinking how secretive they both were about meeting in June at her Paris apartment, and now, everyone in her family knew and seemed to approve. She soon had him maximized, quickly straddled him, and as soon as they were connected, she lay forward on his chest so that he could hold her by her cheeks and begin their love making. He remembered the feel of her and thrilled at how quickly she responded to him. His hands went to the dip in her waist as she adjusted to their embrace. He was fascinated at how she moved on him as her breathing became huskier and he heard the words she liked to whisper to him, "Andre we feel so good together." She wasn't aware of the beginning of her song which sounded like a soft whine deep in her throat, immediately followed by the tensing of her cheeks, then the velvety clenching sensation he could feel around his erection. To these magical sounds and sensations was added the shuddering of her stomach muscles as her climax built. Andre enjoyed this extraordinary pleasure until her spasms began to lessen; she could feel his hands tighten on her and his warm release inside her.

They rolled apart and looked back at each other saying nothing. After they finally caught their breath, Andre sat up on the side of the bed, smoked a few puffs on a joint while trying to compose what he was going to tell her. His head was getting woollier by the moment. He put the remaining joint back into the ashtray and got back under the covers. He looked over at her. She had been watching him. She waited very patiently as she sensed he was going to say something. Elspeth watched him closely and just when she thought he was about to speak, he fell into a deep sleep.

Andre had been felled and carried off by the biggest sleep wave he ever encountered. Elspeth turned toward her love, crooked her elbow under her side, lifted her head up onto her hand and watched him sleep. Andre mumbled something causing an alarming tingle to run up her spine as she clearly heard two of the words: Pelling and ransom.

Elspeth left the bed, went to her bathroom to tidy up, returned to the bedside in her bathrobe and, deep in thought, lit what remained of the joint Andre had started. She sat on the bedroom lounge and drank one of the half-full brandies left on a serving tray. She would finish the other as well as the joint before she returned to bed. She dozed off and slipped into a dream so real and frightening that she woke up soaked in perspiration. It was 2:00AM. Had she really slept for nearly nine hours? She needed desperately to talk with Andre, but he was sleeping so soundly she couldn't bring herself to wake him. She left the bed, sat at her writing desk, took a note book and pen from the drawer and began writing an account of the very vivid dream she had just had.

Elspeth returned to her bed, looked over at Andre's ruggedly handsome face and reached to touch him. She withdrew her hand at the last moment before it made contact, rolled over on her side, with her back to him and tried desperately to force the dream from her mind.

Elspeth didn't realize she had fallen back to sleep, when she experienced a not uncommon phenomena: Chapter two of her dream began.

She and Robert were in a church at a funeral service but she didn't know who the service was for. Elspeth looked in vain through the crowd but could not find Andre, Marta or Tice. She wondered whose bodies were in the two coffins at the altar! Funerals can be heartbreakingly sad and Elspeth's tears were relentless as she scanned the crowd. Robert Bizet stood next to her straight as a pillar and equally as inanimate. He didn't answer her when she asked him where Marta was. Elspeth continued crying uncontrollably for the unknown deceased unable to shake the feeling she was somehow responsible. She awoke and went to the bathroom to dry her tears.

Chapter Thirty Four
The Party's Over

Teddy Pelling and Ida Tesh purchased new clothes at the shopping complex two blocks away from the Hotel Vidalia close to the Royal Bank where they stopped to transfer the fifteen and one half million US dollars in the Linus Svendsen account. Ida, acting as Ruth Werner, transferred the two million in Ruth's account into the Linus Svendsen account. Pelling, was dressed in his new outfit: chocolate colored sport coat, dark blue sport shirt, khaki slacks, dark brown socks and tan loafers. The tan colored Panama hat over his pony tail completed his makeover and made him look exactly like his passport photo of Linus Svendsen that the bank officer only glanced at it for comparison and then watched him carefully as he signed. He ordered five million in cashier's cheques: twelve of two hundred fifty thousand each and twenty of one hundred thousand denominations. The remaining ten million and one half million he transferred to an account they opened for him at their branch in Zurich, Switzerland. They left the bank and headed back to their Hotel, stopping momentarily at a travel agency to purchase an airline ticket to Atlanta for Ida.

Ida thought: *This is as good a time as any. I'd like to see Paris again as long as I'm over here. I wonder would he mind if I went back home to Atlanta via Paris? I'll stay at a hotel in the shopping district and buy myself a few things. No, on second thought, why even ask his permission? I can re-arrange my flight at the airport. He said he wouldn't be coming along to the airport, because it was foolish to risk it. So, he won't be with me. I'll give him a little special lovin' before it's time to leave and see if he changes his mind about seeing me off and then asks for the three million back.*

Back in their hotel room, Teddy handed the airline ticket to Ida along with five thousand in US cash. "Wow! What's all this for, Babe?" Ida asked.

"You will need some going around money until you get your millions re-arranged. Take it! Enjoy!" Pelling said.

Ida thought, Here it comes! He's going to ask me to wire the three million to Linus' account when I get to Atlanta. Ida handed over the portfolio containing Ruth's bank account books and her reconstructed passport.

"This is the end of our little adventure, Ida. You can take a taxi to the airport this evening to meet your flight. I'll use the Mercedes for a little unfinished business I have to take care of and then I'll move on. I'd like you to stay at your present address for at least a week. I'll call you and let you know how to get in touch with me," Pelling instructed.

Teddy was watching Ida very closely as he said this. She listened very intently to him as she slowly began to peel away her clothes while walking back and forth in front of him. It appeared as if she was getting turned on. When she had only her bra and panties left on, she stood in front of him in her high heels. Teddy could see her excitement as her nipples strained against the fabric of the bra.

"Teddy, honey. I've been on a few of these sexy adventures before. Mostly with Ruth, but none as wild and crazy as this one. Be straight with me now, please lover. You will want me to wire you the three million you and Ruthie parked in my new Royal Bank account in Atlanta, correct? You'll contact me in the next week with instructions, right?" Ida arched her back to push out her chest while she smiled knowingly at him sitting on the edge of the bed and trying to look hurt.

Teddy stood up and took off his shirt, then his shoes and sox. While he was undoing his belt he said, "Ida, when I said you had been well paid for your part in this little escapade, I meant the three million dollars. It's all yours as well as the ten thousand we first sent to you and the five more I just gave you. It's ALL yours." Teddy let his trousers and boxer shorts fall around his ankles and stepped away from them. He was naked except for the wide money belt which looked like a corset over his muscular middle.

Ida undid her bra, freeing her breasts with their tiered swollen areolas and extended nipples. She stood tall and tucked her thumbs into the waistband of her panties while wiggling out of them. Stepping away from her panties, she took the remaining steps toward him as he let the money belt drop to the floor. Their genitals met before the embrace and Ida circled her arms around his chiseled upper body, hung on tight, swung herself up to his midsection, wrapping her long legs around him as they joined. They fell back onto the bed, vigorously taking pleasure from each other.

While she was into her optimum level of release, Teddy rolled her over onto her back. Still joined, he kept at her, feeling her orgasm becoming more intense as she writhed under him. Something welled up inside him as his hands went to her throat and began to squeeze the life from her body. Ida started to thrash about, pinned under him. He was, in his mind, with Ursula experiencing the exciting transition from vigorous orgasm to death throes. He had entered a remembered level of excitement as she fought frantically for her life. It had become his ultimate sexual release, but Ida abruptly stopped moving which brought Pelling immediately out of his erotic trance. She could feel his hands loosen around her neck as her bulging eyes seemed to be smiling up at him. When she could finally speak she said, "Lover, you came like a fire hose when you started to choke the life out of me. My God you are intense! Babe you really are something! I knew right away it was really turning you on, feeling me thrash about for air when I was getting off. It was the only thing I could think of to get your attention Sweetie, so I turned myself off, stopped moving and fighting for breath. Wow! What a rush! I've never been so nearly fucked to death, ever! Next time Lover, I'll have to tie your hands to the bed posts, just to be on the safe side. Tell me darlin', how many ladies have you killed that way?" Ida asked.

"Get dressed Ida!" Pelling ordered.

While Ida washed herself clean of the sex, she looked in the mirror at her reflection with the redness beginning to appear on both sides of her neck. She was frightened as she rubbed lotion on her throat thinking she wouldn't be allowed to leave the hotel room now for damn sure. Ida went into her cool zone, dressed in a platinum colored sleeveless blouse of Ruth's that was made of a heavier shiny expensive material with a high turtle neck collar. She wore her own gun metal grey tailored slacks with grey sandals. Ida pushed all the loose clothing on the floor into Ruth's overnight bag and put it by the door.

She waited by the bags as he approached her, not knowing what he would do next but remembering that panic seemed to throw a switch in him. She smiled and concentrated on his naked body. She focused on his marvelous build. What a gorgeous hunk he was!

"Got everything?" Pelling asked.

"Uh huh! Ticket and money in my purse along with my passport. I'm all set!" Ida answered.

He stepped into her space and pulled her to him and kissed her on the lips. Hard. She responded with lots of tongue but didn't let herself go.

"You're going to call me in the next week, right?" Ida said.

"Ida, the sex was terrific! Better even than with Ruth. So, if you really would like to take her place, I'm retired and looking for somewhere to settle in Europe. I'm taking a chance saying goodbye to you now because I don't really know you yet. If we are to be buddies, Ida, I have to prove to you that you really are free to go. So, go on home and do something sensible with your money. Spend some, invest a lot, hide some, whatever, and when you finally realize it's all yours to do with as you like, well, about that time I'll call you and see If you're interested in meeting me somewhere interesting so we can play some more. In other words, the party is over for now and you are free to go. I never meant that you be some captive play-kitten. This way, if you do decide to come stay with me again, you'll be returning of your own free will. It'll be interesting negotiating a fee for your services. I think you know I can pay almost anything you might ask. Whether I choose to or not...we'll just have to wait and see," Pelling said.

"Sounds, interesting and profitable. I'll be waiting for your call, lover." She opened the hotel room door, blew him a kiss and left swinging the expensive overnighter as she made her way to the elevators.

Ida rode the elevator down to the lobby and marched to the front desk where she requested a cab to take her to the airport. She exited the swinging doors to wait on the curb until the summoned cab arrived. The elderly doorman held the taxi door open for her and then put her bags in the trunk. She unconsciously locked her rear doors as she gave the driver her destination. She kept looking at the sweep hand of her watch as she held her breath. Two minutes and six seconds went by before she sucked air. She had done better. Her habit of practicing holding her breath began when they were sixteen during that sexy summer when she and Ruth took the train into Boston on weekends to stay with Bruno. They had doubled back and forth with Bruno and his teammates on the water polo team. She and Ruth had fellated all of Bruno's college chums that fall. Fellatio had become a very accomplished part of their repertoire. Whenever a partner had a particular offensive smell she would simply hold her breath for as long a period as she could. Thank god, she hadn't been completely into the orgasm she was having with Pelling, and quickly figured out that he was getting off on her death struggle. She hadn't panicked: she had turned herself completely off, stiffened like a plank, and after two or three more thrusts, his hands loosened and she felt him come inside her so much it overflowed into the crease of her ass. When she could breathe again, she remained calm and told him how good it had been. *Do the ludicrous recognize the demented?* Ida wondered. *Teddy is a real genuine piece of work, but big-time scary. He would be near-perfect if he had different wiring,* she thought. *Ruth was right though, he was a fuck-and-a-half and Teddy had been her best buddy for a long time. Poor Ruthie, I'm going to miss you darlin'. What a bloody waste! But, it was a stupid accident! And, it could just as easily been me. Good old Teddy just cleaned up the mess like nothing happened. Throwing them both off the jet like that. Incredible but not surprising! Ruth always said he made vulgar amounts of money as a real bad guy.* She could hear Ruth's voice saying, "*He's really a good guy and you'll like him. He's a hunk who knows how to take care of a lady. I ought to know, I taught him most of what he knows from his 17th birthday until now and I know he has turned down a lot of the action that just seems to come his way. He has paid a secret agency for very high priced specially trained young ladies. He's bought a few virgins from these same establishments, they ranged from age 14 up to 18, ten in all so far, he told me. They had all been taught the art of massage, fellatio and masturbation but had not been deflowered. He had to return them after a two week period. They have been his only extravagance and he probably squandered a million dollars over a ten year period on them.*" Of course, after hearing about Teddy over the years, Ida had a built-up-yearning for the guy, but on the three other occasions when she came to Paris as Ruth's guest, she was paired up with clients of Ruth. Teddy never showed up. *Well, I finally met him alright! Didn't I? He's everything Ruth said he was and more! I'll bet he came just as close to killing Ruth as he did me a while ago. If he had strangled me to death what would have been the point? He would have to dispose of my body besides losing any chance of recovering the three million parked in my bank account. All that trouble for what, a few seconds more sex while he watched me die? He didn't really strike me as weirdly kinky but, being the very accomplished stud he is, who knows? Maybe he has a need to star in his own snuff-sex and just got carried away.*

At The Hague Airport, Ida changed her flight to Atlanta via Paris, where she would stay for a few days to shop, then fly home. She promised herself that the first thing she planned was to open an account at a Royal Bank in Paris and transfer some money there. She would make her time in Paris count.

Chapter Thirty Five
Elspeth's Vivid Dream

Pelling retrieved the Gucci bag from the front desk security station, mentioned that he would be back in two days to complete his stay, which he had paid for in advance. In the hotel room he removed all the cash from the bags and rearranged the bills and cashier's cheques. He activated the Linus Svendsen passport which he would need later that day. The portfolio belonging to Ruth now contained only money and cashier's cheques and the Linus Svendsen passport. One Gucci bag contained all the clothes he planned to use, with the George Yaro outfit on top. He spent some time changing his look to that of Linus Svendsen. What money he could not put into Ruth's portfolio went into the other Gucci bag. He swept the room of everything which could identify them as the latest occupants. The suite was paid for four more days but he wouldn't be expected back for another two days. He made his way down the stairs to the parking level and walked the remaining distance to where he had parked the Mercedes.

Pelling had preselected a huge Hotel complex on the outskirts of Voorburg for his next stop. It was a half hour drive to the entrance to the Hotel and Mall. As he approached the unloading area he popped the trunk so that the bell-captain could remove his luggage, then gave him the car keys and asked for valet parking. Pelling checked in to a very expensive suite on the fourth floor as Linus Svendsen and paid for a week's stay with US dollars. When he was shown the room, he tipped the bellhop and asked him to arrange for the Hotel limo to take him into The Hague in half an hour.

***

Lieutenant Robert Bizet had been faxed information from his two sergeants stationed at the Bastille. They were in charge of the ongoing collection of information about the workings of the ETA from Raoul de Vascos. The sergeants, in their faxed reports to their boss, mentioned the terrorist seemed a little less stressed after being moved to a secret holding cell inside the ancient prison. The sergeants: Debois and Pilon, were the only visitors the terrorist had. One would stay stationed outside the cell while the other brought in his food. They would tape record their question and his answers later to be transcribed and faxed to the Lieutenant at the Chateau in Utrecht. They took turns asking the questions of Raoul after the Lieutenant had read the transcriptions and faxed new questions to them. They made daily trips back to their head office to check incoming mail and any faxes that might be of interest to the lieutenant.

One such fax was from the George Town office of the Cayman Constabulary from Captain Lewis announcing his appointment as acting inspector while Inspector Pennington was summoned to London to answer charges of dereliction of duty. Acting Inspector Lewis promised to advise Lieutenant Bizet the results of that investigation.

On the second day of this procedure, Sergeant Pilon was reading the newswire at the Sûreté offices of the Anti-Terrorist Team when he spotted the news release about Ramon Atmos being found dead in a hotel suite in Rome. The sergeant recognized the name of the missing Gulfstream's pilot. The article went on to say his hands had been cut off and he was forced to watch himself bleed to death according to the coroner. Authorities said murder victims found like this were thought to be thieves punished for stealing from organized crime or terrorist factions. Authorities were asking for help in solving the murder.

Later that same afternoon following a telephone call from Lieutenant Bizet, the Gulfstream was located by the Italian Special Squad who had taken two men into custody, one of whom was a certified pilot capable of flying the Gulfstream. Because of the background that the lieutenant had provided the Italian authorities, they were quickly established as ETA agents wanted by both French and Spanish police. The Gulfstream was indeed the jet Teddy Pelling had hijacked and used for his own purposes. The Rome airport said their records from customs officers said the jet arrived with only the pilot. No passengers. Their information was the pilot was to wait at the Rome airport for further instructions from the owner, George Yaro. The last destination stated was Antwerp, Belgium. Further checking had turned up a filed flight plan to Tunis International Airport that had been changed to the Rome Aeroporto in flight. Strange, but not unusual, behavior of the wealthy.

Lieutenant Robert Bizet concentrated his search for the remaining four occupants of the Gulfstream at the Airport in Antwerp, where he was told the pilot Ramon Atmos, the owner George Yaro and a lady friend, Ruth Werner, landed and cleared customs. Yaro and Werner were registered at the Sint Erasmus Gasthaus for a week's stay. Yaro and Werner had left for a motor trip of Belgium and Holland in a rented Mercedes sports car taken out for a week and paid for by Ruth Werner's credit card. The Gulfstream left later the same day with just the pilot Ramon Atmos on board who filed a flight plan to Tunis. The jet had been serviced and paid for with George Yaro's credit card.

In a telephone call, the lieutenant interviewed the desk clerk who registered Yaro and Werner at the Sint Erasmus Gasthaus. After this conversation, Bizet, pre-conditioned to Pelling's penchant for disguises, guessed that George Yaro was really Teddy Pelling. He would know more after he had a look at the airplane registration credentials that the Italian police were faxing to him. He tightened the net to include all the border crossings, airports and bus and train stations in Holland and Belgium. Instructions were issued through Interpol and under Sûreté authority to apprehend anyone using passports in the name of Werner or Meikle (same description) or George Yaro (any description).

While the lieutenant manned his office in the Chateau, a decided coolness had fallen over the relationship of Andre and Elspeth. Elspeth had let Andre read about her dream, then told him the second part. The first part had to do with a rendezvous with the terrorist and herself. The part that had woke her up in a cold sweat was when Pelling had begun to remove her only remaining clothes: her panties. When she returned to her bed and fell back to sleep, part two of the dream began. She was at a funeral for two people but didn't know who they were. And she could not see the twins or Andre.

The details of Elspeth's vivid dream mistakenly suggested to Andre that it would be the right time to give the ransom to her. He presented Elspeth with the four cashier's cheques worth a quarter of a million US each, and told her the whole story about how he had followed Pelling, shot him, tied him and his girl-friend up, left them to be arrested, after stopping the bleeding as best he could. Andre told her how he had taken the four cheques and twenty thousand in US cash from the terrorist and left them neatly trussed up for the police. Elspeth's eyes were widening in terror as he related the encounter in detail to her. She began to shiver with fear, then began to turn angry at his interference. Her emotions were stretched from her concern for her family and the thought of what might have happened to him. Elspeth started to cry. Andre could not understand, thinking she would at least be pleased to have the ransom money back, although this seemed to bother her the most. Finally, she regained enough of her composure to be able to explain to him that she could now be accused of breaking faith with the terrorist who would carry out his threat to kill the twins and them as well. Andre offered reasons why this wouldn't happen but none that made any sense to Elspeth who looked all the world like she was retreating into a depression.

This was not the case, rather than becoming depressed, Elspeth was actually formulating a plan to head off Pelling's attack which she knew was sure to come, but how would she get in touch with him?

Andre was in Elspeth's shower when a phone call came in for her and was transferred upstairs to her suite.

"Elspeth Vander Riis here, who is speaking please?"

"I took you as a woman of honor. Perhaps I was wrong." His distinct voice caused a flush to run up her spine as she swallowed a gasp and made her plea quickly.

"I have your money. It was returned to me this morning. Four cashier's cheques worth $250,000 each. I had nothing at all to do with this or the police or the authorities who are after you. You must believe me. Please don't harm my children, I beg you. It's all a terrible mistake. I want to bring the money to you myself and explain. I am a person of honor," Elspeth said.

The momentary silence before he answered almost caused her to panic.

Finally, he said, "Have your driver bring you to the shopping complex and hotel in Voorburg. Do you know the place?" Pelling asked.

"Yes, I know where it is. Where will I meet you?"

"There is a bistro with outside tables across from the hotel lobby. Sit at one of the tables, order a coffee. Be there in two hours: 10:00AM. When your driver drops you at the entrance, dismiss him. Tell him you will call him when you wish to be picked up. I'll decide after I observe you from my vantage point whether or not you have come alone. Have the money with you and think of a way you can convince me that this matter between us can be concluded." He paused, listening to her nervous breathing.

"I'll come alone," Elspeth promised.

He hung up and Elspeth replaced the receiver, took a deep breath of resignation as she looked toward the bathroom where Andre had begun toweling dry.

Elspeth was already dressed for the day in beige sweater and tailored slacks. Her outfit was meant for Andre as she had wanted his eyes on her. She thought about changing, but decided not to. She put the four cashier's cheques in her purse and called down to Veldhoen, her driver, to bring the Rolls around because she wanted to go into The Hague. She left her suite saying nothing to Andre. Descending the stairs, she didn't encounter any of the others. If she had, she would simply say she was going into the bank and would return shortly. Once she reached the landing she walked quickly along the hallway, poked her head into the library where she saw Robert Bizet bent over an incoming fax. Good! She was glad he was preoccupied. She wouldn't have to lie to him or anyone else. She put on a leather shirt jacket at the front entrance, slipped out the huge oak doors and down the front entrance steps to the driveway. The white Rolls was waiting for her. After seating herself in the rear seat, she instructed Veldhoen to take her to the hotel shopping complex in Voorburg on the way to The Hague. Elspeth had plenty of time before her 10:00 meeting. She looked into her purse to assure herself that the cheques were still there. And his voice came to her again...'and think of a way to convince me that this matter between us can be concluded." Elspeth knew exactly what he was referring to and how she thought she would convince him.

Chapter Thirty Six
Do What You Have To So You Can Do What You Want to

Pelling was on station when the Vander Riis white Rolls Royce pulled to a stop at the entrance to the Hotel mall complex. He watched the widow exit the rear door and walk determinedly toward the entrance. He was at the bank of telephones inside the main lobby dressed as the old man, Adolph Studer. Pelling had decided earlier to book another room in the name of Elspeth Vander Riis who was due to check in just after 10:00 this morning. He glanced at his watch and noted the time was 9:25. The widow was early. She was a fine looking woman dressed in tailored slacks, matching low cut cream colored sweater, over which she had on a taupe leather shirt jacket. Her pumps and purse matched the jacket and identified her as a lady of means and style. Pelling admired how purposeful she moved with the self-assured stride of the affluent. To anyone who noticed her, she appeared to be just another well-to-do shopper, but Pelling knew she was on a mission and followed her from a discreet distance. Elspeth walked past the tables of the Bistro she was to sit at, taking note that only half of the eight tables were occupied. She strolled along the mall-way and into a pharmacy. He took up surveillance in a row of shaving material and, while reading the label on a can of shaving cream, glanced in her direction. She was purchasing items from the pharmacist. Pelling could not see what it was that she paid cash for and put in her purse. He noticed her look at her wrist watch and walk out of the store. She returned to the Bistro and sat at the table closest to the mall traffic. A young waiter appeared at her table and took her order for a coffee, returning with it minutes later.

As Elspeth was putting the cup to her lips a heavy set older man with a slight limp passed close by and dropped an envelope onto her table. Elspeth tried to keep him in sight but lost him in the steadily increasing flow of shoppers. She picked up the envelope which was addressed to her, opened it and read:

> There is a room reserved in your name at the Hotel across from the Bistro where you're sitting. Go and register for a day and then leave an envelope addressed to A. Studer with the cashiers' cheques inside. I'll leave it up to you whether or not you want me to know what room you're in.

Elspeth read the note again then put it back into the envelope and into her purse. She left more than enough for her coffee and walked across to the Hotel lobby. She signed in and gave her American Express card as the deposit. Elspeth asked for an envelope and writing material. The clerk handed her key to room 134 and pointed out an elaborate writing desk to the left of the check-in area. Elspeth made out an envelope addressed to A. Studer and put the four $250,000 US cashier's cheques inside. She paused for only a brief moment and simply wrote 134 on a page, folded it and put it into the envelope as well. She returned to the same clerk who had checked her in and said someone would come and ask if she had left an envelope for A. Studer. The clerk smiled at her and put the envelope in her key slot.

Elspeth made her way to the hallway marked rooms 119-140, and walked quickly to the door of 134. Once inside, she went to the bathroom and took out her drug store purchases and left them on the counter. She looked at her image in the mirror and took a deep breath.

If you are not convincing, he won't buy it. He wants you to offer him sex, why else did he say, "I'll leave it up to you whether or not you tell me your hotel room number." The arrogance of the man!

The knock at the door startled her.

She looked through the peep-hole at the old chap who had dropped the letter of instructions on her table at the bistro. Elspeth opened the door and asked him to come in. Pelling stepped into the room and went to the desk with the big mirror and carefully lifted the wig off of his head exposing his real hair. Elspeth saw that his military hair-cut had grown out.

He got straighter and younger before her eyes. His transformation intrigued her. Pelling removed his suit coat and then his shirt and set them over the back of the nearest chair. He wore a tan colored short sleeved muscle shirt with an exaggerated scooped neckline tucked neatly into his tailored tan slacks. Elspeth watched him carefully, marveling silently at the change in age from the elderly chap to this muscular young man, thinking, *he likes to be looked at.*

"We have something between us which I'd like to settle today so that we can each get on with our lives," Elspeth said.

"I received your envelope with the million in cashier's cheques. So, that concludes our business as far as I'm concerned. But, then, you did leave me this room number didn't you?" Pelling teased.

"Look, my hope is that you get away clean so that you can retire or do whatever it is you have planned. I feel I can count on you to keep our bargain. And I want you to believe once and for all that I do keep my word. After today, we never need to see each other again, but I want you to take something with you that will seal our bargain," Elspeth said.

"Elspeth are you going to seduce me?" Pelling asked.

"I'd like to know why you didn't rape me when you threatened to, when you had the chance?" Elspeth asked.

"Look at me, lady! Do I honestly look like I have to rape anybody to have sex? Hell, I turn it down practically every day," Pelling said.

"I thought as much. I sensed that...you wanted me to come on to you... out of fear...or whatever!" Elspeth stammered.

"Well, it's what usually happens but not out of fear, I can assure you. I knew that you were badly frightened, but then you got angry. Hell, I could understand! I chocked it up to either you were a real cold ass rich bitch or the drugs had affected you adversely, but I took another look at those Polaroid pictures of you with Laurent...and I knew different. You're obviously a very randy lady, Elspeth, and I thought, why not? Sure, I wanted some. When I took off your clothes so you wouldn't get sick all over them in your drugged state, I left you in just your bra and panties...well, let's just say you come in a package that would put most teenagers to shame, lady," Pelling said smiling.

"So, I was right about what you're really after. You do want to have sex with me, but only on your terms. Tell me, did you just watch me masturbate while I was drugged or did you participate?" Elspeth inquired.

"Actually, I just placed you on the berth so that your legs were apart and I could watch you get after yourself through your panties. I might have helped you get it off a bit when I gave you some tongue. Hell, you seemed to really like it," Pelling said.

Elspeth, was sitting on the side of the bed watching him sprawled out in the chair facing her. She made up her mind, stood and undid the belt on her slacks, then the zipper on the side, letting them fall about her ankles. While she stepped away from them, she removed the sweater she was wearing, walked into the bathroom and returned with a package in her hand.

"I would like to have sex with you but I don't want to take any chances on a disease, since you get around so much. Please understand and wear one of these. Elspeth handed him the package of condoms and forced a smile. She sat on the corner of the big bed straddling it. Maintaining eye contact with him, she reached behind her and undid her bra and set it aside. Elspeth leaned back onto the bed spreading her knees in an unmistakable invitation then, bringing herself back up to a sitting position she asked, "Would you like me to put the condom on you or can you manage?"

Pelling stood up and quickly dropped his pants and jockey shorts, kicked off his loafers and stepped to the corner of the bed while he peeled off his skimpy muscle shirt. He handed her the condom and literally posed in front of her face while she undid the package. She held him in one hand and rubbed it over her breasts. The condom fit only three quarters of the way up his shaft. Elspeth licked his encased penis which got him real excited. She looked up to make eye contact with him and went into the scenario she had imagined for this moment: *I picked him up in the bar downstairs, just like the one I'd met and decided I wanted to have sex with. This wouldn't be any different. I'll just stay in control and let it happen. God, he looks even bigger without his clothes on.*

Elspeth said in the most convincing manner she could summon, "Let me slip my underwear off and then I'd like you to show me what you did to me on the SeaOx."

He helped her out of her panties, knelt between her legs and obliged her. His tongue had to compete with her fingers until the guttural sounds in the back of her throat announced her climax was beginning. He entered her, slowly until he was well lubricated. After his initial gentleness with her, he could feel her responding and began more deliberate thrusting which started her to move under him. This is how he always imagined she might respond to him. When she was really into it, Pelling began to stroke her vigorously which had the usual effect of causing much writhing under him. He always knew when they were really liking it, they all went a little nuts. Elspeth seemed to be in a zone of her own and locked her legs around his waist. His hands went around her neck and began to squeeze. Elspeth almost panicked, but instead of continuing her frantic squirming and fighting for air, she reached between them, searching for her target.

The thunderous sound of blood pounding in her ears was drowned out by what sounded like the ringing of the telephone and then his piercing scream. He let go of her neck as her finger nails dug sharply into his scrotum. He smacked her a devastating backhand and rolled off of her, his hands now clutching his genitals. The phone continued to ring. In the bathroom, he removed and flushed the overflowing condom. After a quick soapy suds cleansing of his injured sack, Pelling dressed quickly, found hotel letterhead in the desk and quickly scribbled her a note.

Elspeth was still unconscious when the telephone began to ring again. Pelling closed the door behind him. He thought to himself: *Damn! What a sexy looking woman she is, especially when she's unconscious.*

When Elspeth finally identified the ringing in her ears as the telephone, she rolled to the side of the bed and sat listening to its continuous ringing. The pain in her jaw was excruciating and her throat hurt. She touched her chin and picked up the receiver.

"Hello." She croaked, looked at her watch and noticed the time was 11:30.

"Elspeth are you alright? It's Andre here."

"Andre? Oh Andre! Where are you?" she asked.

"I'm calling from your car. Veldhoen will drop me off at your hotel in fifteen minutes. Your voice sounds strange. Are you sure you're alright?" Andre asked.

"Yes, yes I'm alright Andre. When you get to the hotel come to my room, 134. I'll explain everything. Please darling, hurry."

Elspeth hung up the phone. She made her way, unsteadily, to the door and chained it. Pelling was gone...out of her life forever she prayed. In the bathroom, she set the shower on hot and scrubbed herself clean after which she dressed. Looking at her reflection in the mirror, she noticed the red welt beginning to form across the lower right side of her face and touched her hands to her throat.

Well, I needed to be convincing didn't I? Cripes! I thought I was in control, until he stirred up some real lust inside me. God help me. My body betrayed me, overruled my good intentions and I couldn't help it. I just went with it. Tears of shame began to run down her cheeks. I just couldn't help myself, I was enjoying it until he started to strangle me. Why in the hell did he try and kill me? If Andre hadn't called when he did, I might be dead now. I've got to explain everything that happened to Andre. I just pray to God he understands.

Elspeth was standing in front of the desk mirror combing her hair when she noticed the hand written note addressed to her.

> Elspeth
>
> You are, without a doubt, one of the finest sexual partners I have ever been with. I thought you would be.
>
> When we were really getting into it and you began to rock and roll under me, well that's when I like to choke and the action always goes to another level and it gets so intense I sometimes black out. I did get a bit carried away with you but the ringing telephone was a real turn-off and brought me immediately back to earth. Your very painful way of ending our little romp will undoubtedly leave me on the sidelines for a while. You are one very brave and courageous lady.
>
> I'm out of your life

T.P.

Elspeth read it again, folded it and put it away in her purse. She thought to herself; *Andre will be along shortly. I'll explain everything. I think he'll now understand the dream I had last night. I feel a tremendous burden has been lifted from me.*

The knock at the door must be Andre.

When she opened it to him, she smiled at the troubled look on his face, hugged him fiercely and kissed him hungrily.

"How did you know I was here?" Elspeth asked.

He caught his breath as they sat on the edge of the bed and he answered, "I asked your driver Veldhoen and he told me he had never ever been dismissed by you like this morning and thought something was wrong, so he found a parking space nearby and went into the mall. He spotted you sitting at a table reading a letter and watched you go across to the Hotel and register and then go over to a desk and write a letter which he saw you give to the hotel clerk. You then walked into the hotel like you were going to meet someone. Veldhoen was concerned but thought he might be interfering in a private matter, so he returned to the Chateau. He wasn't sure if he should tell the lieutenant what he had seen, but when I asked him if he had seen you, he told me what he'd seen and I asked him to bring me here. On the way, I called to see if you were registered, they confirmed that you were and rang your room. Elspeth, your face and neck are red and swollen. What the hell happened to you?" Andre asked.

She held his hand in both of hers, smiled at him and began.

"Andre my love, your phone call may very well have saved my life. Please open your heart and your mind and let me explain."

The End

CPSIA information can be obtained at www.ICGtesting.com
Printed in the USA
LVOW07s0039240415

435861LV00001B/87/P